"Brave, gallant men,"

[See page 374]

THE ADVENTURES OF
M. D'HARICOT

❀❀❀❀❀❀❀❀❀❀❀❀❀❀❀❀❀❀❀❀❀

BY

J. STORER CLOUSTON

ILLUSTRATED **BY**

ALBERT LEVERING

❀❀❀❀❀❀❀❀❀❀❀❀❀❀❀❀❀❀❀❀❀

HARPER AND BROTHERS

PUBLISHERS NEW YORK AND LONDON

1902

THE

ADVENTURES OF M. D'HARICOT

Chapter I

"Adieu, the land of my birth!
Henceforth strange faces!"
—Boulevardé.

ON my window-sill lies a faded rose, a rose plucked from an English lane. As I write, my eyes fall upon the gardens, the forests, around my ancestral château, but the faint scent is an English perfume. To the land of that rose, the land that sheltered, befriended, amused me, I dedicate these memoirs of my sojourn there.

They are a record of incidents and impressions that sometimes have little connection one with another beyond the possession of one character in common—myself. I am that individual who with unsteady feet will tread the tight-rope, dance among the eggs, leap through the paper tambourine—in a word, play clown and hero to the melody of the castanets. I hold out my hat that you may drop in a sou should you chance to be amused. To the serious I herewith bid adieu, for instruction, I fear, will be conspicuously absent, unless, indeed, my follies serve as a warning.

And now without further prologue I raise the curtain.

The first scene is a railway carriage swiftly travelling farther and farther from the sea that washes the dear shores of France. Look out of the window and behold the green fields, the heavy hedge-rows enclosing them so tightly, the trees, not in woods, but scattered everywhere as by a restless forester, the brick farms, the hop-fields, the moist, vaporous atmosphere of England.

Cast your eyes within and you will see, wrapped in an ulster of a British pattern concealing all that is not British in his appearance, an exile from his native land. Not to make a mystery of this individual, you will see, indeed, myself. And I— why did I travel thus enshrouded, why did my eye look with melancholy upon this fertile landscape, why did I sit sad and sombre as I travelled through this strange land? There were many things fresh and novel to stir the mind of an adventurer. The name, the platform, the look of every station we sped past, was a little piece of England, curious in its way. Many memories of the people and the places I had known in fiction should surely have been aroused and lit my heart with some enthusiasm. What reason, then, for sadness?

I shall tell you, since the affair is now no secret, and as it hereafter touches my narrative. I was a Royalist, an adherent of the rightful king of France. I am still; I boast it openly. But at that time a demonstration had been premature, a government was alarmed, and I had fled.

why did I travel thus enshrouded

Hereafter I shall tell you more of the secret and formidable society of which I was then a young, enthusiastic member—the Une, Deux, Trois League, or U. D. T's, as we styled ourselves in brief, the forlorn hope of royalty in France. At present it is sufficient to say that we had failed.

Baffled hopes, doubt as to the future, fear for the present, were my companions; and they are not gay, these friends.

I felt—I confess it now mirthfully enough—suspicious of the porter of the train, of the guard, of the people who eyed me.

I was young, and "political offender" had a terrible sound. The Bastile, Siberia, St. Helena; were not these places built, created, discovered, for

3

the sole purpose of returning white-haired, enfeebled unfortunates to their native land, only to find their homes dissolved, their families deceased, themselves forgotten? The truth is that I was already in mourning for myself. The prospect of entering history by the martyr's postern had seemed noble in the heat of action and the excitement of intrigue. Now I only desired my liberty and as little public attention as possible. I commend this personal experience to all conspirators.

Such a frame of mind begets suspicions fast, and when I found myself in the same compartment with a young man who had already glanced at me in the Gare du Nord, and taken a longer look on board the steamboat, I felt, I admit, decidedly uncomfortable. From beneath the shade of my travelling-cap I eyed him for the first half-hour with a deep distrust. Yet since he regarded me with that total lack of interest an Englishman bestows upon the unintroduced, and had, besides, an appearance of honesty written on his countenance, I began to feel somewhat ashamed of my suspicions, until at last I even came to consider him with interest as one type of that strange people among whom for a longer or a shorter time I was doomed to dwell. He differed, it is true, both from the busts of Shakespeare and the statues of Wellington, yet he was far from unpleasing. An athletic form, good features, a steady, blue eye, a complexion rosy as a

4

girl's, fair hair brushed flat across his forehead, thirty years of truth-telling, cricket-playing, and the practice of three or four elementary ethical principles, not to mention an excellent tailor, all went to make this young man a refreshing and an encouraging spectacle.

"Bah!" I said to myself. "My friend may not be the poet-laureate or the philanthropic M. Carnegie, but at least he is no spy."

By nature I am neither bashful nor immoderately timid, and it struck me that some talk with a native might be of service. My spirits, too, were rising fast. The train had not yet been stopped and searched; we were nearing the great London, where he who seeks concealment is as one pin in a trayful; the hour was early in the day, and the sun breaking out made the wet grass glisten.

Yes, it was hard to remain silent on that glorious September morning, even though dark thoughts sat upon the same cushion.

"Monsieur," I said, "the sun is bright."

With this remark he seemed to show his agreement by a slight smile and a murmured phrase. The smile was pleasant, and I felt encouraged to continue.

"Yet it does not always follow that the heart is gay. Indeed, monsieur, how often we see tears on a June morning, and hear laughter in March! It must have struck you often, this want of harmony in the world. Has it not?"

I had been so carried away by my thoughts
that I had failed to observe the lack of sympathy
in my fellow-traveller's countenance.

"Possibly," he remarked, dryly.

"Ah," I said, with a smile, "you do not appreciate. You are English."

" Yet, it does
not always
follow that the
heart is gay."

"I am," he replied. "And you are French, I
suppose?"

At his words, suspicion woke in my heart. It was
only as a Frenchman that I ran the risk of arrest.

"No; I am an American."

This was my first attempt to disclaim my nationality, and each time I denied my country I, like
St. Peter, suffered for it. Fair France, your lovers
should be true! That is the lesson.

"Indeed," was all he said; but I now began to

enjoy my first experience of that disconcerting phenomenon, the English stare. Later on I discovered that this generally means nothing, and is, in fact, merely an inherited relic of the days when each Englishman carried his "knuckle-duster" (a weapon used in boxing), and struck the instant his neighbor's attention was diverted. It is thanks to this peculiarity that they now find themselves in possession of so large a portion of the globe, but the surviving stare is not a reassuring spectacle.

Yet I must not let him see that I was in the slightest inconvenienced by his attitude. The antidote to suspicion is candor. I was candid.

"Yes," I said. "I am told that I do not resemble an American, but my name, at least, is good Anglo-Saxon."

And I handed him a card prepared for such an emergency. On it I had written, "Nelson Bunyan, Esq." If that sounded French, then I had studied philology in vain.

"I am a traveller in search of curios," I added. "And you?"

"I am not," he replied, with a trace of a smile and a humorous look in his blue eyes.

He was quite friendly, perfectly polite, but that was all the information about himself I could extract—"I am not," followed by a commonplace concerning the weather. A singular type! Repressed, self-restrained, reticent, good-humoredly condescending—in a word, British.

We talked of various matters, and I did my best to pick him, like his native winkle, from the shell. Of my success here is a sample. We had (or I had) been talking of the things that were best worth a young man's study.

"And there is love," I said. "What a field for inquiry, what variety of aspects, what practical lessons to be learned!"

He smiled at my ardor.

"Have you ever been in love?" I asked.

"Possibly," he replied, carelessly.

"But devotedly, hopelessly, as a man who would sacrifice heaven for his mistress?"

"Haven't blown my brains out yet," he answered.

"Ah, you have been successful; you have invariably brought your little affairs to a fortunate issue?"

"I don't know that I should call myself a great ladies' man."

"Possibly you are engaged?" I suggested, remembering that I had heard that this operation has a singularly sedative effect upon the English.

"No," he said, with an air of ending the discussion, "I am not."

Again this "I am not," followed by a compression of the lips and a cold glance into vacancy.

"Ah, he is a dolt; a lump of lead!" I said to myself, and I sighed to think of the people I was leaving, the people of spirit, the people of wit. Little did I think how my opinion of my fellow-traveller would one day alter, how my heart would expand.

But now I had something else to catch my attention. I looked out of the window, and, behold, there was nothing to be seen but houses. Below the level of the railway line was spread a sea of dingy brick dwellings, all, save here and there a church-tower, of one uniform height and of one uniform ugliness. Against the houses nearest to the railway were plastered or propped, by way of decoration, vast colored testimonials to the soaps and meat extracts of the country. In lines through this prosaic landscape rose telegraph posts and signals, and trains bustled in every direction.

"Pardon me," I said to my companion, "but I am new to this country. What city is this?"

"London," said he.

London, the far-famed! So this was London. Much need to "paint it red," as the English say of a frolic.

"Is it all like this?" I asked.

"Not quite," he replied, in his good-humored tone.

"Thank God!" I exclaimed, devoutly. "I do not like to speak disrespectfully of any British institution, but this—my faith!"

We crossed the Thames, gray and gleaming in the sunshine, and now I am at Charing Cross. Just as the train was slowing down I turned to my fellow-traveller.

"Have you been vaccinated?" I asked.

9

"I have," said he, in surprise.

You see even reticence has its limits.

"I thank you for the confidence," I replied, gravely.

As he stood up to take his umbrella from the rack he handed me back my card.

"I say," he abruptly remarked, in a tone, I thought, of mingled severity and innuendo, "I should have this legend altered, if I were you. Good-morning."

And with that he was gone, and my doubts had returned. He suspected something! Well, there was nothing to be done but maintain a stout heart and trust to fortune. And it takes much to drive gayety from my spirits for long. I was a fugitive, a stranger, a foreigner, but I hummed a tune cheerfully as I waited my turn for the ordeal of the custom-house. And here came one good omen. My appearance was so deceptively respectable, and my air so easy, that not a question was asked me. One brief glance at my dress-shirts and I was free to drive into the streets and lose myself in the life of London.

Lose myself, do I say? Yes, indeed, and more than myself, too. My friends, my interests, my language, my home; all these were lost as utterly as though I had dropped them overboard in the Channel. I had not time to obtain even one single introduction before I left, or further counsel than I remembered from reading English books. And

I assure you it is not so easy to benefit by the experiences of Mr. Pickwick and Miss Sharp as it may seem. Stories may be true to life, but, alas! life is not so true to stories.

Fortunately, I could talk and read English well—even, I may say, fluently; also I had the spirit of my race; and finally—and, perhaps, most fortunately—I was not too old to learn.

Chapter II

"In that city, sire, even the manner of breathing was different."

—Pizarro.

WAS in London, the vastest collection of people and of houses this world has ever seen; the ganglion, the museum, the axle of the English race; the cradle of much of their genius and most of their fogs; the home of Dr. Johnson, the bishops of Canterbury, the immortal Falstaff, the effigied Fawkes; also the headquarters of all the profitable virtues, all the principles of business. With an abandon and receptivity which I am pleased to think the Creator has reserved as a consolation for the non-English, I had hardly been half an hour in the city before I had become infected with something of its spirit.

"Goddam! What ho!" I said to myself, in the English idiom. "For months, for years, forever, perhaps, I am to live among this incomprehensi-

ble people. Well, I shall strive to learn something, and, by Great Scotland! to enjoy something."
So I turned up my trousers and sallied out of my hotel.

Ah, this was life, indeed, I had come into; not more so than Paris, but differently so. Stolidly, good-naturedly, and rapidly the citizens struggle along through the crowds on the pavement. They seem like helpless straws revolving in a whirlpool. Yet does one of them wish to cross the street? Instantly a constable raises a finger, the traffic of London is stopped, and Mr. Benjamin Bull, youngest and least important son of John, passes uninjured to the farther side.

"What is this street?" I ask one of these officers, as he stands in the midst of a crossing, signalling which cab or dray shall pass him.

"Strand," says he, stopping five omnibuses to give me this information.

"Where does it lead me?"

"Which way do you wish to proceed?" he inquires, politely, still detaining the omnibuses.

"East," I reply, at a venture.

"First to the right, second to the left, third to the right again, and take the blue bus as far as the Elephant and Angel," he answers, without any hesitation.

"A thousand thanks," I gasp. "I think, on the whole, I should be safer to go westward."

He waves his hand, the omnibuses (which by

this time have accumulated to the number of fourteen) proceed upon their journey, and I, had I the key to the cipher, should doubtless be in possession of valuable information. Such is one instance of the way in which the Londoner's substitute for Providence does its business.

I shall not attempt to give at this point an exhaustive description of London. The mandates of fortune sent me at different times to enjoy amusing and embarrassing experiences in various quarters of the city, and these I shall touch upon in their places. It is sufficient to observe at present that London is a name for many cities.

A great town, like a great man, is made up of various characters strung together. Just as the soldier becomes at night the lover and next morning the philosopher, so a city is on the east a factory, on the west a palace, on the north a lodging-house. So it is with Paris, with Berlin, with all. But London is so large, so devoid of system in its creation and in its improvements, so variously populated, that it probably exceeds any in its variety.

No emperor or council of city fathers mapped the streets or regulated the houses. What edifice each man wanted that he built, guided only by the length of his purse and the depth of his barbarism; while the streets on which this arose is either the same roadway as once served the Romans, or else the speculative builder's idea of best advancing the interests of his property. Then some day comes a great company who wish to occupy a hundred metres of frontage and direct attention to their business. So many houses are pulled down and replaced by an erection twice the height of anything else, and designed, as far as possible, to imitate the cries and costume of a bookmaker. And all this time there are surviving, in nooks and corners, picturesque and venerable buildings of a by-gone age, and also, of late, are arising on all sides worthy and dignified new piles.

So that the history of each house and each street, the mental condition of their architects and the financial condition of their occupants, are written upon them plainly with a smoky finger. For you see all this through an atmosphere whose millions of molecules of carbon and of aqueous vapor darken the bricks and the stones, and hang like a veil of fine gauze before them. London is huge, but the eternal mistiness makes it seem huger still, for however high a building you climb, you can see nothing but houses and yet more houses, melting at what looks a vast distance into the blue-and-yellow haze. Really, there may be green woods and the fair slopes of a country-side within a few miles, but since you cannot see them your heart sinks, and you believe that such good things must be many leagues below the brick horizon. More than once upon a Sunday morning, when the air was clear, I have been startled to see from the

Strand itself a glimpse of the Surrey hills quite near and very beautiful, and I have said, "Thank God for this!"

"I ate it till half past two"

It was in the morning that I arrived in London, and my first day I spent in losing my way through the labyrinth of streets, which are set never at a right angle to one another, and are of such different lengths that I could scarcely persuade myself it had not all been specially arranged to mislead me.

About one o'clock I entered a restaurant and ordered a genuine English steak—the porter-house, it was called. In quality, I admit this segment of an ox was admirable; but as for its quantity—my faith! I ate it till half-past two and scarcely had made an impression then. Half stupefied with this orgy, and the British beer I had taken to assist me in the protracted effort, I returned to my hotel,

16

and there began the journal on which these memoirs are founded. As showing my sensations at the time, they are now of curious interest to me. I shall give the extract I wrote then:

"Amusing, absorbing, entertaining as a Chinese puzzle where all the pieces are alive; all these things is the city of London. Why, then, has it already begun to pall upon me? Ah, it is the loneliness of a crowd! In Paris I can walk by the hour and never see a face I know, and yet not feel this sense of desolation. Friends need not be before the eye, but they must be at hand when you wish to call them. For myself, I call them pretty frequently, yet often can remain for a time content to merely know that they are somewhere not too far away. But here — I may turn north, south, east, or west, and walk as far as I like in any direction, and not one should I find!

"Shall I ever make a friend among this old, phlegmatic, business-like people? Some day, perhaps, an acquaintance may be struck with some such reticent and frigid monster as my fair-haired companion of the journey. Would such a one console or cheer or share a single sentiment? Impossible! Mon Dieu! I shall leave this town in three days; I swear it. And where then? The devil knows!"

At this point the writing of these notes was unexpectedly interrupted, only to be resumed, as it chanced, after some adventurous days.

A waiter entered, bearing a letter for me. I sprang up and seized it eagerly. It was addressed to Mr. Nelson Bunyan, Esq., and marked "Immediate and confidential." These words were written in English and execrably misspelled.

It could come from but one source, for who else knew my *nom de plume*, who else would write "Immediate and ·confidential," and, I grieve to say it, who else would take their precautions in such a way as instantly to raise suspicions? Had the secretary of the "Une, Deux, Trois" no English dictionary, that he need make the very waiter stare at this very extraordinary address? I did my best to pass it off lightly.

"From a lady," I said to the man. "One not very well educated, perhaps; but is education all we seek in women?"

"No, sir," said he, replying to my glance with insufferable familiarity, "not all by no means."

Alas that the fugitive cannot afford to take offence!

I opened the letter, and, as I expected, it was headed by the letters U. D. T:

"Go at once to the house of Mr. Frederick Hankey, No. 114 or 115 George Road, Streatham. Knock thrice on the third window, and when he comes say distinctly 'For the King.' He will give directions for your safety."

This missive was only signed F. 11, but, of course, I knew the writer—our most indefatigable, our most enthusiastic, the secretary himself.

Well, here was something to be done; a friend, perhaps, to be made; a spice of interest suddenly thrown into this city of strangers. After my fashion, my spirits rose as quickly as they had fallen. I whistled an air, and began to think this somewhat dreary hotel not a bad place, after all. I should only wait till darkness fell and then set out to interview Mr. Frederick Hankey.

Chapter III

"What door will fit this key?"
—CASTILLO SOPRANI.

S I ate my solitary dinner before *A* starting upon my expedition to Mr. Hankey's house, I began to think less enthusiastically of the adventure. Here was I, comfortable in my hotel, though, I admit, rather lonely; safe, so far, and apparently suspected by none to be other than the blameless Bunyan. Besides, now that I could find a friend for the seeking, my loneliness suddenly diminished. Also I was buoyed by the thought that I was a real adventurer, a romantic exile, as much so, in fact, as Prince Charles of Scotland or my own beloved king. Now I was to knock upon the window of a house that might be either number 114 or 115, and give myself blindfold to strangers.

Yet on second thoughts I reflected that I knew nothing of English laws or English ways. Was

I not in "perfidious Albion," and might I not be
handed over to the French government in defiance
of all treaties, in order to promote the insidious
policy of Chamberlain? Yes, I should go, after
all, and I drank to the success of my adventure
in a bottle of wine that sent me forth to the
station in as gay a spirit as any gallant could
wish.

I had made cautious inquiries, asking of different servants at the hotel, and I had little difficulty
in making my way by train as far as the suburb

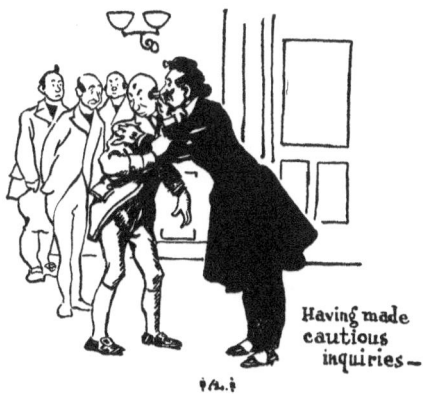

Having made
cautious
inquiries —

in which Mr. Hankey lived. There I encountered
the first disquieting circumstance. Inquiring of
a policeman, I found there was no such place as
George Road, but a St. George's Road was well
known to him. If F. 11 had been so inaccurate

in one statement, might he not be equally so in another?

I may mention here that the name of this road is my own invention. The mistake was a similar one to that I have narrated. In all cases I have altered the names of my friends and their houses, as these events happened so recently that annoyance might be caused, for the English are a reticent nation, and shrink from publicity as M. Zola did from oblivion.

Up an immensely long and very dark road I went, studying the numbers of the houses on either side, and here at once a fresh difficulty presented itself. In an English suburb it is the custom to conceal the number provided by the municipal authorities, and decorate the gates instead with a fanciful or high-sounding title. Thus I passed "Blenheim Lodge," "Strathcory," "Rhododendron Grove," and many other such residences, but only here and there could I find a number to guide me. By counting from 84, I came at last upon two houses standing with their gates close together that must either be 114 and 115, or 115 and 116. I could not be sure which, nor in either case did I know whether the one or the other sheltered the conspiring Hankey. The gate on the left was labelled "Chickawungaree Villa," that on the right "Mount Olympus House." In the house I could see through the trees that all was darkness, and the gate was so shabby as to suggest that no one lived there. In the villa, on the contrary, I saw two or three lighted windows. I determined to try the villa.

The drive wound so as to encircle what appeared in the darkness to be a tennis-court and an arbor, and finally emerged through a clump of trees before a considerable mansion. And here I was confronted by another difficulty. My directions said, knock upon the third window. But there were three on either side of the front door, and then how did I know that Hankey might not prefer me to knock upon his back or his side windows? My friend F. II might be a martyr and a patriot; but business-like? No.

"Blind fortune is the goddess to-night," I said to myself, and with that I tapped gently upon the third window from the door counting towards the right. I have often since consoled myself by thinking that I should have exhibited no greater intuition had I counted towards the left.

I tap three times. No answer. Again three times. Still no answer. It was diabolically dark, and the trees made rustling noises very disconcerting to the nerves of one unaccustomed to practise these preliminaries before calling upon a friend.

"The devil!" I say to myself. "This time I shall make Mr. Hankey hear me."

And so I knocked very sharply and loudly, so sharply that I cracked the pane.

"Unfortunate," I thought; "but why should I

not convert Hankey's misfortune into my advantage?"

With the intention of perhaps obtaining a glimpse into the room, I pushed the pane till, with an alarming crash, a considerable portion fell upon the gravel.

Still no answer

With a start I turned, and there, approaching me from either side, were two men. Hankey had evidently heard me at last.

"Who are you?" said one of them, a stout gentleman, I could see, with a consequential voice.

I came a step towards him.

"For the King," I replied.

He seemed to be staring at me.

"What the devil—?" he exclaimed, in surprise.

My heart began to sink.

"You are Mr. Hankey?" I inquired.

"I am not," he replied, with emphasis.

Here was a delicate predicament!

But I was not yet at the end of my resources.

"May I inquire your name?" I asked, politely.

"My name is Fisher," he said, with a greater air of consequence than ever, but no greater friendliness.

"What, Fisher himself!" I exclaimed, with pretended delight. "This is indeed a fortunate coincidence! How are you, Fisher?"

24

I held out my hand, but this monster of British brutality paid no attention to my overture.

"Who are you?" he asked once more.

Not having yet made up my mind who I was, I thought it better to temporize.

"My explanations will take a few minutes, I am afraid," I answered. "The hour also is late. May I call upon you in the morning?"

"I think you had better step in and explain now," said Fisher, curtly.

They were two to one, and very close to me, while I was hampered with my British ulster. I must trust to my wits to get me safely out of this house again.

"I shall be charmed, if I am not disturbing you."

"You are disturbing me," said the inexorable Fisher. "In fact, you have been causing a considerable disturbance, and I should like to know the reason."

Under these cheerful circumstances I entered Chickawungaree Villa, Fisher preceding me, and the other man, whom I now saw to be his butler, walking uncomfortably close behind.

"Step in here," said Fisher. He showed me into what was evidently his dining-room, and then, after saying a few words in an undertone to his servant, he closed the door, drew forward a chair so as to cut off my possible line of flight, sat upon it, and breathed heavily towards me.

Figure to yourself my situation. A large, red-

25

faced, gray-whiskered individual, in a black morning-coat and red slippers, staring stolidly at me
from a meat-eating eye; name Fisher, but all other
facts concerning him unknown. A stiff, unin-
habited-looking apartment of considerable size,
lit with the electric light, upholstered in light wood

" How are you
Fisher? "

and new red leather, and ornamented by a life-
sized portrait of Fisher himself, this picture being
as uncompromising and apoplectic as the original.
Finally, standing in an artificially easy attitude
before a fireplace containing a frilled arrangement of pink paper, picture an exceedingly uncomfortable Frenchman.

"You scarcely expected me?" I begin, with a
smile.

"I did not," says Fisher.

"I did not expect to see you," I continue; but to this he makes no reply.

"I was looking for the house of Mr. Hankey."

"Were you?" says Fisher.

"Do you know him?" I ask.

"No," says Fisher.

A pause. The campaign has opened badly; no doubt of that. I must try another move.

"You will wonder how I knew him," I say, pleasantly.

Fisher only breathes more heavily.

"Our mutual friend, Smith," I begin, watching closely to see if his mind responds to this name. I know that Smith is common in England, and think he will surely know some one so called. "Smith mentioned you."

But no, there is no gleam of recognition.

"Indeed," is all he remarks, very calmly.

There is no help for it, I must go on.

"I intended to call upon you some day this week. I have heard you highly spoken of—'The great Fisher,' 'The famous Fisher.' Indeed, sir, I assure you, your name is a household word in Scotland."

I choose Scotland because I know its accent is different from English. My own also is different. Therefore I shall be Scotch. Unhappy selection!

"Do you mean to pretend you are Scotch?" says Fisher, frowning as well as breathing at me.

I must withdraw one foot.

"Half Scotch, half Italian," I reply.

Ah, France, why did I deny you? I was afraid to own you, I blush to confess it. And I was righteously punished.

"Italian?" says he, with more interest. "Ah, indeed!"

He stares more intently, frowns more portentously, and respires more loudly than ever.

Do you mean to pretend you are Scotch?

"A charming country," I say.

"No doubt," says Fisher.

At this moment the door opens behind him and a lady appears. She has a puffy cheek, a pale eye, a comfortable figure, a curled fringe of gray hair, and slightly projecting teeth; in a word, the mate of Fisher. There can be no mistake, and I am quick to seize the chance.

"My dear Mrs. Fisher!" I exclaim, advancing towards her.

With a movement like a hippopotamus wallowing, Fisher places himself between us. Does he think I have come to elope with her?

I assume the indignant rôle.

28

"Mr. Fisher!" I cry, much hurt at this want of confidence.

"Who is this gentleman?" asks Mrs. Fisher, looking at me, I think, with a not altogether disapproving glance.

"Ask him," says Fisher.

"Madame," I say, with a bow, "I am an unfortunate stranger, come to pay my respects to Mr. Fisher and his beautiful lady. I wish you could explain my reception."

"What is your name?" says Mrs. Fisher, with comparative graciousness, considering that she is a bourgeois Englishwoman taken by surprise, and fearing both to be cold to a possible man of position and to be friendly with a possible nobody.

A name I must have, and I must also invent it at once, and it must be something both Scotch and Italian. I take the first two that come into my head.

"Dugald Cellarini," I reply.

They look at one another dubiously. I must put them at their ease at any cost.

"A fine picture," I say, indicating the portrait of my host, "and an excellent likeness. Do you not think so, Mrs. Fisher?"

She looks at me as if she had a new thought.

"Are you a friend of the artist?" she asks.

"An intimate," I reply with alacrity.

"We have informed Mr. Benzine that we specially desired him not to bring any more of his

Bohemian acquaintances to our house," says the amiable lady.

I am plunging deeper into the morass! Still, I have at last accounted for my presence.

"Mr. Benzine did not warn me of this, madame," I reply, coldly. "I apologize and I withdraw."

I make a step towards the door, but the large form of Fisher still intervenes.

"Then Benzine sent you?" he says.

"He did, though evidently under a misapprehension."

"And what about Smith?" asks Fisher, with an approach to intelligence in his bovine eye.

"Well, what about him?" I ask, defiantly.

"Did he send you, too?"

"My reception has been such that I decline to give any further explanations."

"That is all very well," says Fisher—"that is all very well—"

He is evidently cogitating what is all very well, when we hear heavy steps in the passage.

"They have come at last!" he exclaims, and opens the door.

"More visitors!" I say to myself, hoping now for a diversion. In another moment I get it. Enter the butler and two gigantic policemen.

Chapter IV

"'Let me out,' said the mouse, 'I do not care for this cheese.'"
—FABLES OF LAETERTIUS.

ICTURE now this comedy and its actors. Fisher of the porpoise habit, Mrs. Fisher of the puffy cheek, poor Dugald Cellarini, and these two vast, blue-coated, thief-catching "bobbies" (as with kindly humor the English term their police); all save Dugald looking terribly solemn and important. He, poor man, strove hard to give the affair a lighter turn, but what is one artist in a herd of Philistines? I was not appreciated; that is the truth. A man may defy an empire, a papal bull, an infectious disease, but a prejudice—never!

"Constable," says Fisher, "I have caught him."

Both bobbies look at me with much the same depressing glance as Fisher himself.

"Yes, sir," says one, in what evidently was intended for a tone of congratulation. "So I see."

The other bobby evidently agrees with this sentiment. Wonderful unanimity! I have noticed it in the Paris gendarmes also, the same quick and intelligent grasp of a situation.

The latter quality was so conspicuous in my two blue-coated friends that I named them instantly Lecoq and Holmes.

Holmes speaks next, after an impressive pause.

"What's he done?"

"That is the point," says Fisher, in a tone of such damaging insinuation that I am spurred to my defence.

"Exactly—what have I done?"

"He has endeavored to effect an entry into my house by removing a pane of glass," says Fisher.

"Pardon me; to call the attention of the servants by rapping upon a pane of glass."

"Come now, none of that!" says Lecoq, with such severity that I see the situation at once. He is jealous. I have cast an imputation on some fair housemaid—the future Mrs. Lecoq, no doubt.

"An assignation, you think?" I ask, with a reassuring smile.

"Sir!" cries Mrs. Fisher, indignantly. "It was my daughter's window you broke!"

Shall I pose as the lover of Miss Fisher? I have heard that unmarried English girls take strange liberties.

"Your fair daughter—" I begin.

"Is a child of fifteen," interrupts virtuous Mrs.

Fisher, "and I am certain knows nothing of this person."

By the expression of their intelligent countenances, Holmes and Lecoq show their concurrence in this opinion.

"Confront her with me!" I demand, folding my arms defiantly.

It has since struck me that this was a happy inspiration, and in the right dramatic key. Unfortunately, it requires an imaginative audience, and I had two Fishers and two bobbies.

Rapidly I had calculated what would happen. The fair and innocent maiden should be aroused from her virgin slumbers; with dishevelled locks, and in a long, loose, and becoming drapery of some soft color (light blue to harmonize with her flaxen hair, for instance), she should be led into this chamber of the inquisition; then my eye should moisten, my voice be as the lute of Apollo, and it would be a thousand francs to a dishonored check that I should melt her into some soft confession. Not that I should ask her to compromise her reputation to save me. Never, on my honor, would I permit that. Indeed, if my plight tempted her to invent a story she might repent of afterwards, I should disavow it with so sincere and honest an air that my captors would exclaim together, "We have misjudged him!"

No, I should merely persuade her to confess that a not ill-looking foreigner had pursued her with glances of chivalrous admiration for some days past, and that from his air of hopeless passion it was not surprising to find him to-night tapping upon her window-pane.

Alas, that so promising a scheme should fail through the incurable poverty of the Fisher spirit! My demand is simply ignored.

"What acquaintance have you with my daughter?" asks Mrs. Fisher, icily.

"You will respect my confidence?" I ask, earnestly.

"We shall use our discretion," replies the virtuous lady.

"Quite so; we shall use our discretion," repeats her unspeakable husband.

"I am satisfied with your assurance," I say. "The discretion of a Fisher is equivalent to the seal of the confessional. I thank you from my heart, and I bow to your judgment."

"What do you know of my daughter?" Mrs. Fisher repeats, quite unmoved by my candor.

"Madame, I was about to tell you. You asked if I was acquainted with that charming, and, I can assure you on my honor, spotless young lady?"

"I did," says Mrs. Fisher; "but I do not require any remarks on her character from you, sir."

"Pardon me; they escaped me inadvertently What I feel deeply I am tempted to say. I do not know Miss Fisher personally. I have not yet ventured to address a word to her, not so much as a

34

syllable, not even a whisper. My respect for her innocence, for her youth, for her parents, has been too great. But this I confess: I have for days, for weeks, for months, followed her loved figure with the eye of chaste devotion! On her walks abroad I have been her silent, frequently her unseen, attendant. Through every street in London I have followed the divine Miss Fisher, as a sailor the polar star! To-night, in a moment of madness, I approached her home; I touched her window that I might afterwards kiss the hand that had come so near her! In my passion I touched too hard, the pane broke, and here I stand before you!"

So completely had I been carried away on the wings of my own fancy that once or twice in the course of this outburst I had committed myself to more than I had any intention of avowing. Be emphatic but never definite, is my counsel to the liar. But I had, unluckily, tied myself to my inventions. The gestures, the intonation, the key of sentiment were beyond criticism; but then I was addressing Mr. and Mrs. Fisher, of Chickawungaree Villa.

They glance at one another, and Lecoq glances at them.

He, honest man, merely touches his head significantly and winks in my direction. The Fishers are not, however, content with this charitable criticism.

"My daughter only returned from her seminary in Switzerland four days ago," says Mrs. Fisher.

"And she has never visited the streets of London except in Mrs. Fisher's company," adds her spouse, with a look of what is either dull hatred or impending apoplexy.

Even at that crisis my wits did not desert me.

"My faith!" I cry, "I must be mistaken! It is not, then, Miss Fisher whom I worship! A thousand pardons, sir, and I beg of you to convey them to the lady whom I disturbed under a misapprehension!"

At this there is a pause, nobody volunteering to run with this message to the bedside of Miss Fisher, though I glance pointedly at Holmes, and even make the money in my pocket jingle. At last comes a sound of stifled air trying to force a passage through something dense. It proceeds, I notice, from my friend Fisher. Then it becomes a more articulate though scarcely less disagreeable noise.

"I do not believe a word you say, sir!" he booms.

"My friend, you are an agnostic," I reply, with a smile.

Fisher only breathes with more apparent difficulty than ever. He is evidently going to deal a heavy blow this time. It falls.

"I charge this person with being concerned in the burglary at Mrs. Thompson's house last night, and with trying to burgle mine," says he.

He pauses, and then delivers another:

"He has confessed to being an Italian."

The constables prick up their ears.

"The organ - grinder!" exclaims Holmes, with more excitement than I had thought him capable of.

"The man as made the butler drunk and gagged the cook!" cries Lecoq.

Here is a fine situation for a political fugitive! I am indignant. I am pathetic. No use. I explain frankly that I came to see Mr. Hankey. That only deepens suspicion, for it seems that the excellent Hankey inhabited Mount Olympus House next door for only three weeks, and departed a month ago without either paying his rent or explaining the odor of dead bodies proceeding from his cellars. Doubtless my French friends had acted for the best in sending me to him, but would that he had taken the trouble to inform them of his change of address! And then, why had I ever thought of being an Italian? It appeared now that a gentleman of that nationality, having won the confidence of the Thompson children and the Thompson servants by his skill upon the hand-organ, had basely misused it in the fashion indicated by Lecoq. Certainly it was hard to see why such a skilled artist should have returned the very next night to a house three doors away, and then bungled his business so shamefully; but that argument is beyond the imagination of my bobbies. In fact, they seem only too pleased to find a thief so ready to meet them half-way.

"Thank you, sir," says Holmes, at the conclusion of the painful scene. "We shouldn't mind a drop."

This means that they are about to be rewarded for their share in the capture by a glass of Fisher's ale. And I? Well, I am not to have any ale, but I am to accompany them to the cells, and next morning make my appearance before the magistrate on one charge of burglary and another of attempted burglary.

I cannot resist one parting shot at my late host.

"Yes, Fisher," I remark, critically, showing no hurry to leave the room, "I like that portrait of you. It has all your plain, well-fed, plum-pudding appearance, without your unpleasant manner of breathing and your ridiculous conversation—and it is not married to Mrs. Fisher."

To this there is no reply. Indeed, I do not think they recovered their senses for at least ten minutes after I left the room.

Chapter V

" The comedy of the law is probably the chief diversion of the angels."
—LA RABIDE.

OVER the rest of that night I shall draw a veil. I was taken to Newgate, immured in the condemned cell, and left to my reflections. They were sombre enough, I assure you. Young, ambitious, ardent, I sat there in that foreign prison, without a friend, without a hope. If I state the truth about myself, this excuse will be seized for sending me back to France. And what then? Another prison! If I keep my identity concealed, how shall I prove that I am not the burgling musician?

As you can well imagine, I slept little and dreamed much. I was only thankful I had no parents to mourn my loss, for by this time I had quite made up my mind that the organ-grinder's antecedents would certainly hang me.

39

I cursed Fisher, I cursed the League, I cursed F. 11, that indefatigable conspirator who had dragged me from a comfortable hotel and a safe alias to—what? The scaffold; ah, yes, the scaffold!

It may sound amusing now, when I am still unhanged; but it was far from amusing then, I assure you.

Well, the morning broke at last, and I was led, strongly escorted by the twins Lecoq and Holmes, towards the venerable law-court at Westminster. I recognized the judge, the jury, the witnesses, and the counsel, though my thoughts were too engrossed to take a careful note of these. In fact, in writing this account I am to some extent dependent on reports of other trials. They are all much the same, I understand, differing chiefly as one or more judges sit upon the bench.

In this case there was only one, a little gentleman with a shrewd eye and a dry voice—a typical hanging judge, I said to myself. I prepared for the worst.

First comes the formal accusation. I, giving the name of Dugald Cellarini, am a blood-thirsty burglar. Such, in brief, is the charge, although its deadly significance is partly obscured by the discreet phraseology of the law.

Then my friend Holmes enters the box, stiff and evidently nervous, and in a halting voice and incoherent manner (which in France would inevitably have led to his being placed in the dock himself) he describes the clever way I was caught by himself and the astute Lecoq. So misleading is his account of my guilty demeanor and suspicious conduct, that I instantly resolve to cross-examine him. Politely but firmly I request the judge's permission. It is granted, and I can see there is a stir of excitement in the court.

"Did I struggle with you?" I ask.

Holmes; turning redder than ever, admits that I did not.

"Did I knock you down? Did I seek to escape?"

No, Holmes was not knocked down, nor had I tried to escape from the representatives of the law.

"And why, if I was a burglar, did I not do these things?"

"You wasn't big enough," says Holmes.

Well, I admit he had the advantage of me there. The court, prejudiced against me as they were, laughed with Holmes, but at the next bout I returned his lunge with interest.

"What did Fisher give you to drink?" I ask.

The question is dismissed by my vindictive judge as irrelevant, but I have thrown Holmes into great confusion and made the court smile with me.

"That is all," I say, in the tone of a conqueror, and thereupon Lecoq takes the place of Holmes, and in precisely the same manner, and with the same criminal look of abasement, repeats almost exactly the same words.

Against him I design a different line of counter-attack. I remember his jealousy when I spoke of the servants, and, if possible, I shall discredit his testimony by an assault upon his character. Assuming an encouraging air, I ask:

"You know the servants at Fisher's house?"

He stammers, "Yes."

"With one in particular you are well acquainted?"

He looks at the judge for protection, but so little is my line of attack suspected that the judge only gazes at us in rapt attention.

"I do," says Lecoq, after a horribly incriminating pause.

"Now tell me this," I demand, sternly. "Have you always behaved towards her as an honorable policeman?"

Would you believe it? This question also is disallowed! But I think I have damaged Lecoq all the same.

Next comes Fisher, red-faced, more pompous than ever, and inspired, I can see, with vindictive hatred towards myself. It appears that he is a London merchant; that his daughter heard a tapping on her window and called her father; that he and his servant caught me in the act of entering the chaste bedchamber through a broken window.

At this point I ask if I may put a question. The judge says yes.

"How much glass fell out?" I ask.

"Half a pane," says he.

"And the rest stayed in?"

He has to admit that it did; very ungraciously, however.

"How many panes to the window?"

He cannot answer this; but the judge, much to my surprise, comes to the rescue and elicits the fact that there are six.

"How far had I gone through a twelfth of your window?" I ask.

His face gets redder, and there is a laugh through the court. I feel that I have "scored a try," as they say, and my spirits begin to rise again.

But, alas! they are soon damped. Mrs. Thompson's butler steps into the witness-box, and a more shameless liar I have never heard. Yes, he remembers an organ-grinder coming to the house on various occasions during the past fortnight. Here I interpose.

"What did he play?" I ask.

"Not being interested in such kinds of music, I cannot say."

"Possibly you have a poor ear?" I suggest.

"My ear is as right as some people's, but it has not been accustomed to the hand-organ," says the butler, with a magnificence that seems to impress even the judge.

43

"You should have it boxed, my friend," I cannot help retorting, though I fear this does not meet the unqualified approval of the judge.

Next he is asked for an account of his dealings with the musician when that gentleman visited the kitchen upon the night of the burglary, and it appears that, shortly after the grinder's departure, he lost consciousness with a completeness and rapidity that can only have been caused by some insidious drug surreptitiously introduced into the glass of beer he happened to be finishing at that moment. He scorns the insinuation (made by myself) that he and the musician were drinking together; he would not so far demean himself. That outcast did, however, on one occasion, approach suspiciously near his half-empty glass.

"Well," I remark, with a smile, "the moral is that next time you should provide your guests with glasses of their own."

Again I score, but quickly he has his revenge. Does he recognize me as the organ-grinder? he is asked. He is not sure of the face, not taking particular notice of persons of that description, but— he is ready to swear to my voice!

It seems, then, that I have the same accent as an Italian organ-grinder! I bow ironically, but the sarcasm, I fear, is lost.

"What is so distinctive about this voice I share with your Italian boon companion?" I inquire, suavely.

He evidently dislikes the innuendo, but, in the presence of so many of his betters, decides to retaliate only by counter-sarcasm. "It's what I call an unedicated voice," says he.

"Uneducated Italian or uneducated English?" I inquire.

"Italian," he replies, with the most consummate assurance.

"You know Italian?"

"Having travelled in Italy, I am not altogether unfamiliar," he answers.

I then put to him a simple Italian sentence.

"What does that mean, and is it educated or uneducated?" I ask.

"It means something that I should not care for his lordship to hear, and is the remark of a thoroughly uneducated person," he retorts.

The court roars, and some even cheer the witness. For myself, I am compelled to join the laughter—the impudence is so colossal.

"My lord," I say to the judge, "this distinguished scholar has so delicate a mind that I should only scandalize him by asking further questions."

So the butler retires with such an air of self-satisfaction that I could have shot him, and the gagged cook takes his place.

This young woman is not ill-looking, and is very abashed at having to make this public appearance. It appears that her glimpse of the burglar was brief, as with commendable prudence he rapidly fastened her night-shift over her head, but in that glimpse she recognized my mustache!

"Could she tell how it felt?" I ask.

The point is appreciated by the court, though not, I fear, by the judge, who looks at me as though calculating the drop he should allow. Yes, it is all very well to jest about my mustache, but to be hanged by it, that is a different affair. And the case is very black against me.

"Has the prisoner any witnesses to call?" asks the judge.

"No," I reply, "but I shall make you a speech."

And thereupon I delight them with the following oration, an oration which should have gone on much longer than it did but for a most unforeseen interruption.

"My lord, the jury, and my peers," I begin—remembering so much from my historical stories—"I am entirely guiltless of this extraordinary and infamous charge. No one but such a man as Fisher would have brought it!" [Here I point my finger at the unhappy tenant of Chickawungaree.] "No one else of the brave English would have stooped to injure an innocent and defenceless stranger! As to the butler and the cook, you have seen their untruthful faces, you have heard their incredible testimony. I say no more regarding them. The policemen have only shown that they found me an unwilling and insulted—though invited—guest of the perfidious Fisher. What harm,

then? Have you never been the unwilling guests
of a distasteful host?

"Who am I? Why did I visit such a person as
Fisher? I shall tell you. I am a French subject,
a traveller in England. Only yesterday I arrived in
London. How can I, then, have burgled Madame
Thompson? Impossible! Absurd! I had not set
my foot upon the shores of England—"

At this point the judge, in his dry voice, interrupts me to ask if I can bring any witnesses to
prove this assertion.

"Witnesses?" I exclaim, not knowing what the
devil to add to this dramatic cry, when, behold!
I see, sent by Providence, a young man rising from
his seat in the court. It is my fair-haired fellow-
passenger!

"May I give evidence?" says he.

"Though your name be Iscariot, yes!" I cry.

The judge frowns, for it seems the demand was
addressed to him and not to me; but he permits
my acquaintance to enter the box. And now a
doubt assails me. What will he say? Add still
more damaging testimony, or prove that I am
the harmless Bunyan?

He does neither, but in a very composed and
assured fashion, that carries conviction with it,
he tells the judge that he travelled with me from
Paris on the very night of the crime, adding that I
had appeared to him a very harmless though somewhat eccentric person. Not the adjectives I should

have chosen myself, perhaps; but, I assure you, I should have let him call me vulgar or dirty without a word of protest.

Of course it follows that I cannot be the musical burglar, while as for my friend Fisher, that worthy gentleman is so disconcerted at the turn things have taken that he seems as anxious to withdraw his share of the charge as he was to make it.

I am saved; the case breaks down.

"How's that?" says the judge.

"Guiltless!" cries the jury.

And so I am a free man once more, and the cook must swear to another mustache.

The first thing I do is to seize my witness and drag him from the court, repeating my thanks all the while.

"But how did you come to be in court?" I ask.

"Oh, I happen to be a barrister," he explains. "I came in about another case, and, finding you'd been burgling, I thought I'd stay and see the fun."

"Your case must take care of itself; come and lunch with me."

Yes, he can escape. His case will not come on to-day, as mine has taken so long; and so we go forth together to begin a friendship that I trust may always endure.

And to this day I have never paid for Fisher's broken pane of glass.

Chapter VI

" On earth men style him 'Richard,'
But the gods hail him 'Dick !'"
—AN ENGLISH POET (ADAPTED).

" *A* FRIEND in need," say the English, "is a friend indeed." And who could be more in need of a friend than I at that moment? It was like the rolling up of London fog-banks and the smile of the sun peeping through at last. No longer was I quite alone in my exile. If you have ever wandered solitary through an unknown city, listened to a foreign tongue and to none other, eaten alien viands, fallen into strange misadventures, and all without a single friendly ear to confide your troubles to, you will sympathize with the joyous swelling of my heart as I faced my barrister at that luncheon.

And he, I assure you, was a very other person from the indifferent Englishman of the journey. The good heart was showing through, still ob-

scured as it was by the self-contained manner and
the remnants of that suspicion with which every
Briton is taught to regard the insinuating European.

I have already given you a sketch of his exterior
—the smooth, fair hair, the ruddy cheek, the clear
eye, and, I should add, the compressed and resolute
mouth; also, not least, the admirable fit of his garments. Now I can fill in the picture: Name, to
begin with, Richard Shafthead; younger son of
honest, conservative baronet; eldest brother provided with an income, I gather, Dick with injunc-
tions to earn one. Hence attendance at courts
of justice, a respectable gravity of apparel, and
that compression of the lips. In speech, courteous
upon a slight acquaintance, though without any
excessive anxiety to please; on greater intimacy,
very much to the point without regarding much
the susceptibilities of his audience. Yet this blunt-
ness was, tempered always by good - fellowship,
and sometimes by a smile; and beneath it flowed,
deep down, and scarcely ever bubbling into the
light of day, a stream of sentiment that linked him
with the poetry of his race. My friend Shafthead
would have laughed outright had you told him
this. Nevertheless this secret is the skeleton in
the respectable English cupboard. Your John
Bull is an edifice of sentiment jealously covered
by a hoarding on which are displayed advertise-
ments of pills and other practical commodities. It

is his one fear lest any one should discover this preposterous and hideous erection is not the real building.

Dick's only comment on the above statement would probably be that I had mixed my metaphors or had exceeded at lunch. But he is shrewd enough to know in his heart that I have but spoken the truth, even though my metaphors were as heterogeneous as the ark of Noah. How else can you explain the astonishing contrast between those who write the songs of England and those whose industry enables them to recompense the singers?

No doubt there is a noticeable difference between the poet and the people in every land and every race, but in England it is so staggering. The hair of the English poet is so very long, his eye so very frenzied, his voice so steeped in emotion, so buoyed by melody. Even his prose appeals to the heart rather than to the head. Thackeray weeps as he writes of good women; Scott blushes as he writes of bad. No one is cynical but the villains. The heroines are all pure as the best cocoa.

Then look at the check suits and the stony eyes of Mr. Cook's protégées. Do they understand what Tennyson has written for them? If not, why do they pay for it?

John Bull and John Milton; William Bull and William Shakespeare; Lord Bull and Lord Byron; Charles Bull and Charles Dickens; how are these couples related? By this religious, moral, sentimental stream; welling in one, hidden in another under ten tons of shyness and roast beef; a torrent here, a trickle there, sometimes almost dry in a dusty season. That is how.

Does Dick again recommend teetotalism as a cure for these speculations? Come with me to your rooms, my friend, and let us glance through your library.

I take up a volume of Shakespeare and find it contains the sonnets.

"Ah, Shakespeare's sonnets," I say, with an air of patronage towards that eminent poet. "You know them?"

"Used to know 'em a little." He is giving me another taste of that characteristic British stare. Evidently he is offended by my tone, and will fall an easy victim to my next move.

"They are much overrated," I say, putting the book away.

"You should write to the *Times* about it," he replies, sarcastically, and then adds, with conviction, "They are about the finest things in English."

"Yet no Englishman reads them," I remark, lightly.

"I used to know half a dozen of 'em by heart," he retorts.

Half a dozen of those miracles of sensuous diction off by heart! Prosaic Briton! I do not say this aloud, but take next the songs of Kipling, and profess not to understand one of them. To convince me it is not mere nonsense, he reads and expounds.

He has been round the world, and shot wild beasts on the veldt and in the jungle, and can explain allusions and share exotic sentiments.

Is this man mere plum-pudding and international perfidy, who feels thus the glamour of the song?

"Ah, here is a novel of Zola!" I exclaim. "You enjoy him, of course?"

"A filthy brute," says Dick. "I read half of that, and I am keeping it now for shaving-papers."

There is perhaps more strength of conviction than critical judgment in this comment. I might retort that all the water in the world neither has been passed through a filter nor foams over a fall, and that the pond and the gutter have their purpose in the world. I do not make this reply, however; I merely note that a strong sentiment must underlie a strong prejudice.

As you will perhaps have gathered, my good Dick had his limitations. He could be sympathetic; if, for instance, he were to see me insulted, beaten, robbed of my purse and my mistress, and blinded in one eye, he would, I am sure, feel for me deeply, and show himself most tactful in his consolation. But it would require some such well-marked instance to open the gates of his heart; and in minor matters I should not dream of applying to him, unless, indeed, it was a practical service he could perform.

He himself had held his peace and confided in no one when his fair cousin married the wealthy manufacturer of soda-water, and his heart had long since healed. In the days of his wild oats, when duns were knocking at his door, he had retired from St. James Street to a modest apartment in the Temple, sold such of his effects as were marketable, and philosophically sought a cheap restaurant and a coarser tobacco. His debts were now paid and all was well again. When he did not get the degree he was expected to at Oxford, he may have said " damn," but I doubt if he enlarged on this observation. What did that disappointment matter to-day? Then why should other people make a fuss if they were hurt?

Yet his heart was as a child's if you could extract it from its wrappings of tin-foil and brown paper, and I am happy I knew him long enough to see him "play the fool," as he would term it.

On that first afternoon of our acquaintance I found him courteous before lunch, genial after (I took care to "make him proud," as the English say). I was perfectly frank; told him my true name, the plot that had miscarried, my flight to England—everything.

"I am not Bunyan, I am not even Cellarini, but merely Augustine d'Haricot, eternally at your service," I said. "You have saved me from prison, perhaps from the scaffold."

He laughed.

"It wouldn't have been as bad as that, but I'm glad to have been of any use."

And then changing the subject, as an Englishman does when complimented (for they hold that either you lie and are a knave, or tell the truth and are a fool), he asked:

"What are you going to do now?"

"That depends upon your advice," I replied. "What is my danger? How wise is it to move freely in this country?"

"There is no danger at all if it is only a political offence," he answered. "Unless you've been picking pockets, or anything else as well."

I answered him I had not, and he promised to inquire into the case and give me a full assurance on the next morning.

"And now," I said, "tell me, my friend, how to live as an Englishman. I do not mean to adopt the English mind, the English sentiment, but only to move in your world, so long as I must live in it. I want to see, I want to hear, I want to record my impressions and my adventures. As the time is not ripe to wield the sword, I shall wield the eyes and the pen. Also, I shall doubtless fall in love, and I should like to hunt a fox and shoot a pheasant."

We laughed together at this programme; in brief, we made a good beginning.

That afternoon we set out together to look for suitable apartments for myself, and by a happy chance we had hardly gone a hundred paces before we spied a gentleman approaching us whom Shafthead declared to be a veritable authority on London life; also a cousin of his own.

"But will he not be busy?" I inquired.

"Young devil," answered Shafthead, "it will serve to keep him out of mischief for an hour or two."

Thereupon I was presented to Mr. Teddy Lumme, a young gentleman of small stature, with a small, cheerful, clean-shaven, dark face, and a large hat that sloped backward and sideways towards a large collar. His elbows moved as though he were driving a cab; his boots shone brightly enough to serve for mirrors; his morning-coat was cut in imitation of the "pink" of a huntsman; a large mass of variegated silk was fastened beneath his collar by a neat pearl pin; in a word, he belonged to a type that is universal, yet this specimen was unmistakably English. In age I learned afterwards that he was just twenty-five, emancipated for little more than a year from the University of Oxford, and still enjoying the relief from the rigorous rules of that institution. No accusation of reticence to be made against Mr. Lumme! He talked all the time, cheerfully and artlessly.

"You want rooms?" he said. "Quelle chose? I mean, don't you know, what kind? I don't know much French, I'm afraid. Oh, you talk English?

Devilish glad to hear it. I say, Dick, you remember that girl I told you of? Well, it's just as I said. I knew, damn it all. What do you want to give?" (This to me.) "You don't care much? That simplifies matters."

In this strain Mr. Lumme entertained us on our way, Shafthead regarding him with a half-amused, half-sardonic grin, of which his relative seemed entirely oblivious, while I enjoyed myself amazingly. I felt like Captain Cook on the gallant *Marchand* palavering with the chiefs of some equatorial state.

"I demand a cold bath and an English servant," I said. "Anything else characteristic you can add, but those are essential."

I do not know whether Lumme quite understood this to be a jest. He took me to three sets of apartments, and at each asked first to be shown the bathroom, and then the servant, after which he inquired the price, and whether a tenant was at liberty to introduce any guest at any hour.

a cold bath and an English servant...

Finally, to end the story of that day, which began in jail and ended so merrily, I found myself the tenant of a highly comfortable set of apartments, with everything but the valet supplied at an astonishingly high price.

"However," I said to myself, "it may be expensive, but it is better than ten years' transportation for burgling Fisher!"

Chapter VII

*" Little, cheerful, and honest—do you not
know the species?"*
—KOVALEFFSKI.

HAD left my hotel and settled in my apartments; the labels with "Nelson Bunyan" were removed from my luggage; I had been assured that so long as I remained on English soil I was safe. Next thing I must find a servant; one who should "know the ropes" of an English life. Lumme had promised to make inquiries for me, and I had impressed upon him that the following things were essential—in fact, I declared that without them I should never entertain an application for one instant. First, he must be of such an appearance as would do me credit, whether equipped in the livery I had already designed for him, in the cast-off suits I should provide him with, or in the guise of an attendant at the chase or upon the moors. Then, that he must be honest enough to trust in the room with a handful of mixed change, sober enough to leave alone with a decanter, discerning enough to arrange an odd lot of sixteen boots into eight pairs, cleanly enough to pack collars without soiling them. Finally, he must be polite, obliging, industrious, discreet, and, if possible, a little religious—not sufficiently so to criticise my conduct, but enough to regulate his own.

I wrote this list down and handed it to the obliging Teddy.

"You will procure him by this afternoon?" I said.

"I know a man who keeps a Methodist footman in his separate establishment," answered Lumme, after a moment's reflection. "That's the kind of article you require, I suppose. If you get 'em too moral there's apt to be a screw loose somewhere, and if you get 'em the other way the spoons go. Well, I can't promise, but I'll do my best."

So this amiable young man departed, and I, to pass the time, walked into Piccadilly, and there took my seat once more upon the top of an omnibus to enjoy the sunshine, and be for a time a spectator of the life in the streets. To obtain a better view I sat down on the front bench close to the driver's elbow, and we had not gone very far before this individual turned to me and remarked with a cordiality that pleased me infinitely, and a perspicacity that astonished me:

"Been long in London, sir?"

"You perceive that I am a stranger, then?" I asked.

"Well," said the man, as he cracked his whip and drove his lumbering coach straight at an orifice between two cabs just wide enough, it seemed to me, for a wheelbarrow, "I'm a observer, I am. When I sees that speckled tie droopin' from a collar of unknown horigin, and them rum kind of boots, I says to myself a Rooshian, for 'alf a sovereign. Come from Rooshia, sir?"

The man's naïveté delighted me.

"I belong to an allied power," I replied, wondering if his powers of observation would enable him to decide my nationality now.

He seemed to debate the question as, with an apropos greeting to each cabman, his 'bus bumped them to the side and sailed down the middle of the street.

"Native o' Manchuria, perhaps?" he hazarded.

"Not quite; try again."

"Siberia?" he suggested next.

Seeing that either his imagination or my appearance confined his speculations to Asia, I told him forthwith that I was French.

"French?" he said. "Well, now I'm surprised to 'ear it, sir. If you'll excuse me saying so, you don't look like no Frenchman."

"Why not?" I asked.

"I always thought they was little chaps, no

bigger than a monkey. Why, you're quite as tall as most Englishmen."

Considering that my friend could not possibly have measured more than five feet, two inches, and that I am five feet, nine inches, in my socks, I was highly diverted by this.

" Have you seen many Frenchmen?" I asked him.

"I knew one once," he replied, after a minute or two's thought, and a brief interruption to invite some ladies on the pavement to enter his 'bus. "'E was a waiter at the Bull's 'Ead, 'Ighbury. I drove a 'bus that way then, and there was a young lady served in the bar 'im and me was both sweet on. Nasty, greasy little man 'e was—meaning no reflection on you, sir. They couldn't make out where the fresh butter went, and when 'e left— which 'e 'ad to for kissing the missis when she wasn't 'erself, 'aving 'ad a drop more than 'er usual—do you know what they found, sir?"

I confessed my inability to guess this secret.

"Why, 'e'd put it all on 'is beastly 'air, two pounds a week, sir, of the very best fresh butter in 'Ighbury. Perhaps, sir, I've been prejudiced against Frenchmen in consequence."

I admitted that he had every excuse, and asked him whether my buttered compatriot had won the maiden's affections in addition to his other offences.

"No, sir," said he, "I'm 'appy to say she 'ad more sense. More sense than to take either of

62

us," he added, with a deep sigh, and then, as if to quench melancholy reflections, hailed another driver who was passing us in the most hilarious fashion.

" 'Old your 'at on, ole man!" he shouted. "Them opera-'ats is getting scarce, you know!"

The other driver, a bottle-nosed man, redeemed only from unusual shabbiness by the head - gear in question, winked, leered, and made some reply about "not 'aving such a fat head underneath it as some people."

" When she wasn't 'erself."

My friend turned to me with a confidential air.

"You saw that gentleman as I addressed?" he said, in an impressive voice. "Well, that man was driving 'is own kerridge not five years ago. On the Stock Exchange 'e was, and worth ten thousand a year if 'e was worth a penny; 'ouse in Park Lane, and married to the daughter of a baronite. 'E's told me all that 'isself, so it's true and no 'umbug.

" 'Ow did 'e lose 'is money? Hunfortunit speculations and consols goin' down; but you, being a furriner, won't likely understand."

Looking as unsophisticated as possible, I pressed

my friend for an explanation of these mysteries.

"Well," said he, "it's something like this: If you goes on the Stock Exchange you buys what they calls consols—that's stocks and shares of va-

"the very best fresh butter in 'Ighbury

rious sorts and kinds, but principally mines in Australia, and inventions for to make things different from what they is at present. That's what's called makin' a corner, which ain't a corner exactly in the usual sense—not as used in England, that's to say, but a kind o' American variety.

"What, O Bill! Bloomin', thank you. 'Ow's yourself?" (This to another driver passed upon the road.)

"As I was sayin', sir, this 'ere pore friend o' mine speculated in consols, and prices being what they calls up, and then shiftin', he loses and the bank wins. Inside o' twenty-four hours that there gentleman was changed from one of the richest men in the city into a pore cove a-looking out for a job like you and me."

"And he chose driving an omnibus?" I asked.

" 'Adn't got no choice. He was too much of a gentleman to sink to a ordinary perfession, and drivin' a pair o' 'orses seems to 'im more in keepin' with 'is position than drivin' one 'orse in a cab, which was the only thing left."

He paused, and then shaking his head with an air of sentiment, continued:

"Wunderful 'ow sensitive he is, sir. He wouldn't part with that there hopera-'at, not if you give him five 'undred pounds; yet he can't a-bear to 'ear it chipped, not except in a kind o' delicate way, same as I did just now. You 'eard me, sir? 'Hopera-'ats is scarce,' says I; but I dursn't sail closer to the wind nor that. 'E'd say, ' 'Old your jaw, Halfred,' or words to that effec', quick enough. Comes o' being bred too fine for the job, I tells 'im often; I says it to 'im straight, sir. 'Comes o' being bred too fine for the job,' says I."

At this point my friend's attention was called from the romantic history of his fellow-driver to the exigencies of their common profession, and I had an opportunity of studying more attentively this entertaining specimen of the cockney.

He was, as I have said, a very short man, from thirty to thirty-five years of age, I judged, red-cheeked and snub-nosed, with a bright, cheerful eye, and the most friendly and patronizing manner. Yet he was perfectly respectful and civil, despite his knowledge of my unfortunate nationality. In fact, it seemed his object to place me as far as possible at my ease, and enable me to forget for a space the blot upon my origin.

"There's some quite clever Frenchmen, I've 'eard tell," he said, presently. "That there 'idrophobia man — and Napoleon Bonyparty, in his way, too, I suppose, though we don't think so much of 'im over 'ere."

"I am sorry to hear that," I said.

"Well, sir," he explained, "we believes in a man 'aving his fair share of what's goin'. Like as if me and a friend goes inter a public 'ouse, and another gentleman he comes in and he says, 'What's it going to be this time?' or, 'Name your gargle, gents,' or words to some such effec'; and we says, 'Right you are, old man,' and 'as a drink at his expense. Now it wouldn't be fair if I says to the young lady, 'I'll 'ave a 'ole bottle of Scotch whiskey, miss, and what I can't drink I'll take 'ome in a noospaper,' and I leaves 'im to pay for all that; would it, sir? Well, that's what Bonyparty done; 'e tried to get more nor his share o' what was goin' in Europe. Not that it affec's us much, we being able to take care of ourselves, but we don't like to see it, sir. That's 'ow it is."

All this time we had been going eastward into the city of London, and now we were arrived at the most extraordinary scene of confusion you can possibly imagine. I should be afraid to say how many 'buses and cabs were struggling and surging in a small open space at the junction of several streets. Foot - passengers in hundreds bustled along the pavements or dodged between the horses, and, immobile in the midst of it, the inevitable policeman appeared actually to be sifting this mob according to some mysterious scheme.

"Cheer-O!" cried my friend upon the box. " 'Ow's the price o' lime-juice this morning?

"That there's wot we calls the Bank, sir, where the Queen keeps 'er money, and the Rothschilds and the like o' them; guarded by seven 'undred of the flower o' the British army, it is, the hofficer bein' hinvariably a millionaire hisself, in case he's tempted to steal. Garn yerself and git yer face syringed with a fire-'ose. You can't clean it no 'ow else. The 'andsome hedifice to your right, sir, is the Mansion 'Ouse; not the station of that name, but the 'ome of the Lord Mayor; kind o' governor of the city, 'e is; 'as a hextraordinary show of 'is own on taking the hoath of hoffice; people comes all the way from Halgiers and San Francisco to see it; camels and 'orses got up like chargers of the holden time, and men disguised so as their own girls wouldn't know 'em. Representing harts, hindustries, and hempire, that's their game. Pleeceman, them there bloomin' whiskers of yours will get mowed off by a four-wheel cab some day, and then 'ow'll you look? Too bloomin' funny, am I?

More'n them whiskers is, hinterfering with the traffic like that.

"Yes, sir, we 'as a rest 'ere for a few minutes; we ain't near at the end yet, though."

I shall leave it to your judgment to guess which of these remarks were addressed to me and which to various of his countrymen in this vortex of wheels and human beings. For a few minutes he now sat at ease in a quieter street (though, my faith! no street in this city of London but would

" then 'ow 'll you look ?"

seem busy in most towns), apparently deliberating what topic to enter upon next. I say apparently deliberating, but on further acquaintance with my good "Halfred," as he called himself (the aspirated form of "Alfred" used by the cockney; Alfred being the name of England's famous monarch), I came to the conclusion that his mind never was known to go through any such process. What came first into his head flew straight to his tongue, till by constant use that organ had got into a state of unstable equilibrium, like the tongue of a toy mandarin, that oscillates for five minutes if you move him ever so gently.

In a word, Halfred was an inveterate chatterbox.

Even had I been that very compatriot of mine who had so deeply, and, I could not but admit, so justly, roused his ire, he would, I am sure, have chattered just as hard.

By the time we were under way again and threading the eastern alleys of the city—for they are called streets only by courtesy—his tongue had started too, and he was talking just as hard as ever. Now, however, his conversation took a more reminiscent and a more personal turn, and this led to such sweeping consequences that I shall keep the last half of our journey together for a separate chapter.

Chapter VIII

"Your valet? Pardon; I thought he had come to measure the gas!"
—HERCULE D'ENVILLE.

O UT of the limits of this city of London we drove into the beginnings of the east. Not the Orient of the poet and the traveller, the land of the thousand - and - one nights, but the miles and miles of brick where some millions of Londoners pass an existence that ages me to think of. Picture to yourself a life more desolate of joys than the Arctic, more crowded with fellow-animals than any ant-heap, uglier than the Great Desert, as poor and as diseased as Job. Not even the wealthy there to gossip about and gape at, no great house to envy and admire, no glitter anywhere to distract, except in the music-halls of an evening. Yet they work on and do not hang themselves—poor devils!

But I grow serious where I had set out to be gay,

70

and thoughtful when you are asking for a somersault. Worse still, I am solemn, sitting at the elbow of my cheerful Halfred.

That genial driver of the omnibus was not one whit depressed upon coming into this region, nor, to tell the truth, was I that morning, for I could not see the backward parts, but only the wide main road, very airy after the lanes of the city, and crowded with quite a different population. No longer the business-man with shining hat, hands in pockets, quick step, and anxious face; no longer the well-dressed woman hurrying likewise through the throng; no longer the jingling hansom; but, instead, the compatriot of the prophets, the costermonger with his barrow, the residue of Hungary and Poland, the pipe of the British workman. Wains of hay in the midst of the road, drays and lorries, and an occasional omnibus jolting at the sides; to be sure there was life enough to look at.

As for my friend, his talk began to turn more upon his own private affairs. Apparently there was less around to catch his attention, and, as I have said, he had to talk, and so spoke of himself. As I sat on the top of that 'bus listening with continuous amusement to his candid reminiscences and naïve philosophy, I studied him more attentively than ever, for, as you shall presently hear, I had more reason. His dress, I noticed, was neat beyond the average of drivers; a coat of box - cloth, once light yellow, now of various shades, but still quite respectable; a felt hat with a flat top, glazed to throw off the rain; a colored scarf around his neck, whether concealing a collar or not I could not say; and something round his knees that might once have been a rug or a horse-cloth, or even a piece of carpet.

"Yus," said Halfred, meditatively, as he cracked his whip and urged his 'bus at headlong speed through a space in the traffic, "it's some rum changes o' luck I've 'ad in my day. My father he give me a surprisin' good eddication for a

— but my 'ead got swelled

hembyro 'bus-driver, meaning me to go into the stevedore business in Lime-'ouse basin, same as 'e was 'imself, but my 'ead got swelled a-talkin' to a most superior policeman what 'ad come down in the world, and nothing would satersfy me but mixin' in 'igh life. So our rector 'e gives me a introduction to a bloomin' aunt o' his in the country what wanted a boy in buttons, and into buttons I goes, and I says to myself, says I, 'Halfred, you're goin' to be a credit to your fam'ly, you are'; that's what I says. Blimy, I often larf now a-thinkin' of it!"

He paused to blow his nose in a primitive but effective fashion, and smiled gently to himself at these recollections of his youthful optimism.

"How long did you remain in these buttons?" I asked him.

"Till I outgrowed them," said Halfred.

"And after that?"

"I was servant to a gentleman what hadvertised for a honest young man, hexperience bein' no hobject."

I asked him how he liked that.

"I was comfertable enough; that I can't deny," said Halfred.

"And why, then, did you leave?"

"The heverlastin' reason w'y I does most foolish things, sir. My 'eart is too suscepterble, and the ladies'-maid was too captivatin'. She wouldn't 'ave nothin' to do with me, so I chucks the 'ole thing up, and, says I, 'I'll be hinderpendent, I will.' 'Ence I'm a-drivin' a 'bus."

"Are you happy now?" I inquired.

"Well," said he, candidly, "I couldn't say as I was exactly *'umped;* but it ain't all bottled beer sittin' in this bloomin' arm-chair with your whiskers froze stiff, and the 'orses' ears out o' sight in the fog. And there ain't much variety in it, nor much chance of becomin' a millionaire. Hoften and hoften I thinks to myself, 'What O for a pair o' trousers to fold, and a good fire in the servants' 'all, and hinderpendence be blowed!'"

I think it was at this moment that an inspiration came into my head. It was rash, you will doubtless say. It was certainly sudden, but then, as perhaps you have discovered ere now, I am not the most prudent of men. This little, cheerful Halfred had taken my fancy enormously, and my heart was warmed towards him.

O, for a pair of trousers to fold —

"Halfred," I asked, abruptly, "are you still an honest young man?"

"I 'ope so, sir," said he, with becoming modesty and evident surprise.

"And now you are experienced?"

"Well, sir," he said, "you've 'ad threepence worth o' this 'ere 'bus, and you 'aven't seed me scrape off no paint yet."

"But, I mean, you are experienced in folding trousers, in packing shirts, in varnishing boots, in all the niceties of your old profession, are you not? You would do credit to a gentleman if he should engage you?"

74

Halfred looked at me sharply, with a true cockney's suspicion of what he feared might be "chaff."

"You ain't a-pulling my leg, sir?" he inquired, guardedly.

"On the contrary, I am taking your hand as an honest and experienced valet, Halfred."

"You knows of a gentleman as wants one?" said he.

"I do," I answered, with conviction.

"It ain't yourself, sir?"

"It is," said I.

"Blimy!" exclaimed Halfred, in an audible aside.

"What about references?" said he.

"Oh, references; yes, I suppose you had better have some references," I replied, though, to tell the truth, I had not thought of them before.

He rubbed his chin with the back of his hand and screwed his rosy face into a deliberative expression, while his eyes twinkled cheerfully.

"I don't mind 'aving a go at the job," he remarked, after a couple of minutes' reflection.

"Apply this evening," I said. "Bring a reference if you have one, and I shall engage you, Halfred!"

For the rest of our journey together his gratitude and pleasure, his curiosity, and his qualms as to how much he remembered and how much he had forgotten of a man-servant's duties, de-

lighted me still further, and made me congratulate
myself upon my discrimination and judgment.

We parted company among the docks and ship-
ping of the very far east of London, and after
rambling for a time by the busy wharves and
breezy harbor basins, and, marvelling again at
the vastness and variety of this city, I mounted
another omnibus and drove back to my rooms.

"A man to see you, sir," said the maid.

Could it be Halfred, already? No, it was a very
different individual; a tall and stately man, with a
prim mouth and an eye of unfathomable discretion. He stood in an attitude denoting at once respect for me and esteem for himself, and followed
me to my room upon a gently creaking boot.

"Well," said I, at a loss to know whether he came
to collect a tax or induce me to order a coffin, "what
can I do for you?"

"Mr. Lumme, sir," said he, in a mincing voice,
"has informed me that you was requiring a man-
servant. Enclosed you will find Mr. Lumme's
recommendation."

He handed me a letter which ran as follows:

"DEAR MONSIEUR,—I have found the very man you
want. He was valet to Lord Pluckham for five years,
and could not have learned more from any one. Pluckham was very particular as to dress, and had many affairs requiring a discreet servant. He only left when
P. went bankrupt, and has had excellent experience
since. Been witness in two divorce cases, and is highly

76

recommended by all; also a primitive Wesleyan by religion, and well educated. You cannot find a better man in London, nor as good, I assure you. His name is John Mingle. Don't lose this chance. I have had some trouble, but am glad to have found the very article.

"Yours truly,

"EDWARD LUMME."

This was a pretty dilemma! The industrious and obliging Lumme had found one jewel, and in the meanwhile I had engaged another. I felt so ungrateful and guilty that I was ashamed to let my good Teddy discover what I had done. So instead of telling Mr. Mingle at once that the place was filled, I resolved to find him deficient in some important point, and decline to engage him on these grounds. Easier said than done.

"Your experience has been wide?" I asked, looking critical and feeling foolish.

"If I may say so, sir, it has," said he, glancing down modestly at the hat he held in his hands.

"You can iron a hat?" I inquired, casting round in my mind for some task too heavy for this Hercules.

He smiled with, I thought, a little pity.

"Oh, certingly, sir."

"Can you cook?"

"I have hitherto stayed at houses where separate cooks was kept," said he; "but if we should happen to be a-camping out in Norway, sir, there isn't nothing but French pastry I won't be happy to oblige with—on a occasion, that's to say, sir."

Not only were Mr. Mingle's accomplishments comprehensive, but he evidently looked upon himself as already engaged by me. Internally cursing his impudence, I asked next if he could sew.

"At a pinch, sir," said he. "That is," he added, correcting this vulgar expression, "if the maids is indisposed, or like as if we was on board your yacht, sir, and there was no hother alternative."

"We" again—and it seemed Mr. Mingle expected me to keep a yacht!

Could he load and clean a gun, saddle a horse, ride a bicycle, oil a motor-car, read a cipher, and manage a camera? Yes; in the absence of the various officials which "our" establishment maintained for these purposes, Mr. Mingle would be able and willing to oblige.

Moreover, he talked with a beautiful accent, and only very occasionally misused an aspirate; and there could be no doubt he would make an impressive appearance in any livery I could design. Even as a Pierrot he would have looked dignified. On what pretext could I reject this paragon?

"Can you drive an omnibus?" I demanded, at last, with a flash of genius.

This time Mr. Mingle looked fairly disconcerted.

"*Drive a homnibus!*" said he. "No, sir; my position and prospec's have always been such that

I am happy to say I have never had the opportunity of practising."

I shook my head.

"I am afraid," I said, "that you won't suit me,
Mingle. It is my
amusement to keep
a private omnibus."

"Oh, private," said
Mr. Mingle, as though
that might make a
difference.

But quickly I add-
ed:

"It is painted and
upholstered just like
the others. In fact,
I buy them second-
hand when beyond
repair. Also I take
poor people from the
work - house for a drive. And you must drive it
in all weathers."

Even
as a
Pierrot

.A.L.

That was the end of Mr. Mingle. In fact, I think
he was glad to find himself safely out of my room
again, and what he thought of my tastes, and
even of my sanity, I think I can guess.

That evening my friend Halfred appeared, bringing a testimonial to his honesty and sobriety from
the proprietor of the stables, and a brief line of
eulogy from the official who collected the pence

and supplied the tickets upon his own 'bus. This last certificate ran thus—I give it exactly as it stood:

" certtifieing alfred Winkes is 1 of The best obligging and You will find him kind to animils yours Sinseerly P. Widdup."

As Halfred explained to me, this was entirely unsolicited, and Mr. Widdup, he was sure, would feel hurt if he learned that it had not been presented.

"You can tell him," I said, "that it has secured the situation for you."

I had just told him that I should expect him to begin his duties upon the following morning, and he was inspecting my apartment with an air of great interest and satisfaction, when there came a knock upon the door, and in walked Mr. Teddy Lumme himself. He was in evening-dress, covered by the most recent design in top-coats and the most spotless of white scarfs. On his head he wore a large opera-hat, tilted at the same angle, and on his feet small and shiny boots.

"Hullo," said he. "Sorry; am I interrupting? Came to see if you'd booked Mingle. I suppose you have."

"A thousand thanks, my friend, for your trouble," I replied, with an earnestness proportionate to my feeling of compunction. "Mingle was, indeed, admirable — exquisite. In fact, he was perfect in every respect save one."

"What's that?" said Teddy, looking a little surprised.

"He could not drive an omnibus."

I am afraid my friend Teddy thought that I was joking. He certainly seemed to have difficulty in finding a reply to this. Then an explanation struck him.

"You mean what we call a coach," he suggested. "Thing with four horses and a toot-toot - toot business — post - horn, we call it. What?"

"I mean an omnibus," I replied. "The elegant, the fascinating, British 'bus. And here I have found a man who can drive me. This is my new servant, Halfred Winkles."

Lumme stared at him, as well he might, for my Halfred cut a very different figure from the grave, polished, quietly attired Mingle. To produce the very best impression possible, he had dressed himself in a suit of conspicuously checkered cloth, very tight in the leg and wide at the foot, and surmounted by a very bright-blue scarf tightly knotted round his neck. In his button-hole was an artificial tulip, in his pocket a wonderful red-and-yellow handkerchief. His ruddy face shone so brightly that I shrewdly suspected his friend Widdup had scrubbed it with a handful of straw, and he held in his hand, pressed against his breast, the same shining waterproof hat beneath which he drove the 'bus.

"Left your last place long?" asked Lumme, of this apparition.

"Gave 'em notice this arternoon, sir," said Halfred.

"Who were you with?"

"London General," replied Halfred.

"London General"

"A London general?" said Teddy. "Sounds all right. He gave you a good character, I suppose?"

"The very best," I interposed.

"Well," said Lumme, dubiously, "I hope you'll turn out all right, and do my friend, the monsieur here, credit."

As he turned to go he added to me, aside:

"Rum - looking chap, he seems to me. Keep an eye on him, I'd advise you. Personally, I'd have chosen Mingle, but o' course you know best. Good-night."

And I was left with the faithful Halfred.

Chapter *IX*

"I often envy the snail. Mon Dieu, think of always travelling beneath the comfortable roof of one's own house!"
—MAXIME ARGON.

ND now I must tell you something *A* about my rooms, the little ledge in London in which I rested, and flapped my wings and preened my feathers. The door of the house rented by Mr. and Mrs. Titch, and disposed of piece-meal to unmarried gentlemen, looked upon a very tiny square opening off a busy street. But my two chambers were at the back, and from their windows I saw nothing of square or street, or any house at all. The green Hyde Park with its trees and grass, and the wide drive where carriages and people aired themselves and lingered, that was what I saw; and often I could fancy myself in the woods and the gardens about a certain house in another land, and then I would shut my eyes and let the picture grow and grow, till I could hear known voices and look upon old faces that perhaps I should never again hear or see in any other fashion. Yes, the exile may be very gay, and jingle the foreign coins in his pocket, and whistle the airs of alien songs, and afterwards write humorously of his adventures; but there are many moments when he and the canary in the cage are very near together.

For myself, I am best, my friends say, when I am laughing at the world and playing somewhat the buffoon. And, of course, I am naturally anxious to appear at my best. Besides, I must confess that I do not think this world is an affair to be treated with a too great gravity; not, at least, if one can help it. Frequently it makes itself ridiculous even in the partial eyes of its own inhabitants. How much more frequently if one could sit outside— upon a passing shower, for instance—and see it as we look upon a play? Ten to one, some of our most sententious friends would seem no different from those amusing sparrows discussing the law of property in a bread-crumb, or from my dog playing the solemn comedy of the buried bone. Therefore I always think it safer to assume that there is some unseen cynic, some creature in the fourth dimension, looking over my shoulder as I write, and exclaiming, when I grow too sensible, "Oh, the wise fool!"

Yet for all this excellent philosophy, and in spite of a most reasonable desire to say those things that are instantly rewarded by a smile, rather than those an audience receives in silence, and perhaps approves, perhaps condemns—despite all this, the rubbing of the world upon a set of nerves does not always make one merry ; and in that humor I should sometimes like to perpetrate a serious sentence. If ever I succumb to this temptation of the writer's devil, please turn the page and do not linger over the indiscretion.

Therefore I shall pass quickly over the thin ice of sentiment, the days when I felt lonely on my comfortable ledge, the hours I spent looking at the fire. More amusing to tell you of the bright lining to my clouds; of the sitting-room, for instance, low in the ceiling, commodious, and shaped, I think, to fit the chimneys or the stairs or the water-butt outside; at any rate, to suit something that required two unequal recesses and three non - rectangular corners. It was on the ground-floor, and had two French windows (of which the adjective cheered me, I think, as much as the noun). These opened upon a little, stone-paved space, shaded by a high tree in the park, and which I called my garden.

Rejecting some articles of my landlord's furniture as too splendid for an untitled tenant—a plush-covered settee, for instance, and an alabaster tea-table, adorned with cut-glass trophies from the drawing-room of a bankrupt alderman—I replaced them by a bookcase, three easy-chairs, and an inviting sofa of my own; I bought substitutes for the engravings of "The Child's First Prayer" and "The Last Kiss," and the colored plates representing idyllic passages from the lives of honest artisans, which had regaled my predecessor; I re-curtained the dear French windows.

Neither Mr. Titch nor his good wife entirely approved of these changes. In fact, I suspect they would have given such a Goth notice to quit in a month had it not been for the reflection that, after all, such eccentricities were only to be expected of a foreigner. The English have a most amusing contempt for the rest of mankind, accompanied by an equally amusing toleration for the peculiarities that are naturally associated with such degenerates. The Chinese, I understand, have an equal national modesty, but their contempt for the foreigner finds expression in a desire to decapitate his mangled remains. John Bull, on the other hand, will not only allow but expect you to walk upon your head, eat rats and mice, maintain a staff of poisonous serpents, and even play the barrel-organ. This goes to such a length that supposing you beat him at something he most prides himself upon, such as rowing, boxing, or manufactures, he will but smile and shake his head and say, "These are, indeed, most remarkable animals."

Mr. and Mrs. Titch were no exceptions to this rule, and I think that in time they even came to have an affection for and a pride in their preposterous tenant, much like an enthusiastic savant who handicaps himself with a half-tamed cobra.

Mr. Titch was a little, gray-haired man, with a respectful manner overlaid upon a consequential air. He had enjoyed varied experience as footman and butler in several families of distinction, and my Halfred had been but a short time in the house before he became tremendously impressed by Mr. Titch's reminiscences of the great, and his vast knowledge of Halfred's own profession.

"Wonderful man, Mr. Titch, sir," he would say to me. "What 'e don't know about our Henglish haristocracy ain't worth knowing. You'd 'ardly believe it, sir, but he seed the Dook of Balham puttin' his arm round Lady Sarah Elcey's waist three months before their engagement was in the papers, and the Dook 'e says to 'im, 'Titch,' says he, ' 'ere's a five-pun' note; you're a man of discretion, you are, and what you sees you keeps to yourself, don't you? I mean no 'arm,' he says. 'I'll hundertake to marry the lady if you only gives me time.' And Mr. Titch, he lay low three 'ole months a-knowing a secret like that."

Mr. Titch's caution and advice were certainly serviceable to Halfred, who was rapidly becoming transformed from the cheerful 'bus-driver into the obliging valet. Whether the world did not lose more than I gained by this change I shall not undertake to say; but I can always console myself for depriving society of a friend, and Halfred of his "hinderpendence," by picturing the little man, poorly protected by his nondescript rug, driving his 'bus all day through the wind and the rain. He, at least, enjoyed the transformation; and one result is worth a hundred admirable theories. Besides, the virtues of Halfred remained the virtues of Halfred through all the polishings of circumstances and Mr. Titch.

For the good Mrs. Titch, my discerning servant expressed a respect only a shade less profound than his homage to her spouse. Now this excellent lady, though motherly in appearance and wonderfully dignified in the black silk in which she rustled to church of a Sunday, was not remarkable either for acuteness of mind or that wide knowledge of the world enjoyed by Mr. Titch. She knew little of the aristocracy except through his reminiscences, though I am bound to say her respect for that august institution was as profound as Major Pendennis himself could have desired. Also her observations on that portion of the world she had met were distinguished by an erroneous and solemn foolishness that cannot have passed unnoticed by Halfred.

Yet he quoted and reverenced her with an inexplicable lack of discrimination.

"Mrs. Titch is what I calls, sir, a genuwine lady in a 'umble sphere," he once remarked to me. "Her delicacy is surprisin'."

Yes, there must be some mysterious glamour about these worthy people, and this glamour I began to have dark suspicions was none other than Miss Aramatilda Titch, daughter of the ex-butler and his genuine lady.

At first I saw this maiden seldom, and then only by glimpses. As more than one of these revealed her in curl-papers, and as I do not appreciate woman thus decked out, I paid her but little attention. But after a week or two had passed I surprised her one afternoon conversing in my sitting-room with the affable Halfred.

"Miss Titch is a-lookin' to see if the windows want cleaning," he explained. Though, as they were standing in the recess farthest removed from the windows, I came to the conclusion that other matters also were being discussed.

It was about this time that I had hired a piano to console my solitude, and a day or two later, as I came towards my room, I heard a tinkle of music. Pushing the door gently open, I saw Miss Aramatilda picking out the air of a polka, and Halfred listening to this melody with the most undisguised admiration.

This time his explanation was more lamely delivered, while Aramatilda showed the liveliest confusion and dismay.

"My dear Miss Titch," I assured her, "by all means practise my piano while I am out—provided, of course, that Mr. Winkles gives you permission.

She asked you, no doubt, if she might play it, Halfred?"

This did not diminish their confusion, I am afraid, and after that their concerts were better protected against surprise.

Not that I should have objected very strongly to take Halfred's place as audience one day, for these further opportunities of seeing Miss Titch roused in me some sympathy with my valet. Aramatilda was undoubtedly attractive with her hair freed from a too severe restraint, a plump, brown-eyed young woman, smiling in the most engaging fashion when politely addressed. Indeed, I should have addressed her more frequently had not Halfred shown such evident interest in her himself. In these matters I have always held it better that master and man should be separately apportioned.

There remains but one other inhabitant of this house who comes into my story, and that was a certain old gentleman living in the rooms immediately over mine. In fact, we two were the only lodgers, and so, having few friends as yet, I began to feel some interest in him.

I had heard him referred to always as "the General," and the few glimpses I had had of him confirmed this title. Figure to yourself an erect man of middle height, white-mustached, quick in his step, with an eye essentially military—that is to say, expressionless in repose, keen when aroused—

and do you not allow that, if he is not a general, he at least ought to be?

"Who is this general?" I asked Halfred one day.

"As rummy a old customer as ever was, sir," said Halfred. "Been here for three years and never 'ad a visitor inside his room all that time, exceptin' one lady."

"A lady?" I said. "His—"

"Don't know, sir. Some says one thing, some says another. Kind o' a hexotic, I calls 'im, sir. Miss Titch she thinks he's 'ad a affair of the 'eart; I think he booses same as a old pal o' mine what kept a chemist's shop in Stepney used to. My friend he locks 'isself up in the back room and puts away morphine and nicotine and strychnine and them things by the 'alf-pint. 'Ole days at it he were, sir, and all the time the small boys a-sneaking cough-drops, and tooth-brushes for to make feathers for their 'ats when playin' at soldiers, and when the doctor he sees 'im at last he says nothing but a hepileptic 'ome wouldn't do 'im any good."

"You think, then, the General drinks?" I said.

"Either that or makes counterfeit coins, sir," said Halfred, with an ominous shake of his bullet head.

I was quite aware of my Halfred's partiality for the melodramatic. Nevertheless there was certainly something unusual in my neighbor's conduct that excited my interest considerably. For I confess I am one of those who are apt to be blind towards the mysteries of the obvious and the miracles of every day, and to revel in the romance of the singular.

Chapter X

*"Seek you wine or seek you maid at the
journey's end?
Give to me at every stage the welcome of
a friend!"*

—Cyd.

D O not think that all this time I had
lost sight of my new friends, the fair-
haired Dick Shafthead and the genial
Teddy Lumme. On the contrary, we
had had more than one merry night
together, and exchanged not a few confidences.
Very soon after I was settled, Dick had come round
to my rooms and criticised everything, from Halfred to the curtains. His tastes were a trifle too
austere to altogether appreciate these latter rather
sumptuous hangings.

"They'll do for waistcoats if you ever go on
the music-hall stage," he observed, sardonically.
"That's why you got 'em, perhaps?"

"The very reason, my friend," I replied. "I

93

cannot afford to get both new waistcoats and new curtains; just as I am compelled to employ the same person to get me out of jail and criticise my furniture."

Dick laughed.

"You are too witty, mossyour." (He came as near the pronunciation of my title as that.) "You should write some of these things down before you forget 'em."

"For the French," I retorted, "that precaution is unnecessary."

For Halfred, I am sorry to say, he did not at first show that appreciation I had expected.

"Your 'bus-man," was the epithet he applied behind his back; though I am bound to say his good-breeding made him so polite that Halfred, on his side, conceived the highest opinion of my friend.

"A real gentleman, Mr. Shafthead is, sir," he confided to me. "What I calls a hunmistakable toff. He hasn't got no side on, and he speaks to one man like as he would to another. In fact, sir, he reminds me of Lord Haugustus I once seed at the Hadelphi; a nobleman what said, 'I treats hevery fellow-Briton as a gentleman so long as Britannia rules the waves and 'e behaves 'isself accordingly.'"

This may seem exaggerated praise, but, indeed, it would be difficult to exaggerate my dear Dick's virtues. Doubtless his faults are being placed in the opposite page of a ledger kept somewhere with his name upon the cover; but that is no business of mine. To paste in parallel columns the virtues of our friends and the faults of ourselves, that may be unpleasant, but it is necessary if we are to turn the search-light inward. Certain weak spots we must not look at too closely if we are to keep our self-respect; but, my faith ! we can well give the most of our humanity an airing now and then; also, if possible, a fumigating. It was Dick Shafthead, more than any other, who took my failings for a walk in the sunshine, and somehow or other they always returned a little abashed.

A very different person was his cousin Teddy Lumme, for whom, by-the-way, I discovered Dick had a real regard carefully concealed behind a most satirical attitude. Teddy was not clever— though shrewd enough within strict limits; he was no moralist, no philosopher; an observer chiefly of the things least worth observing—a performer upon the tin-whistle of life. But, owing to his kindness of heart and ingenuous disposition, he was wonderfully likable.

His leisure moments were devoted, I believe, to the discharge of some duty in the foreign office, though what precisely it was I could never, even by the most ingenious cross-examination, discover. His father held the respectable position of Bishop of Battersea; his mother was the Honorable Mrs. Lumme. These excellent parents had a high regard for Teddy, whom they considered likely to make his mark in the world.

I was taken to the bishopric (*sic*), and discussed with the most venerable Lumme, senior, many points of interest to a foreigner.

Note of a conversation with Bishop of Battersea, taken down from memory a few days after:

Myself. "What is the difference between a High Church and a Low Church?"

Bishop. "A High Church has a high conception of its duties towards mankind, religion, the apostolic succession, and the costume of its clergymen. A Low Church has the opposite."

Myself. "Are you Low Church?"

Bishop. "No."

Myself. "I understand that the conversion of the Pope is one of your objects. Is that so?"

Bishop. "Should the Pope approach us in a proper spirit we should certainly be willing to admit him into our fold."

Myself. "Have you written many theological works?"

Bishop. "I believe tea is ready."

Afterwards further discussion on tithes, doctrine, and the Thirty-nine Articles, of which I forget the details.

My friend Teddy did not live at the bishopric with his parents, but in exceedingly well-appointed chambers near St. James Street. Here I met various other young gentlemen of fortune and promise, who discussed with me many questions of international interest—such as the price of champagne in foreign hotels, the status of the music-hall artiste at home and abroad, the best knot for the full-dress tie, and so forth.

Dick Shafthead did not often appear in this company.

"Can't afford their amusements, and can't be bothered with their conversation," he explained to me. "Look in and have a pipe this evening if you're doing nothing else. If you want cigars, bring your own; I've run out."

And, after all, learning to perform upon the briar-pipe in Dick's society under the old roof of the Temple, applauding or disapproving of our elders and our betters, had infinitely more charm to me than those intellectual conclaves at his cousin's, for six nights in the week at least. A different mood, a different friend. Sometimes one desires in a companion congenial depravity; at others, more points of contact.

This Temple where Dick lived is not a church, though there is a church within it. It is one of those surprising secrets that London keeps and shows you sometimes to reconcile you to her fogs. Out of the heart of the traffic and the noise you turn through an ancient archway into a rabbit warren of venerable and sober red buildings; each court and passage tidy, sedate, and, if I may say it of a personage of brick, thoughtful and kindly disposed to its inhabitants. This is the Temple, once the home of the Knight Templars, now of English law. In one court Dick shared with a friend an austerely furnished office where he received such work as the solicitors sent him, and was ready to receive more. But it was on the top flight of another staircase in another court-yard that he kept his household gods.

He had come there, as I have said before, during a period of financial depression, and there he had stayed ever since. I do not wonder at it; though, to be sure, I think I should find it rather solitary of an evening, when the offices emptied, silence fell upon the stairs and the quadrangles, and there were only left in the whole vast warren the sprinkling of permanent inhabitants who dwelt under the slates. Yet there was I know not quite what about those old rooms, an aroma of the past, a link with romance, that made them lovable. The panelled walls, the undulating floors, the odd angle which held the fireplace, the beam across the ceiling, the old furniture to match these, all had character; and to what but character do we link sentiment?

Also the prospect from the windows was delightful; an open court, a few trees, the angles of other ancient buildings, a glimpse of green turf in a garden, a peep of more stems and branches, with the Thames beyond. Yes, it was quite the neighborhood for a romantic episode to happen. And one day, as you shall hear in time, it happened.

Chapter *XI*

*"And then I came to another castle where
lived a giant whose name was John Bull."*
—MAUNDEVILLE (ADAPTED).

*D*O you dance?" asked Teddy.
"All night, if you will play to me,"
I replied.
"Ride?" said he.
"On a horse? Yes, my friend, I
can even ride a horse."

"Well, then, I say, d' you care to come to a ball
at Seneschal Court, the Trevor-Hudson's place;
meet next day, and that sort of thing? Dick and
I are going. We'll be there about a week."

"But I do not know the — the very excellent
people you have named."

"Oh, that's all right," said Teddy. "They
want a man or two. So few men dance nowadays, .
don't you know. I keep it up myself a little;
girls get sick if I don't hop round with 'em now and
then. Hullo, I see you've got a card from my

99

mater, for the twenty-ninth. Don't go, whatever
you do. Sure to be dull. The mater's shows
always are. What did you think of that girl the
other night? Ha, ha! Told you so; I know all
about women. What's this book you're reading?
French, by Jove! Pretty stiff, isn't it? Oh, o'
course you are French, aren't you? That makes a
difference, I suppose. Well, then, you'll come with
us. Thursday, first. I'll let you know the train."

"May I bring my Halfred?" I inquired.

"Rather. Looks well to have a man with you.
I'd bring mine, only he makes a fuss if he can't
have a bedroom looking south, and one can't insist on people giving him that. Au revoir, mossoo."

This was on Monday, so I had but little time
for preparation.

Halfred was at once taken into consultation.

"I am going to hunt," I said; "also to a ball;
and you are coming with me. Prepare me for the
ballroom and the chase. What do I require beyond the things I already have?"

"A pink coat and a 'ard 'at, sir," said he, with
great confidence. "Likewise top-boots and white
gloves for to dance in, not forgettin' a pair o' spurs
and a whip."

"I shall get the hat, the coat, and the boots.
Gloves I have already. You will buy me the spurs
and the whip. By-the-way, have you ever hunted,
Halfred?"

"Not exactly 'unted myself, sir," said he, "but I've seed the 'unt go by, and knowed a lot o' 'unt-ing - men. Then, bein' connected with hosses so much myself I've naterally took a hinterest in the turf and the racin'-stable."

"You are a judge of horses?" I asked.

"Well, sir, I am generally considered to know

"A pink coat and a 'ard 'at, sir;"

something about 'em. In fact, sir, Mr. Widdup—that's the gentleman what give me the testimonial —he's said to me more nor once, 'Halfred,' says he, 'what you don't know about these 'ere hani-mals would go into a pill-box comfortable.'"

"Good," I said. "Find me two hunters that I can hire for a week."

The little man looked me up and down with a discriminating eye.

"Something that can carry a bit o' weight, sir,

and stand a lot o' 'ard riding; that's what you need, sir.''

Now, I am not heavy, nor had circumstances hitherto given me the opportunity of riding excessively hard, but the notion that I was indeed a gigantic Nimrod tempted my fancy, and I am ashamed to confess that I fell.

Ive seed the 'unt go by

"Yes," I said, "that is exactly what I require."

"Leave it to me, sir," he assured me, with great confidence. "I'll make hall the arrangements."

My mind was now easy, and for the two following days I studied all the English novels treating of field sports, and the articles on hunting in the encyclopædias and almanacs, so that when Thursday arrived and I met my friends at the station I felt myself qualified to take part with some assurance in their arguments on the chase. We are a

receptive race, we French, and the few accomplishments we have not actually created we can at
least quickly comprehend and master.

Next door to us, in a second-class compartment,
Halfred was travelling, and attached to our train
was the horse-box containing the two hunters he
had engaged. I had had one look at these, and
certainly there seemed to be no lack of bone and
muscle.

"Mr. Widdup and me 'ired 'em, sir," said Halfred, "from a particular friend o' ours what can be
trusted. Jumps like fleas, they do, he says, and
'as been known to run for sixty-five miles without
stoppin' more'n once or twice for a drink. 'Ard in
the mouth and 'igh in the temper, says he, but the
very thing for a gentleman in good 'ealth what
doesn't 'unt regular and likes 'is money's worth
when he does."

"You have exactly described me," I replied.

But if I had the advantage over my two friends
in the suite I was taking with me, Teddy Lumme
certainly led the way in conversation. He was
vastly impressed with the importance of our party
(a sentiment he succeeded in communicating to
the guard and the other officials); also with the re-
spectability of the function we were going to attend, and with the inferiority of other travellers
on that railway. This air of triumphal progress
or coronation procession was still further increased
by the indefatigable attentions of Halfred, who

at every station ran to our carriage door, touched
his hat, and made inquiries concerning our comfort and safety; so that more than once a loyal
cheer was raised as the train steamed out again,
and Dick even declared that at an important junction he perceived the Lord Mayor's daughter ap-

"Jumps like fleas"

proaching with a basket of flowers. Unfortunately, however, she did not reach our carriage in time.

The glories of this pageant he was partaking in
filled Teddy's mind with reminiscences of other
scenes where he had played an equally distinguished part.

"I remember one day with the Quorn last year,"
he remarked. "Devil of a run we had; seventy-

five minutes without a check. When we'd killed, I said to a man, 'Got anything to drink?' It was Pluckham. You know Lord Pluckham, Dick?"

"His bankruptcy case went through our chambers," said Dick, dryly.

"Dashed hard lines that was," said Teddy. "He's a good chap, is Pluckham; kept the best whiskey in England. By Jove! I never had a drink like that. A man needs one after riding with the Quorn."

And Teddy puffed his cigar and chewed the cud of that proud moment.

"Where are your horses, Teddy?" asked Dick. "Coming down by a special train?"

"Oh, they are mounting me," said Teddy. "Trevor-Hudson always keeps a couple of his best for me. What are you doing?"

"Following on a bicycle," replied Dick. "My five grooms and six horses haven't turned up."

"My dear Shafthead," said I, "I shall lend you one of mine."

"Many thanks," he answered, with gratitude, no doubt, but with less enthusiasm than I should have expected. "Unfortunately I've seen 'em."

"And do you not care to ride them?" I asked, with some disappointment, I confess.

"Not alone," said Dick. "If you'll lend me Halfred to sit behind and keep the beast steady I don't mind trying."

"Very well," I said, with a shrug.

This strain of a brutality that is peculiarly British occasionally disfigures my dear Dick. Yet I continue to love him—judge, then, of his virtues.

"Are they good fencers?" asked Lumme.

"I have not yet seen them with the foils," I replied, smiling politely at what seemed a foolish joke.

"I mean," said he, "do they take their jumps well?"

"Pardon," I laughed. "Yes, I am told they are excellent—if the wall is not too high. We shall not find them more than six feet?"

But I was assured that obstacles of more than this elevation would not be met frequently.

"Do they take water all right?" asked the inquisitive Teddy again.

"Both that and corn," I replied. "But Halfred will attend to these matters."

English humor is peculiar. I had not meant to make a jest, yet I was applauded for this simple answer.

"Tell me what to look for in my hosts," I said to Dick, presently.

"Money and money's worth," he replied.

"What we call the nouveau riche?" I asked.

"On the contrary, what is called a long pedigree, nowadays—two generations of squires, two of captains of industry (I think that is the proper term), and before that the imagination of the Herald's Office. There is also a pretty daughter—isn't there, Teddy?"

"Quite a nice little thing," said Lumme, graciously.

"I thought you rather fancied her."

"I'm off women at present," the venerable *roué* declared.

Dick's grin at hearing this sentiment was more eloquent than any comment.

But now we had reached our destination. Halfred and a very stately footman, assisted by the station-master, the ticket-collector, and all the porters, transferred our luggage to a handsome private omnibus; then, Halfred having arranged that the horses should be taken to stables in the village (since my host's were full), we all bowled off between the hedge-rows.

It was a beautiful October evening, still clear overhead and red in the west; the plumage of the trees had just begun to turn a russet brown; the air was very fresh after the streets of London; our horses rattled at a most exhilarating pace.

"My faith," I exclaimed, "this is next to heaven! I shall be buried in the country."

"Those hunters of yours ought to manage it for you," observed Dick.

Yet I forgave him again.

We turned through an imposing gateway, and now we were in a wide and charming English park. Undulating turf and stately trees spread all round us and ended only in the dusk of the evening; a herd of deer galloped from our path;

rooks cawed in the branches overhead; a gorgeous pheasant ran for shelter towards a thicket. Then, on one side, came an ivy-covered wall over whose top high, dark evergreens stood up like Ethiopian giants. Evidently these were the gardens, and in a moment more we were before the house itself.

As I went from the carriage to the door I had just time and light to see that it was a very great mansion, not old, apparently, but tempered enough by time to inspire a kindly feeling of respect. A high tower rose over the door, and along the front, on either side, creepers climbed between the windows, and these gave an impression at once of stateliness and home.

By the aid of two servants, who were nearly as tall as the tower, we were led first through an ample vestibule adorned with a warlike array of spears. These, I was informed, belonged to the body-guard of my host when he was high sheriff of his county, and this explanation, though it took from them the romance of antiquity, gave me, nevertheless, a pleasanter sensation than if they had been brandished at Flodden. They were a relic not of a dead but a living feudalism, a symbol that a sovereign still ruled this land. And this reminded me of the reason I was here and the cause for which I still hoped to fight; and for a moment it saddened me.

But again I commit the crime of being serious; also the still less pardonable offence of leaving my two friends standing outside the doors of the hall.

Hastily I rejoin them; the doors open, a buzz of talk within suddenly subsides, and we march across the hall in single file to greet our host and hostess. What I see during this brief procession is a wide and high room, a gallery running round it, a great fireplace at the farther end, and a company of nearly twenty people sitting or standing near the fire and engaged in the consumption of tea and the English crumpet.

I am presented, received in a very off-hand fashion, told to help myself to tea and crumpet, and then left to my own devices. Lumme and Shafthead each find an acquaintance to speak to, my host and hostess turn to their other guests, and, with melted butter oozing from my crumpet into my tea, I do my best to appear oblivious of the glances which I feel are being directed at me. I look irresolutely towards my hostess. She is faded, affected, and talkative; but her talk is not for me, and, in fact, she has already turned her back. And my host? He is indeed looking at me fixedly out of a somewhat bloodshot eye, while he stuffs tea-cake into a capacious mouth; but when I meet his gaze, he averts his eyes. A cheerful couple; a kindly reception! "What does it mean?" I ask myself. "Has Lumme exceeded his powers in bringing me here?" I remember that at his instigation Mrs. Trevor-Hudson sent me a brief note of invitation, but possibly she repented afterwards. Or is my appearance so unpleasant? In France, I tell myself, it was not generally considered repulsive. In fact, I can console myself with several instances to the contrary; but possibly English standards of taste are different.

At last I venture to accost a gentleman who, at the moment, is also silent.

"Have you also come from London?" I ask.

"I? No. Live near here," he says, and turns to resume his conversation with a lady.

I am seriously thinking of taking my departure before there is any active outbreak of hostilities, when I see a stout gentleman, with a very red face, approaching me from the farther side of the fireplace. I have noticed him staring at me with, it seemed, undisguised animosity, and I am preparing the retort with which I shall answer his request to immediately leave the house, when he remarks, in a bluff, cheerful voice, as he advances:

"Bringin' your horses, I hear."

"I am, sir," I reply, in great surprise.

"Lumme was tellin' me," he adds, genially. "Ever hunted this country before?"

And in a moment I find myself engaged in a friendly conversation, which is as suddenly interrupted by a very beautifully dressed apparition with a very long mustache, who calls my short friend "Sir Henry," and consults him about an accident that has befallen his horse. But I began

to see the theory of this reception. It is an Englishman's idea of making you—and himself—feel at
home. You eat as much cake as you please, talk
to anybody you please, remain silent as long as

" Bringin' your horses I hear "

you please, leave the company if you please and
smoke a pipe, and you are not interfered with by
any one while doing these things. To introduce
you to somebody might bore you; you may not
be a conversationalist, and may prefer to stand
and stare like a surfeited ox. Well, if such are
your tastes it would be interfering with the

111

liberty of the subject to cross them. What was the use of King John signing the Magna Charta if an Englishman finds himself compelled to be agreeable?

This idea having dawned upon me and my courage returned, I cast my eyes round the company, and selecting the prettiest girl made straight at her. She received me with a smiling eye and the most delightful manner possible, and as she talked and I looked more closely at her, I saw that she was even fairer than I had thought.

Picture a slim figure, rather under middle height, a bright eye that sparkled as though there was dew upon it, piquant little features that all joined in a frequent and quite irresistible smile; and, finally, dress this dainty *demoiselle* in the most fascinating costume you can imagine. Need it be said that I was soon emboldened to talk quite frankly and presently to ask her who some of the company were? "Sir Henry" turned out to be Sir Henry Horley, a prosperous baronet, who scarcely ever left the saddle; the gentleman with the long mustache, to be Lord Thane, an elder son with political aspirations; while the man I had first accosted was no less a person than Mr. H. Y. Tonks, the celebrated cricketer.

"And now will you point out to me Miss Trevor-Hudson?" I asked. "I hear she is very beautiful."

"Who told you that?" she inquired, with a more charming smile than ever.

"Her admirers," I answered.

The girl raised her eyebrows, shot me the archest glance in the world, and pointing her finger to her own breast, said, simply:

"There she is."

I said to myself that though my friend Teddy Lumme was "off women," I, at any rate, was not.

Chapter XII

*"Our language is needlessly complicated.
Why, for instance, have two such words as
'woman' and 'discord,' when one would
serve?"*

—LA RABIDE.

RESENTLY the men retired to smoke,
and for an hour or two I had to tear
P myself from the smiles of Miss Trevor-
Hudson. The smoking-room opened
into the billiard-room, and some played
pool while the rest of us sat about the fire and discussed agriculture, the preservation of pheasants,
and, principally, horses, hounds, and foxes. A
short fragment will show you the standard of eloquence to which we attained. It is founded, I
admit, more on imagination than memory, but is
sufficiently accurate for the purpose of illustra-
tion. As to who the different speakers were you
can please your fancy.

First Sportsman. " Are your turnips large?"

114

Second Sportsman. "Not so devilish bad. Did you go to the meet on Tuesday?"

First Sportsman. "Yes, and I noticed Charley Tootle there."

Third Sportsman. "Ridin' his bay horse or his black?"

First Sportsman. "The bay."

Fourth Sportsman. "Oats make better feeding."

Second Sportsman. "My man prefers straw."

First Sportsman. "Did you fish this summer?"

Third Sportsman. "No; I shot buffaloes instead."

First Sportsman. "Where—Kamchatka or Japan?"

Third Sportsman. "Japan. Kamchatka's getting overshot."

Fifth Sportsman. "Do you supply your pheasants with warm water?"

Second Sportsman. "I am having it laid on."

Fifth Sportsman. "What system do you use?"

Second Sportsman. "Two-inch pipes attached by a rotatory tap to the conservatory cistern."

Fifth Sportsman. "Sounds a devilish good notion."

First Sportsman. "Now, let me tell you my experience of those self-lengthening stirrups."

And so on till the booming of a gong summoned us to dress for dinner.

"Well," said Dick, as we went to our rooms,

115

"you looked as though your mind was being improved."

"It is trying to become adjusted," I replied.

On our way we passed along the gallery overlooking the hall, and suddenly I was struck by the contrast between this house and its inhabitants: on the one hand the splendid proportions and dignity of this great hall, dark under the oak beams of the roof, fire-light and lamp-light falling below upon polished floor and carpets of the East; the library lined with what was best in English literature, the walls with the worthiest in English art; on the other, my heavy-eyed host full of port and prejudices, and as meshed about by unimaginative limitations as any strawberry-bed. Possibly I am too foreign, and only see the surface, but then how is one to suspect a gold-mine beneath a vegetable garden?

At dinner I found myself seated between Lady Thane and Miss Rosalie Horley. Lady Thane, wife to the nobleman with the long mustache, had an attractive face, but took herself seriously. In man this is dangerous, in woman fatal. I turned to my other neighbor and partially obtained my consolation there. She was young, highly colored, hearty, and ingenuous, and proved so appreciative a listener as nearly to suffocate herself with an oyster-paté when I told her how I had burgled Fisher. The remainder of my consolation I obtained from the prospect, directly opposite, of Miss

Trevor-Hudson. She was sitting next to Teddy Lumme, and if it had not been for his express declaration to the contrary I should have said he was far from insusceptible to her charms. Yet, since I knew his real sentiments, I did not hesitate to distract her glance when possible.

After dinner a great bustling among the ladies, a great putting on of overcoats and lighting of cigars among the men, and then we all embarked in an immense omnibus and clattered off to the ball. This dance was being held in the county town some miles away, so that for more than half an hour I sat between Dick and Teddy on a seat behind the driver's, my cigar between my teeth, a very excellent dinner beneath my overcoat, and my heart as light as a sparrow's. On either side the rays of our lamps danced like fire-flies along the woods and hedge-rows, but my fancy seemed to run still faster than these meteor companions, and already I pictured myself claiming six dances from Miss Trevor-Hudson.

But now other lights began to appear, twinkling through trees before us, and presently we were clattering up the high street of the market-town. Other carriages were already congregated about the assembly rooms at the Checkered Boar, a crowd of spectators had gathered before the door to stare at visions of lace and jewelry, the strains of the band came through an open window, and altogether there was an air of revelry that I suppose only visited the little borough once a year. Inside the doors, waiters with shining heads and ruddy faces waved us on up and down stairs and along passages, where, at intervals, we met other guests as resplendent as ourselves, till at last we reached the ballroom itself. This was a long, low room with a shining floor, an old-fashioned wall-paper decorated with a pattern of pink roses, and a great blaze of candles to light it up. It was evident that many generations of squires must have danced beneath those candles and between the rose-covered walls, and this suggestion of old-worldness had a singularly pleasant flavor.

In a recess about the middle of the room the orchestra were tuning up for another waltz; at one end the more important families were assembling; at the other, the lesser. Need I say that we joined the former group?

In English country dances it usually is the custom to have programmes on which you write the names of your partners for the evening. I now looked round to secure one particular partner, but she was not to be seen. The waltz had begun; I scanned the dancers. There was Shafthead tearing round with Miss Horley, his athletic figure moving well, his good features lit by a smile he could assume most agreeably when on his best behavior. There was the stout Sir Henry revolving with the more deliberate pomp of sixty summers. But where were the bright eyes? Suddenly I spied the skirt of a light-blue dress through the opening of a doorway. I rushed for it, and there, out in the passage, was the misogamist Lumme evidently entreating Miss Trevor-Hudson for more dances than she was willing to surrender. For her sake this must be stopped.

"I have come to make a modest request," I said. "Will you give me a dance—or possibly two?"

With the sweetest air she took her programme from the disconcerted, and I do not think very amiable, Teddy, and handed it to me.

"I have taken three, seven, and fourteen," I said, giving it back to her.

"Fourteen is mine," cried Teddy.

"Not now," I said, smiling.

"I had booked it," said he.

"Your name was not there," I replied. "And now, Miss Hudson, if you are not dancing this dance will you finish it with me?"

She took my arm, and the baffled despiser of women was left in the passage.

This may sound hard treatment to be dealt out to a friend, and, indeed, I fear that though outwardly calm, and even polite to exaggeration, my indignation had somewhat run away with me. Had I any excuse? Yes; two eyes that, as I have said, were bright as the dew, and a smile not to be resisted.

She danced divinely, she let me clasp her hand tenderly yet firmly, and she smiled at me when

she was dancing with others. I noticed once or
twice when we danced together that Lumme also
smiled at her, but I was convinced she did not reply to this. In fact, his whole conduct seemed to
me merely presumptuous and impertinent. How
mine seemed to him I cannot tell you.

the
baffled
despiser
of
women

He had secured the advantage of engaging several dances before I had time to interfere, and also
possessed one other—a scarlet evening-coat, the
uniform of the hunt. But I glanced in the mirror,
and said to myself that I did not grudge him this
adornment, while as for my fewer number of
dances, I found my partner quite willing to allow
me others to which I was not legally entitled. In
this way I obtained number thirteen, to the det-

riment of Mr. Tonks, and was just prepared to embark upon number fourteen when Lumme approached us with an air I did not approve of.

"This is my dance," he said, in a manner inexcusable in the presence of a lady.

"Pardon," I replied. "It is mine."

Miss Hudson looked from one to the other of us with a delighfully perplexed expression, but, I fear, with a little wickedness in her brown eye.

"What am I to do?" she said, with a shrug of her shoulders.

"It is my dance," repeated Teddy, glaring fixedly at me.

I shrugged my shoulders, smiled, and offered her my arm to lead her away.

"I am sorry, Mr. Lumme," said the cause of this strife, sweetly, "but I am afraid Mr. D'Haricot's name is on my programme."

Teddy made a tragic bow that would have done credit to a dyspeptic frog, and I danced off with my prize. At the end of the waltz he came up to me with a carefully concocted sneer.

"You know how to sneak dances, moshyour," he observed. "Do you do everything else as well?"

I kept my temper and replied, suavely, "Yes, I shoot tolerably with the pistol, and can use the foils."

"Like your cab-horses?" sneered Teddy, taking no notice, however, of the implied invitation to console himself if aggrieved. "I'm keen to see how long you stick on top of those beasts."

"Good, my friend," I replied, "I take that as a challenge to ride a race. We shall see to-morrow who first catches the fox!"

Chapter XIII

"With his horse and his hounds in the morning!"
—ENGLISH BALLAD.

HEN I awoke next morning, my first thoughts were of a pair of brown eyes, dainty features that smiled up at me, and a voice that whispered as we danced for the last time together, "No, I shall not forget you when you are gone."

Then, quickly, I remembered the sport before me, and the challenge to ride to the death with the rival who had crossed my path.

"Halfred," I said.

The little man looked up from the pile of clothes he was folding in the early morning light, and stopped the gentle hissing that accompanied, and doubtless lightened, every task.

"Fasten my spurs on firmly," I said. "I shall ride hard to-day."

He cannot have noticed the grave note in my

123

voice, for he replied, in his customary cheerful fashion, "If heverything sticks on as well as the spurs, sir, you won't 'ave nothin' to complain of."

"I shall ride very hard, Halfred."

"'Arder nor usual, sir?" he asked, with a look of greater interest.

"Vastly, immeasurably!"

"What's hup, sir?" he exclaimed, in some concern now.

"I have made a little bet with Mr. Lumme," I answered in a serious voice, "a small wager that I shall be the first to catch the fox. If you can make a suggestion that may help me to win, I shall be happy to listen to it."

"Catch the fox, sir? he repeated, thoughtfully, scratching his head. "Well, sir, it seems to me there's nothin' for it but starting hoff first and not lettin' 'im catch you up. I 'aven't 'unted myself, sir, but I've 'eard tell as 'ow a sharp gent sometimes spots the fox afore any of the hothers. That's 'ow to do it, in my opinion."

I thought this over and the scheme seemed excellent.

"We shall arrange it thus," I said: "You will mount one horse and I the other. We shall ride together and look for the fox."

Conceive of my servant's delight. I do not believe that if I had offered him a hundred pounds he would have felt so much joy.

I dressed myself with the most scrupulous accuracy, for I was resolved that nothing about me should suggest the novice. My pink coat fitted to within half a little wrinkle in an inconspicuous place, my breeches were a miracle of sartorial art, the reflection from my top-boots perceptibly lightened the room. No one at the breakfast-table cut more dash. I had secured a seat beside Miss Trevor-Hudson and we jested together with a friendliness that must have disturbed Lumme, for he watched us furtively, with a dark look on his face, and never addressed a word to a soul all the time.

"I shall expect you to give me a lead to-day," she said to me.

"Are you well mounted?" I asked.

"I am riding my favorite gray."

"Ride hard, then," I said, loud enough for Lumme
to hear me. "The lead I give will be a fast one!"

Before breakfast was over we had been joined
by guest after guest who had come for the meet.
Outside the house carriages and dog-carts, spectators on foot, grooms with horses, and sportsmen who had already breakfasted were assembled
in dozens, and the crowd was growing greater
every moment. I adjusted my shining hat upon
my head and went out to look for Halfred. There
he was, the centre evidently of considerable interest and admiration, perched high upon one of the
gigantic and noble quadrupeds, and grasping
the other by the reins. His livery of deep-plum
color, relieved by yellow cording, easily distinguished him from all other grooms, while my two
steeds appeared scarcely to be able to restrain their
generous impatience, for it required three villagers
at the head of each to control their exhilaration.

"I congratulate you," I said to my servant.
"The tout ensemble is excellent."

At that moment his mount began to plunge
like a ship at sea, and the little man went up and
down at such a rate that he could only gasp:

"'Old 'im, you there chaw-bacons! 'Old 'im
tight! 'E won't 'urt you!"

In response to this petition the villagers leaped
out of range and uttered incomprehensible sounds,
much to my amusement. This, however, was

quickly changed to concern when I observed my own steed suddenly stand upon end and flourish his fore-legs like a heraldic emblem.

"You have overfed them with oats," I said to Halfred, severely.

"Oats be—" he began, and then pitched on to the mane, "oats be—" and here he just clutched

" Oats be _"

the saddle in time to save himself from retiring over the tail—"oats be blowed!"

"It ain't oats that's the matter with 'em," said a bluff voice behind me.

I turned and saw Sir Henry looking with an experienced eye at this performance.

"What is it?" I inquired.

"Vice," said he. "I know that fiddle-headed brute well; no mistakin' him. It's the beast that broke poor Oswald's neck last season. His widow sold him to a dealer at Rugby for fifteen pounds, and, by Jove! here he is again, just waitin' for a chance to break yours!"

He turned his critical eye to Halfred's refractory steed.

" And I think I remember that dancin' stallion, too," he added, grimly. "Gad! you'll have some fun to-day, monsieur!"

This was cheerful, but there was no getting out of it now. Indeed, the huntsman and the pack were already leading the way to the first covert and everybody was on the move behind them. I mounted my homicide during one of its calmer intervals, the villagers bolted out of the way, and in a moment we were clearing a course through the throng like a charge of cavalry.

"Steady there, steady!" bawled the master of the hunt. "Keep back, will you?"

With some difficulty I managed to take my mount plunging and sidling out to where Halfred was galloping in circles at a little distance from the rest of the field.

"Where are the hounds?" I cried. "Where is the fox?"

"In among them trees," replied Halfred, as we galloped together towards the master.

"Let us go after them!" I exclaimed. "Lumme waits behind with the others. Now is our chance!"

"Come on, sir!" said Halfred, and we dashed past the master at a pace that scarcely gave us time to hear the encouraging cry with which he greeted us.

The wood was small, but the trees were densely

packed, and it was only by the most miraculous good luck, aided also by skilful management, that we avoided injury from the branches. Somewhere before us we could hear the baying of the hounds, and we directed our course accordingly. Suddenly there arose a louder clamor and we caught a glimpse of white and tan forms leaping towards us But we scarcely noticed these, for at that same instant we had espied a small, brown animal slipping away almost under our horses' feet.

"The fox!" cried Halfred.

"The fox!" I shouted, bending forward and aiming a blow at it with my whip.

With a loud cheer we turned and burst through the covert in hot pursuit, and, easily out-distancing the hounds, broke into the open with nothing before us but Reynard himself. Figure to yourself the sensation!

Ah, that I could inoculate you with some potent fluid that should set your blood on fire and make you feel the intoxication of that chase as you read my poor, bald words! Over a fence we went and descended on the other side, myself hatless, Halfred no longer perched upon the saddle, but clinging manfully to the more forward portions of his steed. Then, through a wide field of grass we tore. This field was lined all down the farther side by a hedge of thorns quite forty feet high, which the English call a "bulrush." At one corner I observed a gate, and having never before charged such a barrier,

I endeavored to direct my horse towards this. But no! He had seen the fox go through the hedge, and I believe he was inspired by as eager a desire to catch it as I was myself. I shut my eyes, I lowered my head, I felt my cheek torn by something sharp and heard a great crash of breaking branches,

Figure to yourself the Sensation!

and then, behold! I was on the farther side! My spurs had instinctively been driven harder into my horse's flank, and though I had long since dropped my whip, they proved sufficient to encourage him to still greater exertions.

Finding that he was capable of directing his course unassisted, and perceiving also that he had taken the bit so firmly between his teeth as to preclude the possibility of my guiding him with any certainty, I discarded the reins (which of course were now unnecessary), and confined my attention to seeing that he should not be hampered by my slipping on my saddle. One brief glance over my shoulder showed me his stable companion following hard, in spite of the inconvenience of having to support his rider up on his neck, and racing alongside came the foremost hounds. Behind the pack were scattered in a long procession pink coats and galloping horses, dark habits and more galloping horses. I tried to pick out my rival, but at that instant my horse rose to another fence and my attention was distracted.

Another field, this time ploughed, and a stiffer job now for my good horse. Yet he would certainly have overtaken our quarry in a few minutes longer had he selected that part of the next fence I wished him to jump. But, alas! he must take it at its highest, and the ploughed field had proved too exhausting. We rose, there was a crash, and I have a dim recollection of wondering on which portion of my frame I should fall.

Then I knew no more till I found myself in the arms of the faithful Halfred, with neither horse, hounds, fox, nor huntsmen in sight.

"Did you catch it?" I asked.

"No, sir," said he, "but I give it a rare fright."

But I had scarcely heard these consoling words before I swooned again.

Chapter XIV

"You feel yourself insulted? That is fortunate, for otherwise I should have been compelled to!"

—HERCULE D'ENVILLE.

PICTURE me now, stretched upon a sofa in the very charming morning-room of Seneschal Court, a little bruised, a little shaken still, but making a quick progress towards recovery. Exasperating, no doubt, to be inactive and an invalid when others are well and spending the day in hunting and shooting, but I had two consolations. First of all, Lumme had not beaten me. He, too, had been dismounted a few fields farther on, and though he had ridden farthest, yet I had gone fastest, and could fairly claim to have at least divided the honors. But consolation number two would, I think, have atoned even in the absence of consolation number one. In two words, this comfort was my nurse. Yes, you can picture Amy Trevor - Hudson sitting by the side of that sofa, intent upon a piece of fancy-work that progresses at the rate of six stitches a day, yet not so intent as to be unable to converse with her guest and patient.

"You are really feeling better to-day?" she asks, with that sparkling glance of her brown eyes that accompanies every word, however trivial.

"Thank you; I have eaten two eggs and a plate of bacon for breakfast, and should doubtless be looking forward now to lunch if my thoughts were not so much more pleasantly employed."

"Are you thinking, then, that you will soon be well enough to go away?"

"I am thinking," I reply, "that for some days I shall still be invalid enough to lie here and talk to you."

She does not look up at this, but I can see a charming smile steal over her face and stay there while I look at her.

"Who did you say these things to last?" she inquires, presently, still looking at her work.

"What things? That I am fond of luncheon— or that I am fond of you?"

"I meant," she replies, looking at me this time with the archest glance, "what girl did you last tell that you were fond of her?"

Now, honestly, I cannot answer this question off-hand with accuracy. I should have to think, and that is not good for an invalid.

"I cannot tell you, because I do not remember her," I reply.

She puts a wrong construction on this—as I had anticipated.

"I don't believe you," she says. "I am sure you must have said these things before."

"If you think my words are false, how can I help myself?" I ask, with the air of one impaled upon an ignited stake, yet resigned to this position. "I dare not dispute with you, even to save my character, for fear you become angry and leave me."

She smiles again, gives me another dazzling glance, and then, with the elusiveness of woman, turns the subject to this wonderful piece of work that she is doing.

"What do you think of this flower?" she asks.

To obtain the critical reply she desires entails her coming to the side of the couch and holding one edge of the work while I hold the other. Then I endeavor to hold both edges and somehow find myself holding her hand as well. It happens so naturally that she takes no notice of this occurrence but stands there smiling down at me and talking of this flower while I look up at her face and talk also of the flower. In fact, she seems first conscious of that chance encounter of hands when a step is heard in the passage. Then, indeed, she withdraws to her seat and the very faintest rise in color might be distinguished by one who had acquired the habit of looking at her closely.

It was Dick Shafthead who entered, in riding-breeches and top-boots. I may say, by-the-way, that he had not been reduced to a bicycle. On the contrary, he made an excellent display upon a horse for one who affected to be too poor to ride.

"My horse went lame," he explained, "so I thought I'd come back and have a look at the patient."

From his look I could see that he was unprepared to find me already provided with a nurse. Not that it was the first time she had been here—but then I did not happen to have mentioned that to Dick. In a few moments Amy left us and he looked with a quizzical smile first at the door through which she had gone and then at me.

"You take it turn about, I see," he said. "I didn't know the arrangement or I shouldn't have interrupted."

"I beg your pardon?" I replied. "Either my head is still somewhat confused or I do not understand English as well as I thought."

"I imagined Teddy was having a walk-over," said he, with a laugh.

None are so quick of apprehension as the jealous. Already a dark suspicion smote me.

"Do you allude to Miss Trevor-Hudson?" I asked.

"Who else?"

"And you thought Teddy was having what you call a walk-over?"

"I did," said Dick. "But it is none of my business."

"It is my business," I replied, "to see that this charming lady does not have her name associated with a man she only regards as the merest acquaintance."

"Has she told you that is how she looks on Teddy?"

"She has."

Dick laughed outright.

"What are your hours?" he asked. "When does Miss Hudson visit the sick-bed?"

"If you must know," I replied, "she has had the kindness to visit me every morning; also in the evening."

"Then Teddy has the afternoons," said he.

"But he has been hunting."

"He comes home after lunch, I notice," laughed Dick.

I became angry.

"Do you mean that Miss Hudson—"

"Is an incorrigible flirt? Yes," said he.

"Shafthead, you go too far!" I cried.

"My dear monsieur, I withdraw and I apologize," he answers, with his most disarming smile. "Have it as you wish. Only—don't let her make a fool of you."

He turned and walked out of the room whistling, and I was left to digest this dark thought.

Certainly it was true that I did not see much of her in the afternoons, but then, I argued, she had doubtless household duties. Her mother was an affected woman who loved posing as an invalid and had stayed in her room ever since the ball. Therefore she had to entertain the guests; and, now I came to think of it, Lumme would naturally press his suit whenever he saw a chance, and how could she protect herself? Certainly she could never compare that ridiculous little man with—well, with any one you please. It was absurd! I laughed at the thought. Yet I became particularly anxious to see her again.

In the evening she came for a few minutes to cheer my solitude. She could not stay; yet she sat down. I must be very sensible; yet she listened to my compliments with a smile. She was ravishing in her simple dress of white, that cost, I should like to wager, some fabulous price in Paris; she was charming; she was kind. Yes, she had been created to be a temptation to man, like the diamonds in her hair; and she perfectly understood her mission. Inevitably man must wish to play with her, to caress her, to have her all to himself; and inevitably he must get into that state when he is willing to pay any price for this possession. And she was willing to make him—and not unwilling to make another pay also. Indeed, I do not think she could conceivably have had too many admirers.

But I did not criticise her thus philosophically that evening. Instead, I said to her:

"I was afraid I should not see you till to-morrow—and perhaps not to-morrow."

"Not to-morrow?" she asked. "Are you going away, after all?"

"I shall be here; but you?"

"And I suppose I must visit my patient."

"But if Mr. Lumme does not go hunting—will you then have time to spare?"

She rose and said, as if offended, "I don't think you want to see me very much."

Yet she did not go. On the contrary, she stood so close to me that I was able to seize her hand and draw her towards me.

"Ah, no!" I cried. "Give me my turn!"

"Your turn?" she asked, drawing away a little.

"Yes; what can I hope for but a brief turn? I am but one of your admirers, and if you are kind to all—"

I paused. She gave me a bright glance, a little smile that drove away all prudence.

"Amy!" I cried; "I have something to give you!"

And I gave her—a kiss.

She protested, but not very stoutly.

It is a legend

"I have something else," I said. And I was about to present her with a very similar offering—indeed, I was almost in the act of presentation, when she started from me with a cry of, "Let me go!" and before I could detain her she had fled from the room. In her flight she passed a man who was standing at the door, and it was he who spoke next.

139

"You damned, scoundrelly frog-eater*!" he re-marked.

It was the voice of my rival, Lumme!

"Ah, monsieur!" I exclaimed, springing up. "You have come to act the spy, I see."

"I haven't," he replied. "I came for Miss Hudson—and I came just in time, too!"

"No," I said, "not just; half a minute after."

It was the voice of my rival, Lumme!

"You dirty, sneaky, French beast!" he cried. "I bring you to a decent house—the first you've ever been to—and you go shamming sick to get a chance of insulting a virtuous girl!"

"Shamming!" I cried. "Insulting! What words are these?"

"Do you mean to say you aren't shamming? You can walk as well as me!"

* It is a legend among the English that we subsist principally upon frogs.—D'H.

Unquestionably I was more recovered than I had admitted to myself while convalescence was so pleasant, and now I had risen from my couch I discovered, to my surprise, that there seemed little the matter with me. That, however, could not excuse the imputation. Besides, I had been addressed by several epithets, each one of which conveyed an insult.

"You vile, low, little English pig!" I replied; "you know the consequences of your language, I suppose?"

"I'm glad to see it makes you sit up," he replied.

I advanced a step and struck him on the face, and then, seeing that he was about to assault me with his fists, I laid him on the floor with a well-directed kick on the chest.

"Now," I said, as he rose, "will you fight, or are you afraid?"

"Fight?" he screamed. "Yes; if you'll fight fair, you kicking froggy!"

"As to the weapons," I replied, "I am willing to leave that question in the hands of our seconds—swords or pistols—it is all the same to me."

He looked for a moment a little taken aback by my readiness.

"Ah," I smiled, "you do not enjoy the prospect very much?"

"If you think I'm going to funk you with any dashed weapons, you are mistaken," said Teddy, hotly. "We don't fight like that in England,

141

but I won't stand upon that. My second is Dick Shafthead."

"And I shall request Mr. Tonks to act for me," I replied. "The sooner the better, I presume?"

"To-morrow morning will suit me," said he.

"Very well," I answered. "I shall now send a note by my servant to Mr. Tonks."

I bowed with scrupulous politeness, and he, with an endeavor to imitate this courtesy, withdrew.

Then I rang for Halfred.

Chapter XV

"An animal I should define as a man who fights in a sensible way for a reasonable end."

—LA RABIDE.

EXTRACT from my journal at this time:

"Wednesday Night.

" All is arranged. Tonks and Shafthead have endeavored to dissuade us, but words have passed that cannot be overlooked, and Lumme is as resolute to fight as I. I must do him that credit. At last, seeing that we are determined, they have consented to act if we will leave all arrangements in their hands. We are both of us willing, and all we know is that we meet at daybreak to-morrow in a place to be selected by our seconds. Even the weapons have not yet been decided. Should I fall and this writing pass into the hands of others, I wish them to know that these two gentlemen, Mr.

143

Shafthead and Mr. Tonks, have done their best
to procure a bloodless issue. In these circumstances I also wish Mr. Lumme to know that I
fully forgive him.

"My will is now made, and Halfred is remembered in it. Another, too, will not find herself forgotten. My watch and chain and my signet-ring I
hav bequeathed to Amy. Farewell, dear maiden!
Do not altogether forget me!

"Halfred is perturbed, poor fellow, at the chance
of losing a master whom, I think, he has already
learned to venerate. Yet he has a fine spirit, and
it is his chief regret that the etiquette of the duel
will not permit him to be a spectator.

"'Aim at 'is wind, sir,' he advised me. 'That
oughter double 'im up if you gets 'im fair. And
perhaps, sir, if you was to give 'im the second
barrel somewhere about the point of 'is jaw, sir,
things would be made more certain-like.'

"'And what if he aims at these places himself?'
I asked.

"'Duck, sir, the minute you see 'im a-pulling
of his trigger—like this, sir.'

"He showed me how to 'duck' scientifically,
and I gravely thanked him. I had not the heart
to tell how different are the fatal circumstances of
the duel, his devotion touched me so. I have told
him to lay out my best dark suit, a white shirt, my
patent-leather boots, and a black tie that will not
make a mark for the bullet. He is engaged at

present in packing the rest of my things, for, whatever the issue, I cannot stay longer here. Farewell again. Amy! Now I shall write to my friends in France, and warn them of the possibilities that may arise. Then to bed!''

I have given this extract at length, that it may be seen how grave we all considered the situation, and also to disprove the common idea that Englishmen do not regard the duel seriously. They are, however, a nation of sportsmen, whose warfare is waged against the "furs and feathers," and the refinements of single combat practised elsewhere are little appreciated, as will presently appear.

It was scarcely yet daylight when I left my room, and with a little difficulty made my way along dim corridors and down shadowy stairs to the garden door, by which it had been decided we could most stealthily escape to the rendezvous. Through the trimmed evergreens and the paths where the leaf-fall of the night still lay unswept I picked my course upon a quiet foot that left plain traces in the dew, but made no sound to rouse the sleeping house. A wicket-gate led me out into the park, and there I followed a path towards an oak paling that formed the boundary along that side. At the end of this path a gate in the paling took me into a narrow lane, and this gate was to be our rendezvous.

As I advanced, I saw between the trees a solitary figure leaning against the paling, and I was assured that my adversary at least had not failed me. Looking back, I next caught sight of the seconds following me, and I delayed my steps so that I only reached Lumme a minute or so before them. We raised our hats and bowed in silence. He looked pale, but I could not deny that his expression was full of spirit, and I felt for him that respect which a brave man always inspires in one of my martial race.

His costume I certainly took exception to, for, instead of the decorous garments called for by the occasion, he was attired in a light check suit, with leather leggings and a pale-blue waistcoat, and, indeed, rather suggested a morning's sport than the business we had come upon. This, however, might be set down to his inexperience, and, as a matter of fact, he was outdone by our seconds, for, in addition to wearing somewhat similar clothes, they each carried a gun and a cartridge-bag. Evidently, I thought, they had brought these to disarm suspicion in case the party were observed. Their demeanor was beyond reproach, and, indeed, surprising, considering that they had never before acted either as principals or seconds. They raised their hats and bowed with formality.

"Good-morning, gentlemen," said Shafthead.

He took the lead throughout, my second, Tonks, concurring in everything he said.

"You still wish to fight?"

Lumme and I both bowed.

"You both refuse to settle your differences amicably?"

"I refuse," replied Lumme.

"And I, certainly," I said.

"Very well," said Dick, "it only remains to assure you that the loser will be decently interred."

Here both he and Tonks were obviously affected by a very natural emotion; with a distinct effort he cleared his throat and resumed:

"And to tell you the conditions of the combat. Here are the weapons."

Conceive our astonishment when we were each solemnly handed a double-barrelled shot-gun and a bagful of No. 5 cartridges! Even Lumme recognized the unsuitability of these firearms.

"I say, hang it!" he exclaimed; "I'm not going to fight with these!"

"Tonks, I protest!" I said, warmly. "This is absurd."

"Only things you're going to get," replied Tonks, stolidly.

"Gentlemen," said Shafthead, with more courtesy, "you have agreed to fight in any method we decide. If you back out now we can only suppose that you are afraid of getting hurt—and in that case why do you fight at all?"

"All right, then," replied Lumme, with an *élan* I must give him every credit for; "I'm game."

"And I am in your hands," said I, with a shrug that was intended to protest, not against the danger, but the absurdity of the weapons. "At what distance do we stand?"

"In that matter we propose to introduce another novelty," replied Dick.

"To make it more sporting," explained Tonks.

"Just so," said Dick. "You see that plantation? We are going to put one of you in one end and the other in the other; you have each fifty cartridges, and you can fire as soon as you meet and as often as you please. One of the seconds will remain at either end to welcome the survivor."

"Oh, that's not a bad idea," said Lumme, brightening up.

I had my own opinion on this unheard-of innovation, but I kept it to myself.

"Now you toss for ends," said Tonks. "Call."

He spun a shilling, and Lumme called "Heads."

"Heads it is," said Tonks. "Which end?"

"It doesn't make much difference, I suppose," replied Teddy. "I'll start from this end."

"Right you are," said Dick. "Au revoir, monsieur. When you are ready to enter the wood fire a cartridge to let us know. Here is an extra one I have left for signalling."

I bowed and followed my second across the lane and through a narrow gate in a high hedge that bounded the side farthest from the park. Lumme was left with Shafthead in the lane to make his

way to the nearest end of the wood, so that I should
see no more of him till we met gun to shoulder in
the thickets. I confess that at that moment I could
think only of our past friendship and his genial
virtues, and it was with a great effort that I forced
myself to recall his insults and harden my heart.

We now walked down a long field shut in by
trees on either hand. At the farther end from the
lane these plantations almost met, so that they
and the hedge enclosed the field all the way round
except for one narrow gap. Here Tonks stopped
and turned.

"You enter here," he said, indicating the wood
on the right-hand side of this gap, "and you work
your way back till you meet him. By-the-way,
if you happen to hear shots anywhere else pay
no attention. The keeper often comes out after rab-
bits in the early morning."

"But if he hears us?" I asked.

"Oh, we've made that right. He knows we are
out shooting. Good luck."

I would at least have clasped the hand of possibly the last man I should ever talk with. I
should have left some message, said something;
but with the phlegmatic coolness of his nation
he had turned away before I had time to reply.
For a moment I watched him strolling noncha-
lantly from me with his hands in his pockets, and
then I fired my gun in the air and stepped into
the trees.

Well, it might be an unorthodox method of duelling, but there could be no questioning the element of hazard and excitement. Here was I at one end of a narrow belt of trees, not thirty yards wide and nearly a quarter of a mile in length, and from the other came a man seeking my life. Every moment must bring us nearer together, till before long each thicket, each tree-stem, might conceal the muzzle of his gun. And the trees and undergrowth were dense enough to afford shelter to a whole company.

Three plans only were possible. First, I might remain where I was and trust to catching him unnerved, and perhaps careless, at the end of a long and fruitless search. But this I dismissed at once as unworthy of a man of spirit, and, indeed, impossible for my temperament. Secondly, I might advance at an even pace and probably meet him about the middle. This also I dismissed as being the procedure he would naturally expect me to adopt. Finally, I might advance with alacrity and encounter him before I was expected. And this was the scheme I adopted.

At a good pace I pushed my way through the branches and the thorns, wishing now, I must confess, that I had adopted a costume more suitable for this kind of warfare, till I had turned the corner of the field and advanced for a little distance up the long side. While I was walking down with Tonks I had taken the precaution of noting a particularly large pine which seemed as nearly as possible the half-way mark, but now a disconcerting reflection struck me. That pine was, indeed, half-way down the side of the field, but I had also had half of the end to traverse, so that the point at which we should meet, going at a similar pace, would be considerably nearer than I had calculated. Supposing, then, that Lumme was also hastening to meet me, he might even now be close at hand! I crouched behind a thorn-bush and listened.

It was a still, delightful morning; the sun just risen; the air fresh; no motion in the branches. Every little sound could be distinctly heard, and presently I heard one; a something moving in another thicket not ten paces away. I raised my gun, aimed carefully, and pulled the trigger.

The stealthy sound ceased, and instead a pheasant flew screaming out of the wood. No longer could there be any doubt of my position. I executed a strategic retreat for a short distance to upset my enemy's calculations and waited for his approach. But I heard nothing except two or three shots from the plantation across the field, where the keeper had evidently begun his shooting. I advanced again, though more cautiously, but in a very short time was brought to a sudden stand-still by a movement in a branch overhead. The diabolical thought flashed through my mind, "He is aiming at me from a tree!"

Instantly I raised my gun and discharged both barrels into the leaves. There came down, not Lumme, but a squirrel; yet the incident inspired me with an idea. I chose a suitable tree, and, having scrambled up with some difficulty (which was not lessened by the thought that I might be shot in the act), I waited for my rival to pass below.

Five minutes passed — ten — fifteen. I heard more shots from the keeper's gun. I slew two foxes and a pheasant which were ill-advised enough to make a suspicious stir in the undergrowth; but not a sign of Lumme. I had not even heard him fire one shot since the duel began. Some mystery here, evidently. Perhaps he was waiting patiently for me to approach within a few paces of the lane whence he started. And I—should I court his cartidges by falling into a trap I had thought of laying myself?

Yet one of us must move, or we should be the laughing-stock of the country-side, and if one of two must attack, the brave man can be in no doubt as to which that is. I descended, and with infinite precautions slowly pushed my way forward, raking with my shot every bush that might conceal a foe. Suddenly between the trees I saw a man—undoubtedly a man this time. I put my hand in my cartridge-bag. One cartridge remaining, besides two in my chambers; three cartridges against a man who had still left fifty! Yet

152

three would be sufficient if I could but get them home.

Carefully I crept on my hands and knees to within a dozen paces; then I raised my head, and

I slew two foxes and a pheasant.

behold! it was Tonks I saw standing in the lane leaning against the paling of the park! But Lumme? Ah, I had it. He had fled!

Shouldering my gun, I stepped out of the wood.

"Hillo!" cried Tonks. "Bagged him?"

"No," I said.

"Been hit?" he asked. "You look in rather a mess."

And indeed I did, for my clothes had been rent by the thorns, my face and my hands torn, and doubtless I showed also some mental signs of the ordeal I had been through. For remember that though I had not met an adversary, I had braved the risk of it at every step. And I had made those steps.

"No," I replied. "I have not even been fired at."

"I heard a regular cannonade," he said.

"Forty-seven times have I fired at a venture," I answered. "And I have not been inaccurate in my aim. In that wood you will find the bodies of four squirrels, five pheasants, and two foxes."

"But where is Lumme?" he inquired.

"Fled," I replied, with an intonation of contempt I could not conceal.

"What! funked it?"

"I saw no sign of him."

"By Jove! that's bad," said Tonks, though in so matter-of-course a tone that I was astonished. A man of a sluggish spirit, I fear, was my cricketing second.

"Let us call Shafthead," I said. "For myself, my honor is satisfied, and I shall leave him and you to deal with the runaway."

We walked together along the lane till we came to the gate in the hedge through which we had started for the wood. Through this we could see right down the field, and there, coming towards us, walked Shafthead and Lumme.

"The devil!" I exclaimed.

"By Jove!" said Tonks.

"Can you explain this?" I asked him.

"I? No; unless you passed each other."

"Passed!" I cried, scornfully.

I threw the gate open and advanced to meet them. To my surprise, Lumme looked at me with no sign of shame, but rather with indignation.

"Well," he cried to me, "you're a fine man to fight a duel. Been in a ditch?"

"Poltroon!" I replied. "Where did you hide yourself?"

"I hide?" said he. "Where have you been hiding?"

"Do you mean to tell me that you men never met?" asked Shafthead.

"Never!" we cried together.

"Tonks," said he, "into which plantation did you put your man?"

"The right-hand one," said Tonks.

"The right!" exclaimed Dick. "Then you have been in different woods! Oh, Tonks, this is scandalous!"

But my second had already turned his head away, and seemed so bowed by contrition that my natural anger somewhat relented.

"Possibly your own directions were not clear," I suggested.

"Ah," said Dick, "I see how it was! He must

have turned round, and that made his right hand
his left."

"Well," said Lumme, "you've made a nice mess
of it. What's to be done now?"

"I am in my second's hands," I replied.

"And I think you've fought enough," said

bowed by
contrition

Tonks. "How many cartridges did you fire,
Lumme?"

"Thirty-two," said he.

"Well, hang it, you've loosed seventy-nine cartridges between you, and that's more than any
other duellists I ever heard of. Let's pull up the
sticks* and come in to breakfast."

"Is honor satisfied?" asked Dick, who had more
appreciation of the delicacies of such a sentiment
than my prosaic second.

Lumme and I glanced at each other, and we

* "Pull up sticks"—a football metaphor.—D'H.

remembered now our past intimacy; also, perhaps, the strain of that fruitless search for each other among those thorny woods.

"Mine is," said Lumme.

"Mine also," said I.

And thus ended what so nearly was a fatal encounter.

Chapter XVI

"Heed my words! Beware of women,
  Shallowest when overbrimmin',
  Deepest when they wish you well!
  Tears and trifles, lace and laughter,
  The Deuce alone knows what they're
    after—
  And he's too much involved to tell."
                                        —ANON.

WE all walked back from the field of battle in a highly amicable frame of mind. Going across the park, Lumme and I fell a little behind our seconds and conversed with the friendliness of two men who have learned to respect each other. We had cordially shaken hands, we laughed, we even jested about the hazards we had escaped—one would think that no more complete understanding could be desired. Yet there was still a little thorn pricking us both, a thorn that did not come from the woods in which we had waged battle, but lived in the peaceful house before us. Our talk flagged; we were silent. Then Teddy abruptly remarked:

"I say, I don't want to rake up by-gones and that sort of thing, don't you know, but—er—you mustn't try to kiss her again, d'Haricot."

"Try?" I replied, a little nettled at this aspersion on my abilities. "Why not say, 'You must not kiss her again'?"

"By Jove! did you?" cried Teddy, stopping.

I shrugged my shoulders.

"My dear Lumme, the successful man is he who lies about himself and holds his tongue about women."

"Be hanged!" he exclaimed.

"Well, why not be?" I inquired, placidly.

"I don't believe it," he asserted.

"Continue a sceptic," I counselled.

"She told me she had never kissed any one else," he blurted out.

It was now my turn to start.

"Except whom?" I asked.

"Me—if you must know," said Teddy.

"You kissed her?" I cried.

"Well, it doesn't matter to you."

"Nor does it matter to you that I did," I retorted.

"But did you?" he asked, with such a painful look of inquiry that my indignation melted into humor.

"My dear friend," I replied, "I see it all now. She has deceived us both! We are in the same

159

ship, as you would say; two of those fools that women make to pass a wet afternoon."

"You mean that she has been flirting with me?" he asked, with a woe-begone countenance.

"Also with me," I answered, cheerfully. For a false woman, like spilled cream, is not a matter worth lament.

"I shall ask her," he said, after a minute or two.

"Have you ever known a woman before?" I asked.

"I've known dozens of 'em," he replied, with some indignation.

"And yet you propose to ask one whether she has been true to you?"

"Why shouldn't I?"

"Because, my friend, you will receive such an answer as a minister gives to a deputation."

"But they might both tell the truth."

"Neither ever lies," I replied. "Diplomacy and Eve were invented to obviate the necessity."

This aphorism appeared to give him some food for reflection—or possibly he was merely silenced by a British disgust for anything that was not the roast beef of conversation.

We had come among the terraces and the trim yews and hollies of the garden. The long west wing of Seneschal Court with the high tower above it were close before us. Suddenly he stopped behind the shelter of a pruned and castellated

hedge, and, with the air of a lost traveller seeking
for guidance, asked me,

"I say, what are you going to do?"

"Return to London this morning."

"Why?"

"For the same reason that I leave the table
when dinner is over."

"You won't see her again?"

"See her? Yes, as I should see the remains

of my meal were I to pass through the dining-
room. But I shall not sit down again."

I do not think Teddy quite appreciated this
metaphor.

"Don't you think she is—" he began, but had
some difficulty in finding a word.

"Well served?" I suggested.

"No."

"Digestible, then? No, my friend. I do not

think she is very digestible either for you or for
me. We get pains inside and little nourishment."

"I like her awfully," said poor Teddy.

"Who would not?" I replied. "If a girl is beautiful, charming, not too chary of her favors, and
yet not inartistically lavish; if she knows how
to let a smile spring gently from an artless dim-
ple, how to aim a bright eye and shake a light
curl; and if she is not too fully occupied with
others to spare one an hour or two of these charms,
who would not like her? Personally, I should
adore her—while it lasted."

"Do you really think she isn't all she seems?"
he asked, in a doleful voice.

"On the contrary, I think she is more; considerably more. My dear Lumme, I have studied
this girl dispassionately, critically, as I would a
work of art offered me for sale, and I pronounce
my opinion in three words—she is false! I counsel you, my friend, to leave with me this morning."

"And I should advise you to take this *gentleman's* advice," exclaimed a voice behind us, in a
tone that I cannot call friendly. We turned, possibly with more precipitation than dignity, to see
Miss Amy herself within five paces of us. Evidently she had just appeared round the edge of
the castellated hedge, though how long she had
been standing on the other side I cannot pretend
to guess. Long enough, at any rate, to give her
a very flushed face and an eye that sparkled more

brightly than ever. Indeed, I never saw her to more advantage.

"How dare you!" she cried, tears threatening in her voice; "how *dare* you—talk of me so!"

"Mademoiselle—" I began, with conciliatory humility.

"Don't speak to me!" she interrupted, and turned her brown eyes to Lumme. Undoubted tears glistened in them now.

"So you have been listening to this—this *person's* slanders? And you are going away now because you have learned that I am false? I have been offered for sale like a work of art! He has studied me dispassionately!"

Here she gave me a look whose wrathful significance I will leave you to imagine.

"Go! Go with him! You may be sure that *I* sha'n't ask either of you to stay!"

Never had two men a better case against a woman, and never, I am sure, have two men taken less advantage of it.

"Miss Hudson; I say—" began poor Teddy, in the tone rather of the condemned murderer than the inexorable judge.

"Don't answer me!" she cried, and turned the eyes back to me.

The tears still glistened, but anger shone through them.

"As for you— You—you—*brute!*"

"Pardon me," I replied, in a reasonable tone,

"the conversation you overheard was intended for another."

"Yes," she exclaimed, "while you are trying to force your odious attentions on me, you are attacking me all the time behind my back."

"Behind a hedge," I corrected, as pleasantly as possible.

But this did not appear to mollify her.

"You think every woman you meet is in love with you, I suppose," she sneered. "Well, you may be interested to know that we all think you simply a ridiculous little Frenchman."

"Little!" I exclaimed, justly incensed at this unprovoked and untrue attack. "What do you then call my friend?"

For Lumme was considerably smaller than I, and might indeed have been termed short.

"He knows what I think of him," she answered; and with this ambiguous remark (accompanied by an equally ambiguous flash of her brown eyes at Teddy), she turned scornfully and hurried to the house.

For a moment we stood silent, looking somewhat foolishly at each other.

"You've done it now," said Teddy, at length.

"I have," I replied, my equanimity returning.

"I suppose I'll have to clear out too. Hang it, you needn't have got me into a mess like this," said he, in an injured tone.

"Better a mess than a snare," I retorted. "Let

164

us look up a good train, eat some breakfast, and shake the dust of this house from our feet."

He made no answer, and when we got to the house he tacitly agreed to accompany Shafthead and myself by the 11.25 train.

My things were packed. Halfred and a footman were even piling them on the carriage, and I was making my adieux, when I observed this dismissed suitor enter the hall with his customary cheerful air and no sign of departure about him.

"Are you ready?" I asked him.

"They've asked me to stay till to-morrow,"

he replied, with a conscious look he could not conceal, "and—er—well, there's really no necessity for going to-day. Good-bye—see you soon in town."

"Good-bye," said Amy, sweetly, but with a look in her eyes that belied her voice. "I am so glad we have been able to persuade *one* of you to stay a little longer."

"Better a little fish than an empty dish," I said to myself, and revolving this useful maxim in my mind I departed from Seneschal Court.

Chapter XVII

*"I tell thee in thine ear, he is a man
'Tis wiser thou shouldst drink with than
affront!"*

—BEN VERULAM.

"BUT what is in it?"

"I don't know, sir," said Mr. Titch.
I had just got back to my rooms and stood facing a gigantic packing-case that had appeared in my absence. It was labelled, "For Mr. Balfour, care of M. d'Haricot. Not to be opened." Not another word of explanation, not a letter, not a message, nothing to throw light on the mystery. The three Titches and Halfred stood beside me also gazing at this strange offering.

"Could it be fruit, sir?" suggested Mrs. Titch, in her foolishly wise fashion.

"Fruit!" said Aramatilda, scornfully. "It must weigh near on a ton."

"You 'aven't ordered any furniture inadvertent-

ly, as it were, sir?" asked Halfred, scratching his
head, sagely.

"If anybody has ordered this it is evidently Mr.
Balfour," I replied.

"Who is Mr. Balfour, sir?" said Aramatilda.

"Do you know?" I asked Mr. Titch.

My landlord looked solemn, as he always did
when speaking of the great.

"There is the Right Honorable Arthur Balfour,
nephew to the Marquis—"

"Yes, yes," I interrupted; "but I do not think
that admirable statesman would confide his pur-
chases to me."

"Then, sir," said Mr. Titch, with an air of wash-
ing his hands of all lesser personages, "I give it
up."

"I wish you could," I replied, "but I fear it must
remain here for the present."

They left my room casting lingering glances
at the monstrosity, and once I was alone my curiosity quickly died away. I felt lonely and depressed. Parting from a houseful of guests and
the cheerful air of a country-house, I realized how
foreign, after all, this city was to me. I had acquaintances; I could find my way through the
streets; but what else? Ah, if I were in Paris
now! That name spelled Heaven as I said it over
and over to myself.

I said it the oftener that I might not say "woman." What mockery in that word! Yet I felt

that I must find relief. I opened my journal and this is what I wrote:

"To d'Haricot from d'Haricot.—Foolish friend, beware of those things they call eyes, of that substance they term hair, of that abstraction known as a smile, and, above all, beware of those twin lies styled lips. They kiss but in the intervals of kissing others; they speak but to deceive. Nevermore shall I regard a woman more seriously than I do this pretty, revolving ring of cigarette smoke.

"I am twenty-five, and romance is over. Follow thou my counsel and my example."

Outside it rained—hard, continuously, without room for a hope of sunshine, as it only rains in England, I think. Perhaps I may be unjust, but certainly never before have I been so wet through to the soul. I threw down my pen, I went to the piano, and I began to play "L'Air Bassinette" of Verdi. Gently at first I played, and then more loudly and yet more loudly. So carried away was I that I began to sing.

Now at last the rain is inaudible; my heart is growing light again, when above my melody I hear a most determined knocking on the door. Before I have time to rise, it opens, and there enters—my neighbor, the old General. Is it that he loves music so much? No, I scarcely think so. His face is not that of the ravished dolphin; on the contrary, his eyes are bright with an emotion that is not pleasure, his face is brilliant with a choleric flush. I turn and face him.

"Pray do not stop your pandemonium on my account," he says, with sarcastic politeness. "I have endured it for half an hour, and I now purpose to leave this house and not return till you are exhausted, sir."

"I am obliged to you for your permission," I reply, with equal politeness, "and I shall now endeavor to win my bet."

"Your bet, sir?" he inquires, with scarcely stifled indignation.

"I have made a bet that I shall play and sing for thirty-six consecutive hours," I explain.

"Then, sir, I shall interdict you, as sure as there is law in England!"

"Have you now explained the object of this visit?" I inquire.

"No, sir, I have not. I came in here to request you to make yourself personally known to your disreputable confederates in order that they may not mistake *me* for a damned Bulgarian anarchist —or whatever your country and profession happen to be."

"May I ask you to explain this courteous yet ambiguous demand?"

"Certainly, sir; and I trust you may see fit to put an end to the nuisance. Two days ago I was accosted as I was leaving this house—leaving the

door of my own house, sir, I would have you remark! A dashed half-hanged scoundrel came up
to me and had the impudence to tell me he wanted
to speak to me. 'Well,' I said, 'what is your
business, sir?'

"'My name is Hankey,' said he."

"Hankey!" I exclaimed.

"Yes, sir, Hankey. You know him, then?"

"By name only."

"Then, sir, I had the advantage over you,"
said the General, irately. "I didn't know the
scoundrel from Beelzebub—and I told him so.
Upon that, sir, he had the audacity to throw out
a hint that my friends—as he called his dashed
gang of cut-throats—were keeping an eye on me.
I pass the hint on to you, sir, having no acquaintance myself with such gentry!"

"And was that all that passed?" I asked, feeling too amazed and too interested to take offence.

"No, sir, not all—but quite enough for my taste,
I assure you. I said to him, 'Sir,' I said, 'I know
your dashed name and I may now tell you that
mine is General Sholto; that I am not the man
to be humbugged like this, and that I propose to
introduce you to the first policeman I see.' Gad,
you should have seen the rogue jump! Then it
seemed that he had done me the honor of mistaking me for you, sir, and I must ask you to have
the kindness to take such steps as will enable your
confederates to know you when they see you, or,

by George! I'll put the whole business into the hands of the police!"

I felt strongly tempted to let my indignant fellow-lodger adopt this course, for my feelings towards the absentee tenant of Mount Olympus House could not be described as cordial, and the impudence of his attempt to threaten me took my breath away; but then the thought struck me, "This man is an agent—though I fear an unworthy one—of the Cause. I must sink my own grievances!" Accordingly, with a polite air, I endeavored to lull my neighbor's suspicions, assuring him that it was only a tailor's debt the conspiring Hankey sought from me, and that I would settle the account and abate the nuisance that very afternoon.

He seemed a little mollified; to the extent, at least, that his thunder became a more distant rumble.

"I don't want to ask too many favors at once, sir," he said; "but I fear I must also request you to remove your piano to the basement for the next six-and-thirty hours. I shall not stand it, sir, I warn you!"

"My dear sir," I cried, "that was but a—how does the immortal Shakespeare call it?—a countercheck quarrelsome — that was all. I should not have sung at all had I known you disliked music."

"Music! music!" exclaimed my visitor, with

an expressive blending of contempt and indignation. Then, in a milder tone, yet with the most crushing irony, continued: "I go to every musical piece in London—and enjoy 'em sir; all of 'em. I've even sat out a concert in the Albert Hall; so if I'm not musical, what the deuce am I?"

"It is evident," I replied.

"I might even appreciate your efforts, sir. Very possibly I would, very possibly, supposing I heard 'em at a reasonable hour," said the General, with magnanimity that will one day send him to heaven. "But it is my habit, sir, to take a—ah—a rest in the afternoon, and—er—er—well, it's deuced disturbing."

This is but the echo of the storm among the hills. The wrath of my gallant neighbor is evidently all but evaporated.

"A thousand apologies, sir. If you will be good enough to tell me at what hours my playing is disturbing to you, I shall regulate my melody accordingly."

"Much obliged; much obliged. I don't want to stop you altogether, don't you know," says my visitor, and abruptly inquires, "Professional musician, I presume?"

"Did I sound like it?"

"Beg pardon; being a foreigner, I fancied you'd probably be—er—" He evidently wants to say "a Bohemian," but fears to wound my feelings.

"'A damned Bulgarian anarchist,'" I suggest.

173

He snorts, laughs, and apparently is already inclined to smile at his recent heat.

"I'm a bad-tempered old boy," he says. "Pardon, mossoo."

He is ashamed, I can see, that John Bull should have condescended to lose his temper with a mere foreigner. This point of view is not flattering; but the naïveté of the old boy amuses me.

"Take a seat, sir," I now venture to suggest, "and allow me to offer you a little whiskey and a little soda water."

He hesitates for a moment, for he has not intended that pacification should go to this length; but his kindness of heart prevails. He has erred and he feels he must do this penance for his lack of discretion. So he says, "Thank you," and down he sits.

And that was the beginning of my acquaintance with my martial neighbor, General Sholto. In half an hour we were talking away like old friends; indeed, I soon began to suspect that the old gentleman felt as pleased as I did to have company on that wet afternoon.

"I understand that you adorn the British army," I remark.

"I was a soldier, sir; I was a soldier. I would be now if I'd had the luck of some fellows. A superannuated fossil; that's what I am, mossoo; an old wreck, no use to any one."

As he says this, he draws himself up to show

that the wreck still contains beans, as the English proverb expresses it, but the next moment the fire dies out of his eyes and he sits meditatively, looking suddenly ten years older. He did not intend me to believe his words, but to himself they have a meaning.

I am silent.

"I am one of the unemployed," he adds, in a minute.

"I also," I reply.

I like my neighbor; I am in need of a companion; and I tell him frankly my story. His sympathies are entirely with me.

"I'm happy to meet a young man who sticks up for the decencies nowadays," he says. "Bring back your King, sir, give him a free hand, and set us an example in veneration and respect and all the rest of it. You'll make a clean sweep, I suppose. Guillotine, eh? Not a bad thing if used on the proper people."

I am ashamed to confess how half-hearted my own theories of restoration are, compared with this out-and-out suggestion. I can but twist my mustache, and, looking as truculent as possible, mutter:

"Well, well, we shall see when the time comes.

When at last he rises to leave me, he repeats with emphasis his conviction that republicanism should be trodden out under a heavy boot, and so mollified is he by my tactful treatment that as we part he even invites me into that carefully guarded room of his. It is not yet a specific invitation.

"Some day soon I'll hope to see you in my own den, mossoo. Au revoir, sir; happy to have met you."

Yet I cannot help thinking that even this is a triumph of diplomacy. My spirits rise; my ridiculous humors have been charmed quite away. As for woman, she seems not even worth cynical comment in my journal. "Give me man!" I say to myself.

Chapter XVIII

*"A drop of water on a petal in the sun-
shine; that same drop down thy neck in
a cavern. Both are woman; thy mood and
the occasion make the sole difference."*
                                    —CERVANTO Y'ALVEZ.

RECORD of an episode taken from my
journal, and written upon the evening
following my first meeting with the
General:

"This afternoon I decide to go to the Temple
and see Dick Shafthead. We shall dine together
quietly, and I shall vent what is left of my humors and be refreshed by his good-humored rail-
lery. The afternoon is fading into evening as I
mount his stairs; the lamps are being lit; by this
hour he should have returned. But no; I knock
and knock again, and get no answer.

"'Well,' I say to myself, 'he cannot be long.
I shall wait for him outside.'

"I descend again to wait in that quiet and soothing court, where the fountain plays and the gold-
fish swim and the autumn leaves tremble overhead. Now and then one of these drops stealthily
upon the pavement; the pigeons flit by, settle,
fly off again; people pass occasionally; but at first
that is all that happens. At last there enters a
woman, who does not pass through, but loiters on
the farther side of the fountain as though she were
meditating—or waiting for somebody. So far as
I can judge in the half-light and at a little distance,
she is young, and her outline is attractive; therefore I conclude she is not meditating.

"She does not see me, but I should like to see
more of her. I walk round the fountain and come
up behind her. She hears my step, turns sharply,
and approaches, evidently prepared to greet me.
Words are on the tip of her tongue, when abruptly
she starts back. She does not know me, after all.
But quickly, before she has time to recover herself,
I raise my hat and say:

"'I cannot be mistaken. We have met at the
bishop's?'

"It is a happy inspiration, I think, to choose so
respectable a host, and for a moment she is staggered. Probably she does actually know a bishop, and may have met a not ill-looking gentleman
somewhat resembling myself at his house. In this
moment I perceive that she is certainly young and
very far removed, indeed, from being unattractive.

"To me, meeting her dark eyes for an instant, and then seeing the fair, full face turn to a fair profile as she looks away in some confusion, she seems beyond doubt very beautiful. A simple straw hat covers her dark coil of hair and slopes arrogantly forward over a luminous and brilliant

she hears my step

eye; her nose is straight, her mouth small, suggesting decision and a little petulance, her chin deep and finely moulded, her complexion delicate as a rare piece of alabaster, while her figure matches these distracting charms.

"I make these notes so full that I may the better summon her to my memory. Also I note that the colors she wears are rich and bright; there is red and there is dark green; and they seem to make her beauty stand out with a boldness that corresponds to the dark glance of her eye. Not that she

is anything but most modest in her demeanor,
but, ah! that eye! Its glow betrays a fire deep
underneath.

"Her eye meets mine again, then she says:

"'I—I don't know you. I thought you were—
I mean I don't know why you spoke to me.'

"Evidently she does not quite know how to
meet the situation.

"I decide that it is the duty of a gentleman to
assist her.

"'I spoke because I thought I knew you, and
hoped for an instant I was remembered.'

"'You had no business to,' she replies. Her
air is haughty, but a little theatrical. I mean
that she does not entirely convince me of her displeasure.

"'Mademoiselle, I offer you a thousand apologies. I see now that if I had really met you before
I could not possibly confuse your face with another's. Doubtless I ought to have been more
cautious, but as you perhaps guess, I am a foreigner, and I do not understand the English
customs in these matters.'

"She receives this speech with so much com-
plaisance that I feel emboldened to continue.

"'I am also solitary, and meeting with a face I
thought I knew seemed providential. Do you
grant me your pardon?'

"She gives a little laugh that is more than half
friendly.

"'Of course—if it was a mistake.'

"'Such a pleasant mistake that I should like to continue in error,' I reply.

"But at this she draws back, and her expression changes a little. It does not become altogether hostile, but it undoubtedly changes.

"'May I ask you a favor?' I say, quickly, and with a modest air. 'I was looking for a friend and have become lost in this Temple. Can you tell me where number thirty-four is?'

"'Yes,' she replies, with a look that penetrates, and, I think, rather enjoys, this simple ruse, 'it is next to number thirty-three.' And with that she turns to go, so abruptly that I cannot help suspecting she also desires to hide a smile.

"But observing that I, too, shall not waste more time here, I also turn, and as she does not actually order me away, I walk by her side, studying her afresh from the corner of my eye. She is of middle height, or perhaps an inch above it; she walks with a peculiar swing that seems to say, "I do not care one damn for anybody'; and the expression of her eyes and mouth bear out this sentiment.

"Does she resent my conduct?

"Yes, probably she does, though my demeanor is humility itself.

"'You came to enjoy the quiet of the Temple, mademoiselle?'

"'I was enjoying it—till I was interrupted,' she answers, still smiling, though not in my direction.

"I notice that she again casts her eye round the court, and I make a reckless shot.

"'Perhaps you, too, expected to see a friend?'

"The eyes blaze at me for an instant.

"'No, I did not,' she says, abruptly, and mends her pace still further.

"'I noticed another lady here before you came,' I say, mendaciously, and with a careless air, as though I thought it most natural that two ladies should rendezvous at that hour in the Temple. She gives me a quick glance, which I meet unruffled.

"We pass through a gate and into a side street, and here, by the most evil fortune, a cab was standing.

"'Cabman,' says the lady, abruptly, 'are you engaged?'

"The next moment she has sprung into the cab, bade me a 'good-bye' that seems compounded of annoyance and of laughter, with perhaps a touch of kindness added, thrown me a swift glance of her brilliant eyes, and jingled out of my sight. And I have not even learned her name.

"This exit of the fair Miss Unknown is made so suddenly that for half a minute I stand with my hat in my hand still, foolishly smiling.

"Then I give an exclamation that might be deemed profane, rush round a corner and up a street, catch a glimpse of the back of a cab disappearing into the traffic of the Strand, leap into another, and bid my driver pursue that hansom in front.

" Well, I had a spirited chase while it lasted, for my quarry had a swift steed, and there were many other cabs in the Strand that would have confused the scent for any but the most relentless sleuth-hound. It ended in Pall Mall, where I had the satisfaction of seeing the flying chariot deposit a stout gentleman before a most respectable club.

" I drove to my rooms with my ardor cooled and my cynicism fast returning, and had almost landed at my door when a most surprising coincidence occurred, so surprising that I suspect it was the contrivance of either Providence or the devil. A cab left the door just as I drove up, and in it sat Miss Unknown! I was too dumfounded to turn in pursuit, and, besides, I was too curious to learn the reason of this visit.

" By the greatest good luck the door was opened by Halfred, who in his obliging way lent his services now and then when the maid was out.

"'Did she leave her name?' I cried.

"'Beg pardon, sir?' said Halfred, in astonishment.

"'I mean the lady who just called for me.'

"'She hasked for General Sholto, sir.'

" My face fell.

"'The devil she did!' I exclaimed.

"'Yes, sir,' said he; 'that's the lady as visits 'im sometimes.'

183

"I whistled.

"'Was the General at home?'

"'No, sir, but she left a message as 'ow she'd call again to-morrow morning.'

"'Halfred,' I said, 'do not deliver that message. I shall see to it myself.'

"And so Miss Unknown is the gay General's mysterious visitor. And I caught her at another rendezvous. But she denied this. Bah! I do not believe her. I trust no woman.

"On my mind is left a curious impression from this brief passage—an impression of a beautiful wild animal, half shy, half bold, dreading the cage, but not so much, I think, the chase. Yes, decidedly there was something untamed in her air, in her eye, in her devil-may-care walk. For myself a savage queen has few charms, especially if she have merely the cannibal habit without the simplicity of attire.

"Yet, mon Dieu, I have but seen her once! Come, to-morrow may show her in a better light. Ah, my gay dog of a General! It is unfortunate for you that you were so anxious to make my acquaintance!"

Here ends the entry in my journal. You shall now see with what tact and acumen I pursued this entertaining intrigue.

Chapter XIX

*"Introduce you to my mistress? I should
as soon think of lending you my umbrella!"*
—HERCULE D'ENVILLE.

OOD - MORNING, General. I have come to return your call."

"G" The General stood in the door of his room, holding it half closed behind him. He wore a very old shooting-coat, smeared with many curious stains. Evidently he was engaged upon some unclean work, and evidently, also, he would have preferred me to call at some other hour. I remembered, now, Halfred's dark hints as to his occupation; but I remembered still more distinctly the dark eyes of Miss Unknown, and, whether he desired my company or not, I was determined to spend that morning in his room.

"Morning, mossoo," he said. "Glad to see you, but—er—I'm afraid I'm rather in a mess at present."

"You are the better company, then, for a conspirator who is never out of one," I replied, gayly.
Still he hesitated.

"My dear General, positively I shall not permit you to treat me with such ceremony," I insisted. "I shall empty your ink-pot over my coat to keep you company if you persist in considering me too respectable."

Well, who could withstand so importunate a visitor? I entered the carefully guarded chamber, smiling at myself at the little dénouement that was to follow, and curious in the mean time to see what kind of a den it was that this amorous dragon dwelt in. The first glance solved the mystery of his labors. An easel stood in one corner, a palette and brushes lay on a table, a canvas rested upon the easel; in a word, my neighbor pursued the arts!

He looked at me a little awkwardly as I glanced round at these things.

"Fact is, I dabble a bit in art," he explained. "I have nothing to do, don't you know, and—er— I always felt drawn to the arts. Amateur work —mere amateur work, as you can see for yourself, but I flatter myself this ain't so bad, eh? Miss Ara—Ara—what the devil's her name?—Titch. Done from memory, of course; I don't want these busybodies here to know what I'm doing."

"You keep your proficiency a secret, then?" I said, gazing politely at this wonderful work of memory. It was not very like nor very artistic, and I wished to avoid passing any opinion.

"Never told a soul but you, mossoo, and—er—well, there's only one other in the secret."

Again I smiled to myself.

"Fact is I dabble a bit in Art."

"It must be delightful to perpetuate the faces of your lady friends," I remarked.

The old boy smiled with some complacency.

"That's rather my forte, I consider," he replied.

"You are fortunate!" I cried. "I would that I had such an excuse for my gallantries!"

"Come now, mossoo, I'm an old boy, remember!" he protested, though he did not seem at all displeased by this innuendo.

"You are at the most dangerous age for a woman's peace of mind."

187

"Tuts—nonsense!" said he. "Twenty years ago, I don't mind admitting—er—"

"I understand! And twenty years subsequent to that? Ah, General!'

He laughed good-humoredly. He admitted that for his years he was certainly as youthful as most men. He had become in an excellent temper both with himself and his guest, when suddenly our conversation was interrupted by a knocking at the door. He barely had time to open it when the dénouement arrived. In other words, Miss Unknown stepped into the room. Yet at the threshold she paused, for I could see that at the first glance she recognized me and knew not what to make of this remarkable coincidence.

As she stood there she made a picture that put into the shade anything a much greater artist than the General could have painted, with her deep, finely turned chin cast a little upward and her dark, glowing eyes looking half arrogantly, half doubtingly, round the room. I noted again the petulant, wilful expression in the small mouth and the indescribable, untamed air. As before, she was dressed in bright colors, that set her off as a heavy gold frame sets off a picture; only her color this time was a vivid shade of purple.

She paused but for a moment, and then she evidently made up her mind to treat me as a stranger, for she turned her glance indifferently to my host and asked, in an off-hand tone,

"Didn't you know I was coming this morning?"

"I? No," said he, with an air as embarrassed as I could have wished.

"I left a message yesterday afternoon."

"I never got it."

"You mean you forgot it."

"I mean I never got it," he repeated, irately this time.

She made a grimace, as much as to say, "Don't lose your temper," and glanced again at me.

"My niece, Miss Kerry," said he, hurriedly, introducing me with a jerk of his hand.

His "niece"! I smiled to myself at this euphonism, but bowed as deferentially as if I had really believed her to be his near relation, for I have always believed that the flattery of respect paves the way more readily than any other.

She smiled charmingly, while I by my glance endeavored further to assure her that my discretion was complete.

We exchanged a few polite words, and then she turned contemptuously to the canvas.

"Are you still at this nonsense?" she asked, with a smile, it is true, but not a very flattering one.

"Still at it, Kate," he replied, looking highly annoyed with her tone.

Evidently this hobby of his was a sore subject between them and one which did not raise him in her estimation. For a moment I was assailed by compunction at having thus let her convict him in the ridiculous act. "Yet, after all, they are May and December," I reflected, "and if the worst comes to the worst, I can find a much more suitable friend for this 'niece.'"

With a movement that was graceful in spite of its free and easy absence of restraint, she rummaged first for and then in her pocket and produced a letter which she handed to her "uncle," asking,

"What is the meaning of this beastly thing?"

Yes, unquestionably her language, like her carriage and her eyes, had something of the savage queen.

The General read the missive with a frown and glanced in my direction uncomfortably as he answered,

"It is obviously—er—"

"Oh, it's by way of being a bill," she interrupted. "I don't need to be told that. But what am I to do?"

"Pay it."

"Well, then, I'll need—" She stopped, glanced at me, and then, with a defiantly careless laugh, said, boldly, "I'll need an advance."

"The deuce you will!" said the General. "At this moment I can scarcely go into—"

"Don't trouble," she interrupted. "Just write me a check, please."

Without a word, but with a very sulky expression, the General banged open a writing-desk and hastily scribbled in his check-book, while the undutiful Miss Kerry turned to me as graciously as ever. But I thought I had carried my plot far enough for the present. Besides, she must come down-stairs, and my room was on the ground floor.

"I fear I must leave you, General," I said.

"I must go, too," said Miss Kerry, as I turned to make my adieux to her. "Good-bye, uncle. Much obliged for this."

It seemed to my ear that there was a laugh in that word "uncle," and as I saw the unfortunate warrior watch our exit with a face as purple as his "niece's" dress, I heartily pitied the foiled Adonis. Yet if fortune chose so to redistribute her gifts, was it for me to complain?

"May I accompany you for a short distance this time?" I asked.

And a couple of minutes later I was gayly walking with her from the house, prepared to hail a cab and hurry away my prize upon the first sign of pursuit. No appearance, however, of a bereaved general officer running hatless and distraught with jealousy behind us. Evidently he had resigned himself to his fate—or did he place such reliance in the fidelity and devotion of his " niece "? Well, we should see about that!

"Then you remembered me?" I said.

"How do you know?"

"By that question. Ah, it has betrayed you!

Yes, you do remember the ignorant and importunate foreigner who pursued you with his unpleasing attentions?''

"But it was a mistake, you said," she replied, with a flash of her eyes that seemed to mean much.

"A mistake, of course," I said. "And now let us take a cab and have some lunch."

She appeared a little surprised at this bold suggestion, and recollecting that an appearance of propriety is very rigorously observed in England, often where one would least expect it, I modified my *élan* to a more formal gallantry, and very quickly persuaded her to accompany me to the most fashionable restaurant in Piccadilly.

Even then, though she was generous of her smiles and those flashing glances that I could well imagine kindling the gallant heart of General Sholto, and though her talk was dashed with slang and marked with a straightforward freedom, yet she always maintained a sufficient dignity to check any too presumptuous advances. But by this time all compunction for my gallant neighbor had vanished in the delights of Miss Kerry's society, and I was not to be balked so easily.

"To-night I wish you to do me a favor," I said, earnestly.

"Yes? What is it?" she smiled.

"I have a box at the Gaiety Theatre, and I should

like a friend to dine with me first, and then see
the play."

As a matter of fact the box was not yet taken,
but how was she to know that?

"And I am to be the friend?" she asked.

"If you will be so kind?"

"My uncle is coming, of course?"

I smiled at her, and she beamed back at me.

"We understand each other," I thought. "But,
my faith, how persistently she keeps up this little
farce!"

Aloud I said:

"Of course. Without an uncle by my side I
should not even venture to turn out the gas.
Would you?"

"Of course not!" she replied.

And so it was arranged that at half-past seven
we were to meet at this same restaurant. In the
mean time what dreams of happiness!

13

Chapter XX

"Virtue is our euphonism for reaction."
—LA RABIDE.

ALF-PAST seven had just struck upon a church clock close by. Five minutes passed, ten minutes, and then she appeared, more beautiful than ever—irresistible, in fact.

"But is this a private room?" she asked, as she surveyed the comfortable little apartment with the dinner laid for two, and the discreet waiter opening the wine.

"It could not be more so, I assure you."

She glanced at the two places. "Isn't my uncle coming?" she demanded.

I was prepared for this little formality, which, it seemed, spiced the adventure for her.

"At the last moment he was indisposed," I explained, gravely; "but he will join us for dessert."

The impossibility of gainsaying this, and the attractiveness of the present circumstances—such as they were without an uncle—quickly induced her to accept this untoward accident with resignation, and in a few minutes we were as merry a party of two as you could wish to find. Our jests began to have a more and more friendly sound.

"You do not care for this entrée?" I asked.

"It is rather hot for my taste."

"Not so warm as my heart at this moment," I declared.

"What nonsense you talk!" she cried. "It has some meaning in French, though, I suppose.

Yet she laughed delightfully.

"Much meaning," I assured her.

"When was my uncle taken ill?" she asked, once.

Our eyes met and we mutually smiled.

"When you left his room with me," I replied.

And this answer seemed perfectly to satisfy her.

"What do you do with yourself all day?" I asked.

Again she laughed.

"You will only laugh," she said.

"I shall be as solemn as a judge, a jury, and three expert witnesses," I assured her.

"A friend and I are starting a women's mission."

I certainly became solemn — dumfounded, for one instant, in fact. Then a light dawned upon me.

"Your friend is a clergyman, I presume?" I asked.

I had noticed the poster of an evening paper with the words "Clerical Scandal," and I suppose that put this solution into my head.

"My friend is a she," she replied, with a laugh. "Clergyman? No, thanks! We are doing it all ourselves."

"Ha, ha!" I laughed. "I see now what you mean! Excellent! Forgive my stupidity."

I did not see at all, but I supposed that there must be some English idiom which I did not understand. Doubtless I had lost an innuendo, but then one must expect leakage somewhere. Surely I was obtaining enough and could afford to lack a little.

At last we arrived at dessert.

"I wonder if my uncle has come?" she said.

"I have just been visited by a presentiment," I replied. "General Sholto has retired to bed. This information has been conveyed to me by a spirit—the spirit of love!"

She looked at me with a new expression. Ought I to have restrained my ardor a little longer?

"Does he know I am here?" she asked, quickly.

"I assure you, on my honor, he has not the least notion!" I declared, emphatically.

"Then—" she began, but words seemed to fail her. "Good-night," she said, dramatically, but with unmistakable emphasis.

She rose and stepped towards the door with the air of a tragedy queen.

A thought, too horrible to be true, rushed into my heated brain.

"Stop, one moment!" I implored her. "Do you mean to say that—that he is *really* your uncle?"

Her look of indignant consternation answered the question.

I sank into my chair, and, seeing me in this plight, she paused to complete my downfall.

"What did you imagine?" she asked.

I endeavored to collect my wits.

"Who did you think I was?" she demanded.

what did you imagine?

"Mademoiselle," I replied, "behold a crushed, a penitent, a ridiculous figure. I am even more ignorant of your virtuous country than I imagined. Forgive me, I implore you! I shall endow your mission with fifty pounds; I shall walk home

197

barefoot; you have but to name my penance and I shall undergo it!"

Whether it was that my contrition was so complete or for some more flattering reason that I may not hint at, I cannot tell you to this day, but certainly Miss Kerry proved more lenient than I had any right to expect. Not that she did not give me as unpleasant a quarter of an hour as I have ever tingled through. I, indeed, got "what for," as the English say. But before she left she had actually smiled upon me again and very graciously uttered the words, "I forgive you."

As for myself, I became filled with a glow of penitence and admiration; the admiration being a kind of moral atonement which I felt I owed to this virtuous and beautiful girl. At that moment the seven virtues seemed incarnate in her, and the seven deadly sins in myself. I was in the mood to pay her some exaggerated homage; I had also consumed an entire bottle of champagne, and I offered her—my services in her mission to woman! I should be her secretary, I vowed. Touched by my earnestness, she at last accepted my offer, and when we parted and I walked home in the moonlight, I hummed an air from a splendid oratorio.

Though the hour was somewhat late when I got in, it seemed to me the commonest courtesy to pay another call upon General Sholto and inquire—after his health, for example. I called, I found him in, and not yet gone to bed as my presentiment had advised me, and in two minutes we happened to be talking about his niece.

It appeared that she was the orphan and only child of his sister, and that for some years Kate and her not inconsiderable fortune had been left in his charge, but from the first I fear that she had proved rather a handful for the old boy to manage.

"A fine girl, sir; a handsome girl," he declared, "but a rum 'un if ever there was. I'd once thought of living together, making a home and all that; but, as I said, mossoo, she's a rum girl. You noticed her temper this morning? Hang it, I was ashamed of her!"

"Where is she, then?" I asked.

"Living in a flat of her own with another woman. She is great on her independence, mossoo. Fine spirit, no doubt, but—er—just a little dull for me sometimes."

"She is young," I urged, for I seemed to see only Miss Kerry's side of the argument. "And you, General—"

"Am old," he said. "Hang it, she doesn't let me forget that."

Evidently, I thought, my neighbor was feeling out of sorts, or he would never show so little appreciation of his charming niece. I must take up my arms on behalf of maligned virtue.

"I am certain she regards you with a deep

though possibly not a demonstrative affection,"
I declared. "She does not know how to ex-
press it; that is all. She is love inarticulate,
General!"

"It hasn't taken you long to find that out,"
said he; but observing the confusion into which,
I fear, this threw me, he hastened to add, with a
graver air: "Young women, mossoo, and young
men too, for the matter of that, have to get tired
of 'emselves before they waste much affection
on any one else."

I protested so warmly that the General's smile
became humorous again.

"You forget the grand passion!" I exclaimed.
"Your niece is at the age of love."

"Possibly a young man might—er—do the trick
and that kind of thing," he replied. "But I don't
think Kate is very likely to fall in love at present
—unless it's with one of her own notions."

"Her own notions?" I asked.

"Well," he explained, "the kind of man I'd
back for a place would be a good-looking cabby
or a long-haired fiddler. She'd rig him out with
a soul, and so forth, to suit her fancy — and a
deuce of a life they'd lead!"

No use in continuing this discussion with such
an unsympathetic and unappreciative critic. He
was unworthy to be her uncle, I said to myself.

When I returned to my own rooms, I opened my
journal and wrote this striking passage:

"Illusion gone, clear sight returns. I have found a woman worthy of homage, of admiration, of friendship. Love (if, indeed, I ever felt that sacred emotion for any) has departed to make room for a worthier tenant. Reason rules my heart. I see dispassionately the virtues of Kate Kerry; I regard them as the mariner regards the polar star."

I reproduce this extract for the benefit of the young, just as—to pursue my original and nautical metaphor — they put buoys above a dangerous wreck or mark a reef in the chart. It is on the same principle as the awful example who (I am told) accompanies the Scottish temperance lecturer.

Chapter XXI

"If you would improve their lot,
Put a penny in the slot!"
—ENGLISH SONG (ADAPTED).

ERTAINLY John Bull is a singularly sentimental animal. I have said so before, but I should like to repeat it now with additional emphasis. I do not believe that he ever sold his wife at Smithfield, or, if he did, he became dreadfully penitent immediately after and forthwith purchased a new one. He is not a socialist; that is a too horribly and coldly logical creed for him, but he enjoys stepping forth from the seclusion of that well-furnished castle which every Englishman is so proud of, and dutifully endeavoring to ameliorate the condition of the working-classes.

"England expects every man to do his duty," he repeats, as he puts his hand into his capacious pocket and provides half a dozen mendicants with the means of becoming intoxicated.

Oh yes, my kind English friends, I admit that I am putting it strongly; but again let me remind you (in case you ever see these words) that if I begin to be quite serious I shall cease to be quite readable. The working-man, I quite allow, is provided with the opportunity of learning the violin and the geography of South America and the Thirty-nine Articles of the Anglican Church, besides obtaining many other substantial advantages from the spread of the Altruistic Idea. You are wiser than I am (certainly more serious), and you have done these deeds. For my part, I shall now confine myself to recording my own share in one of them. Only I must beg you to remember that for a time I was actually a philanthropist myself, and as a mere chronicler write with some authority.

The mission of which I now found myself unpaid and unqualified secretary was a recently born but vigorous infant; considering the sex for which it catered, I think this simile is both appropriate and encouraging. The credit of the inspiring idea belonged to Miss Clibborn, the friend with whom my dark-eyed divinity shared a flat; the funds were supplied by both these ladies and from the purses of such of their friends as admired inspiring ideas or intoxicating glances; the office was in an East London street of so dingy an aspect that I felt some small peccadillo atoned for every time I walked along its savory pavements. By the time I had spent a day in that office I could with confidence have murdered a member of Parliament or abducted a clergyman's wife; so much, I was sure, must have been placed to the credit side of my account, that these crimes would be cancelled at once.

Yet can I call it drudgery or penance to sit in the same room with Kate Kerry, to discuss with her whether Mrs. Smith should receive a mangle or Mrs. Brown a roll of flannel and two overshoes, to admonish her extravagance or elicit her smiles? Scarcely, I fear, and I must base my claims to any credit from this adventure upon the hours when she happened to be absent and I had to amuse myself by abortive efforts to mesmerize a peculiarly unsusceptible office cat.

From this you will perhaps surmise that there was no great press of business in our mission; and, indeed, there was not, or I should not have been permitted to conduct its affairs so long; for I spent nearly three weeks in furthering the cause of woman. As for our work, it was really too comprehensive to describe in detail. All women in the district, as they were informed by a notice outside our door, were free to come in. Advice in all cases, assistance in some, was to be given gratuitously. In time, when the mission had thoroughly established its position and influence, these women were to be formed into a league having for its objects female franchise, a thorough reform of the marriage laws, and the opening of all professions and occupations whatsoever to the gentler but, my employers were convinced, more capable sex. In a word, we were the thin end of the Amazonian wedge.

The strong brain which had devised this far-reaching scheme resided in the head of Miss Clib-

when she happened
to be absent.

born. Concerning her I need only tell you that she was a pale little woman with an intense expression, a sad lack of humor, and an extreme distrust of myself. She did not amuse me in the least, and I was relieved to find that her duties consisted chiefly in propagating her ideas in the homes of the women of that and other neighborhoods.

As for Kate, she had entered upon the undertaking with a high spirit, a full purse, and a strong conviction that woman was a finer animal than man and that something should be done in consequence. In the course of a week or two, however, the spirit began to weary a little, the purse was becoming decidedly more empty; and, though the conviction remained as strong as ever, one can think of other things surprisingly well in spite of a conviction, and Miss Kerry's thoughts began to get a little distracted by her secretary, I am afraid, while his became even more distracted by Miss Kerry.

Plato; that was the theme on which we spoke. A platonic friendship—magnificent and original idea! We should show the astonished world what could be done in that line of enterprise. How eloquently I talked to her on this profound subject! On her part, she listened, she threw me more dazzling smiles and captivating glances, she delivered delightfully unconsidered opinions with the most dashing assurance, she smoked my cigarettes and we opened the window afterwards. This was philanthropy, indeed.

Do you think I was unreasonably prejudiced in this lady's favor? Picture to yourself soft lashes fringing white lids that would hide for a while and then suddenly reveal two dark stars glowing with possibilities of romance; set these in the midst of the ebb and flow of sudden smiles and passing moods; crown all this with rich coils of deep-brown hair, and frame it in soft colors and textures chosen, I used to think, by some sprite who wished to bring distraction among men. Then sit by the hour beside this siren who treats you with the kind confidence of a friend, who attracts and eludes, perplexes and delights you, suggesting by her glance more than she says, recompensing by her smile for half an hour's perversity. Do this before judging me.

But I am now the annalist of a mission, and I must narrate one incident in our work that proved to have a very momentous bearing on that generous inspiration of two women's minds.

Kate and I had been talking together for the greater part of a profitable morning, when a woman entered our austere apartment.

She was one of our few regular applicants; a not ill-looking, plausible, tidily dressed widow who confessed to thirty and probably was five years older.

"Good-morning, Mrs. Martin," said Kate, with a haughty, off-hand graciousness that, I fear, intimidated these poor people more than it flattered them. "What do you want?"

"Please, mum," said Mrs. Martin, glancing from one to the other of us and beginning an effective little dry cough, "my 'ealth is a-suffering dreadful from this weather. The doctor 'e says nothink but a change of hair won't do any good. I was that bad last night, miss, I scarcely thought I'd see the morning."

And here the good lady stopped to cough again.

"Well," said Kate, "what can we do?"

"If I 'ad the means to get to the seaside for a week, miss, my 'ealth would benefit extraordinary; the doctor 'e says Margate, sir, would set me up wonderful."

"You had better see the doctor, Miss Kerry," I suggested.

"Oh, I can't be bothered. I've seen him before; he's a stupid little fool. Give her a pound."

"A pound, mum—" began Mrs. Martin, in a tone of decorous expostulation.

"A pound, Mum—"

"Oh, give her three, then," said Kate, impatiently.

Just as the grateful recipient of woman's generosity to her sex was retiring with her booty, Miss Clibborn returned from her round of duty. She was the business partner, with the shrewd head, the judgment comparatively unbiassed, the true soul of the missionary. I give her full credit for all these virtues in spite of her antipathy to myself.

She overheard the last words of the effusive Mrs. Martin, demanded an explanation from us, and frowned when she got it.

"You had much better have investigated the case, Kate," she observed, in a tone of rebuke.

"So I did," replied Kate, with charming insolence. "I asked her whether she went to church and why she wore feathers in her hat, and if she had pawned her watch—all the usual idiotic questions."

"Kate," said her friend severely, "this spirit is fatal to our success."

"Spirit be bothered!" retorted the more mundane partner.

"Ladies," I interposed amicably, "I have in my overcoat pocket a box of chocolate creams. Honor me by accepting them!"

Not even this overture could mollify Miss Clibborn, and presently she departed again with a sad glance at her lukewarm ally and frivolous secretary.

Ah, how divine Kate looked as she consumed those bonbons and our talk turned back to Plato! So divine, indeed, that I felt suddenly impelled to ask a question, to solve a little lingering doubt that sometimes would persist in coming to poison my faith in my friend.

"I have been wondering," I said, after a pause.

"Wondering what?"

"You remember that evening I met you in the Temple? I was wondering what rendezvous you were keeping."

"What a funny idea!" she laughed. "I took a fancy to walk in the Temple; that was all."

"And expected no one?"

"Of course not!"

At last I was entirely satisfied, so satisfied that I felt a strong and sudden desire to fervently embrace this lovely, pure-hearted creature.

But no; it would be sacrilege! I said to myself. She would never forgive me. Our friendship would be at an end. The rules of Plato do not permit such liberties. Alas!

Chapter XXII

" To the foolish give counsel from the
head; to the wise from the heart!"
—CERVANTO Y'ALVEZ.

VER since I became secretary I had
been as one dead to my friends. Except the General, I had seen none of
them. One or two, including Dick
Shafthead, had called upon me, only
to be told that I might not return until long after
midnight (for I was occasionally in the habit of
dining with one of my employers after my labors).
When I thought of Dick, my conscience smote
me. I intended always to write to him, and also
to Lumme, to explain my disappearance, but never
took pen in hand. I heard nothing from France,
nothing about the packing-case; nor did I trouble
my head about this silence. The present moment was enough for me. To Halfred I had
only mentioned that I was busily employed in a
distant part of London, and I fear my servant's

vivid imagination troubled him considerably, for he was earnestly solicitous about my welfare.

"It ain't nothing I can lend a 'and in, sir?" he inquired one day.

"I am afraid not," I replied.

He hesitated, uncertain how best to express his doubts politely and indicate a general warning.

"You'll excuse me, sir, for saying so," he remarked at last, "but Mr. Titch 'e says that fur-riners sometimes gets themselves into trouble without knowing as 'ow they are doing anything wrong."

"Tell Mr. Titch, with my compliments, to go to the devil and mind his own business," I replied, with, I think, pardonable wrath.

Tell Mr. Titch ....
to go to the Devil.

"Yes, sir; very good, sir," said Halfred, hastily; but I do not know that his doubts were removed. However I consoled myself for my want of confidence in him by thinking that he had now a fair field with Aramatilda.

On the evening of that day when we had despatched Mrs. Martin to the seaside, I returned earlier than usual and sat in my easy-chair ruminating on the joys and drawbacks of platonic friendship. "Yes," I said to myself, "it is pleasant, it is pure—devilish pure—and it is elevating. But altogether satisfactory? No, to be candid; something begins to be lacking. If I had had the audacity this morning—what would she have said? Despised me? Alas, no doubt! Yet, is there not something delicate, ideal, out of all ordinary experience in our relations? And would I risk the loss of this? Never!"

At this point there came a knock upon the door, and in walked my dear Dick Shafthead.

"Found you at last," he said. "Well, monsieur, give an account of yourself. What have you been doing—burgling or duelling or what?"

His manner was as cool and unpretentiously friendly as ever; he was the same, yet with a subtle difference I was instantly conscious of. There was I know not what of kindness in his eye, of greater courtesy in his voice. Somehow there seemed a more sympathetic air about him. Slight though it was, this something insensibly drew forth my confidence. Naturally, I should have hesitated to confess my little experiment in Plato and my improbable vocation to such a satirical

critic. I could picture the grim smile with which
he would listen, the dry comments he would make.
But this evening I was emboldened to make a
clean breast of it, and, though his smile was certainly sometimes a little more humorous than
sympathetic, yet he heard me with a surprising
appearance of interest.

"Then she's deuced pretty and embarrassingly
proper?" he said, when I had finished the outline
of my story.

"Indeed, my friend, she is both."

"Novel experience?" he suggested.

"Entirely novel."

"And what's to be the end of it?"

I shrugged my shoulders.

"Going to marry her?"

"Marry!" I exclaimed. "I have told you we are
not even lovers. Dick, I cannot tell you what my feeling is towards her, because I do not know it myself.
Yes, perhaps it is love. She has virtues; I have
told you them—her truth, her high spirit, her—"

"Yes, yes," interrupted Dick, with something
of his old brutality, "you've given me the list already. Let's hear her faults."

"She is so full of delightful faults I know not
where to begin. Perverse, sometimes inconsider-
ate, without knowledge of herself. Divide these
up into the little faults they give rise to in different circumstances, and you get a picture of an
imperfect but charming woman."

"It is evident *you* don't know what falling in love means," said Dick.

I looked at him hard.

"Do you?" I asked.

Dick actually blushed.

"Well," he replied, with a smile that had a little tenderness as well as humor, "since you are a man of feeling, monsieur, and by way of being—don't you know?—yourself, I might as well tell you. I've rather played the fool, I expect."

He said this with an air of sincerity, but it was clear he did not think himself so very stupid in the matter.

"My dear friend," I cried, "I am all ears and sympathy—also intelligent advice."

And then the story came out. I shall not give it in Dick's words, for these were not selected with a view to romantic effect, and the story deserves better treatment.

It appeared that, some twenty years before, a cousin of Lady Shafthead's had taken a step which forever disgraced her in the eyes of her impecunious but ancient family. She had, in fact, married the local attorney, a vulgar but insinuating person with a doubtful reputation for honesty and industry. The consequences bore out the warnings of her family; he went from bad to worse, and she from discomfort to misery, until, at last, they both died, leaving not a single penny in the world, but, instead, a little orphan daughter. Of all the scandalized relations, Lady Shafthead had alone come to the rescue. She had the girl educated in a respectable school, and now, when she was nineteen years of age, gave her a home until she could find a profession for herself.

This latter step did not meet with Sir Philip's approval. He had lent the father money, and in return had had his name forged for a considerable amount; besides, he did not approve of bourgeois relations. However, he had reluctantly enough consented to let Miss Agnes Grey spend a few months at his house on the understanding that, as soon as an occupation was found, that was to be the last of the unworthy connection.

At this stage in the story—about a fortnight ago—fate and a short-sighted guest put a charge of shot into the baronet's left shoulder. At first it was feared the accident might be dangerous; Dick was hurriedly summoned home, and there he found Miss Agnes Grey grown (so he assured me) into one of the most charming girls imaginable. He had known her and been fond of her, in a patronizing way, for some years. Now he saw her with tears in her voice, anxious about his father, devoted to his mother, and all the time feeling herself a forlorn and superfluous dependant. What would any chivalrous young man, with an unattached heart, have done under these circumstances? What would I have done myself? Fallen in love, of course —or something like it.

216

Well, Dick did not do things by halves. He fell completely in love; circumstances hurried matters to an issue, and he discovered himself beloved in turn. Little was said, and little was done; but quite enough to enable a discerning eye to see at the first glance that something had happened to Dick.

And here he sat, with his blue eyes looking far through the walls of my room, and his mouth compressed, giving his confidence not to one of his oldest and most discreet friends, but to one who could share a sentiment. A strange state of things for Dick Shafthead!

"It is an honorable passion?" I asked.

"What the devil—" began Dick.

"Pardon," I interposed. "I believe you. But the world is complex, and I merely asked. You are then engaged?"

Dick frowned.

"We haven't used that word," he replied.

"But you intend to be?"

He was silent for a little, and then, with some bitterness, said: "My earnings for the last three years average £37, 11s., 4d. I have had two briefs precisely this term, and I am thirty years old. It would be an excellent thing to get engaged."

"But your father; he will surely help you?"

"He will see me damned first."

"Then he will not approve of Miss Grey?"

"He will not."

"Have you asked him?"

"No."

Again Dick was silent for a minute, and then he went on: "Look here, d'Haricot, old man, this is how it is. I know my father; he's one of the best, but if I've got any prejudices I inherit them honestly. What he likes he likes, and what he doesn't like he doesn't like. He doesn't like Agnes, he doesn't like her family — or didn't like 'em. He doesn't like younger sons marrying poor girls. On the other hand, he does like the 'right kind of people,' as he calls 'em, and the right sort of marriage, and he does like me too well, I think, to see me doing what he doesn't like. I have only a hundred a year of my own, and expectations from an aunt of fifty-two who has never had a day's illness in her life. You see?"

"What will you do?" I asked.

"What can I do?" he replied, and added, "it is pleasant folly."

His brows were knitted, his mouth shut tight, his eyes hard. He had come down to stern realities and the mood of tenderness had passed.

"But you really love her?" I said.

His face lit up for a moment. "I do," he answered, and then quickly the face clouded again.

"My friend," I said, "I, too, have a friend—a girl, whom I place before the rest of the world; I share your sentiments and I judge your case for you. What is life without woman, without love?

Would you place your income, your prospects, the sordid aspects of your life, even the displeasure of relations, before the most sacred passion of your heart? Dick, if you do not say to this dear girl, 'I love you; let the devil himself try to part us!' I shall not think of you as the same friend."

He gave a quick glance, and in his eye I saw that my audience was with me in spirit.

"And my father? Tell him that too?" he said, dryly in tone, but not unmoved, I was sure.

"Tell him that your veneration, your homage, belongs to him, but that your soul is your own! Tell him that you are not afraid to take some risk for one you love! Are you afraid, Dick?"

He gave a short laugh.

"I'd risk something," he replied.

"Only something? And for Agnes Grey, Dick? Think of the future without her, the life you have been leading repeated from day to day, now that you have known her. Is that pleasant? Is she not worth some risk—a good deal of risk?"

He rose and then he smiled; and he had a very pleasant smile.

"Thanks," he said; "you're a good chap, monsieur. I wish you had to tackle the governor, though."

"Let me!" I exclaimed.

"Well," he said, "if I want an eloquent counsel I know where to look for one. Good-night."

"You will dare it?" I asked, as he went towards the door.

"Shouldn't be surprised," he answered, and with a friendly nod was gone.

I said to myself that I had done a splendid night's work. Also I began to apply my principles to my own case.

Chapter XXIII

*" Old friends for me! I then know what
folly to expect."*

—La Rabide.

N the following morning Kate and I
met as usual in the office of the mission; and as usual she appeared three
quarters of an hour after the time she
was nominally to be expected. She
looked more ravishing than ever; the art that
conceals art had never more inconspicuously per-
vaded every line and shade of her garments, every
tress of her hair; her smile opened up a long vista
of possibilities. Again I strongly felt the sentiments that had inspired me overnight; I could
have closed the desk on the spot and seized her
hands; but I restrained myself and merely asked
instead what had become of her fellow-missionary.
She was indisposed, it appeared, and could not
come to-day.

"She's rather worried about our finances," said

221

Kate, though not in a tone that seemed to share the anxiety.

I had more than once wondered where the money was coming from and how long it would last, but hitherto I had avoided this sordid aspect of the crusade.

"We can't go on any longer unless we get some more money," she added. "What with all my other expenses I can't run to much more, and Miss Clibborn isn't very well off."

"My own purse—" I began.

"Oh," she interrupted, "we want a capitalist to finance us regularly, and Miss Clibborn has found a man who may help if he approves of our work. He is coming down this morning."

"What!" I exclaimed. "We are to be inspected by a philanthropist any moment?"

"Yes," she said, with a laugh. "So you had better get out your papers and look busy."

"Who is this benefactor?" I inquired, as I hastily made the most of our slender correspondence.

"I can't remember his name; but he is something in the city. Very rich, of course."

"And if he refuses to help?"

"Then we must shut up shop, I suppose," she answered, with a smile that was very charming even if somewhat inappropriate to this sad contingency. "Shall you be sorry?"

"Disconsolate!" I said, with more emotion than my employer had shown.

The door opened and the head of our grimy caretaker appeared.

"A gentleman to see you, miss," she said.

"Show him in," said Kate.

"The philanthropist!" I exclaimed, dipping my pen in the ink and taking in my other hand the gas bill.

A heavy step sounded in the passage, mingled with a strangely familiar sound of puffing, and then in walked a stout, gray-whiskered, red-faced gentleman whose apoplectic presence could never be forgotten by me. It was my old friend, Mr. Fisher, of Chickawungaree Villa!

"You are—ah—Miss Kerry?" he said, heavily, but with politeness.

As she held out her hand I could see even upon his stolid features unmistakable evidence of surprise and admiration at meeting this apparition in the dinginess of East London.

"Yes," she said. "And you, I suppose, are—"

"Mr. Fisher—a fisher of—ha, ha!—women, it seems, down here."

The old Gorgon was actually jesting with a pretty girl! As I thought of him in his dining-room I could scarcely believe my senses.

"And this gentleman," he said, turning towards me, "is, I suppose—"

He paused; his eyes had met mine, and I fear I was somewhat unsuccessfully endeavoring to conceal a smile.

"Fisher!" I said, holding out my hand. "How do you do?"

He did not, however, take it; yet he evidently did not know what to do instead.

"Then you know Mr. Fisher?" said Kate.

"We have met," I replied, "and we could give you some entertaining reminiscences of our meeting. Could we not, Mr. Fisher?"

"What are you doing here?" said Fisher, slowly.

"Atoning for the errors of a profligate youth," I replied, "and assisting in the education and advancement of woman."

For some reason he did not appear to take this statement quite seriously. In England, when you tell the truth it must be told with a solemn countenance; no expression in the face, nothing but a simple yet sufficient movement of the jaws, as though you were masticating a real turtle. A smile, a relieving touch of lightness in your words, and you are instantly set down as an irreverent jester.

"Miss Kerry," he said, sententiously, "I warn you against this person."

"But—why?" exclaimed the astonished Kate.

"I say no more. I warn you," said Mr. Fisher, with a dull glance at me.

"Come, now," I said, pleasantly, for I recollected that the mission depended on this monster's good-humor, "let us bury the pick-axe, as you would say. The truth is, Miss Kerry, that Mr. Fisher

and I once had a merry evening together, but, unluckily, towards midnight we fell out about some
trifle; it matters not what; some matter of gallantry that sometimes for a moment separates friends.
She preferred him; but I bear no grudge. That
is all, is it not, Fisher?"

And I gave him a surreptitious wink to indicate
that he should endorse this innocent version of our
encounter.

Unluckily, at this point Kate turned her back
and began to titter.

The overfed eye of Fisher moved slowly from
one to the other of us.

"I came down here," he said, "at my friend
Miss Clibborn's request to—ah—satisfy myself of
the usefulness of her mission. Is this a mission
—or what is it?"

"It is a mission," replied Kate, trying hard to
sober herself. "We are doing ex — ex — cellent
work."

But at that point she had recourse to her handkerchief.

"Our work, sir," I interposed, "is doing an incalculable amount of benefit. It is the most philanthropic, the most judicious—"

I stopped for the good reason that I could no
longer make myself heard. There was a noise
of altercation and scuffling outside our door that
startled even the phlegmatic Fisher.

"What on earth is this?" he demanded.

The door opened violently.

"I can't 'old 'er no longer," wailed the voice of our caretaker, and in a moment more there entered as perfect a specimen of one of the Furies as it has ever been my lot to meet.

She was a woman we had never seen before, a huge creature with a bloated face adorned by the traces of a recently blacked eye; her bonnet had

"I can't 'old 'er no longer,"

been knocked over one ear in the scuffle with the caretaker, and her raw hands still clutched two curling-pins with the adjacent locks detached from her adversary's head.

"Madam," I said, "what can we do for you?"

I was determined to let Fisher see the business-like style in which we conducted our philanthropic operations.

"Where is he? Where the bloomin' blankness is he?" thundered the virago.

Poor Kate gave a little exclamation.

"Leave her to me," I said, reassuringly. "Where is who, my good woman?"

"My 'usband. You've gone and stole my 'usband away! But I'll have the law on yer! I'll make it blooming hot for yer!" (Only "blooming" was not the adjective she employed.)

"Who are you, and what do you want?" said Fisher.

There was something so ponderous in his accents that our visitor was impressed in spite of herself.

"My name is Mrs. Fulcher, and I wants my 'usband. Them there lydies wot's come 'ere to mike mischief in the 'omes of pore, hinnercent wimmen, they've give Mrs. Martin the money to do it."

"To do what?" said Fisher.

"To go for a 'oliday to the seaside, and she's took my 'usband with her!"

"Taken your husband!" I exclaimed. "Why should she do that?"

"Because she ain't got no 'usband of her own, and never 'ad. *Missis* Martin, indeed! Needin' a 'oliday for 'er 'ealth! That's wot yer calls helevatin' wimmen! 'Elpin' himmorality, I calls it!"

"This is a nice business, young man!" said Fisher, turning to me.

Unfortunately for himself he had the ill-taste to smile at this triumph over his ex-burglar.

"Oh, you'd larf, would yer!" shrieked the deserted spouse. "You hold proflergate, I believe you done it on purpose!"

"Me?" gasped Fisher. "You ill-tempered, noisy—"

But before he could finish this impeachment he received Mrs. Fulcher's right fist on his nose, followed by a fierce charge of her whole massive person; and in another moment the office of the women's mission was the scene of as desperate a conflict as the bastion of the Malakoff. Kate screamed once and then shut her lips, and watched the struggle with a very pale face, while I hurled myself impetuously upon the Amazon and endeavored to seize her arms.

"Police! Call the police!" shouted Fisher.

"Perlice, perlice," echoed his enemy. "I'll perlice yer, yer dirty, himmoral hold 'ulk!"

And bang, bang, went her fists against the side of his head.

"Idiot, virago, stop!" I cried, compressing her swinging arm to her side at last.

"Send for the police!" boomed the hapless Fisher.

"Police!" came the frenzied voice of the caretaker at the front door.

"I'll smash yer bloomin' 'ead like a bloomin' cocoanut!" shouted Mrs. Fulcher, bringing the other arm into play.

"Compress her wind-pipe, Fisher," I advised. "Tap her claret! Hold her legs! She kicks!"

228

"Compress her windpipe, Fisher"

Such a contest was too fierce to last; her vigor relaxed; Fisher was enabled to thrust her head beneath his arm, and I to lift her by the knees, so that by the time the policemen arrived all they had to do was to raise our foe from the floor and bear her away still kicking freely and calling down the vengeance of Heaven upon us.

My first thought was for the unfortunate witness of this engagement.

"You are upset, Miss Kerry; you are disturbed, I fear. Let me bring you water."

"I'm all right, thanks," she replied, with wonderful composure, though she was pale as a sheet by now.

"But what is this?" I cried, pointing to a mark on her face. "Were you struck?"

"It's nothing," she replied, feeling for her handkerchief. "She hit me by mistake."

So engrossed was I that I had quite forgotten Fisher; but now I was reminded by the sound of a stentorian grunt.

"Ugh!" he groaned. "Get me a cab; fetch me a cab, some one."

Blood was dripping from his nose; his collar was torn, his cheeks scarred by the nails of his foe; everything, even his whiskers, seemed to have suffered. It would not be easy to persuade this victim of the wars to patronize our mission now, but for Kate's sake I thought I must try.

"Well, Fisher," I said, heartily, "you are a

sportsman! Your spirit and your vigor, my dear sir, were quite admirable."

For reply he only snorted again and repeated his demand for a cab. Well, I sent one of a large crowd of boys who had collected outside the mission to fetch one, and suavely returned to the attack. It was not certainly encouraging to find that he and Kate had evidently exchanged no amenities while I was out of the room, but, ignoring this air of constraint, I said to him:

"We shall see you soon again, I trust? We depend upon your aid, you know. You have shown us your martial ardor! let us benefit equally by your pacific virtues!"

"I shall see myself—" began Fisher. Then he glanced at Kate and altered his original design into, "a very long way before I return to this office. It is disgraceful, sir; madam, I say it is disgraceful."

"But what is?" I asked.

"Everything about this place, sir. Mission? I call it a bear-garden, that's what I call it."

"I am sorry, Mr. Fisher," began Kate, but our patron was already on his way out without another word to either of us. And I had been his rescuer! He slammed the door behind him, and that was the last of my friend Fisher.

For a moment or two we remained silent.

"Well," said Kate, with a little laugh, "that's the end of our mission."

"The end, I fear," I replied.

Chapter XXIV

*"Do I love you? Mon Dieu! I am too
engrossed in this bonnet to say."*
—HERCULE D'ENVILLE.

AN hour has passed since the departure
of Fisher; the crowd outside, after
cheering each of the combatants down
the street, has at last dispersed; the
notice at the door informing all females
of our patronage and assistance has been removed;
the mission has become only a matter for the local
historian, yet we two still linger over the office
fire. Kate says little, but in her mind, it seems
to me, there must be many thoughts. She has
recovered her composure and reflections have had
time to come. I, with surprising acumen and confidence, speculate on the nature of these. Disillusionment, the collapse of hopes, and the chilly
thaw that leaves only the dripping and fast-van-
ishing remnants of ideals; these are surely what
she feels. As I watch her, also saying little, her

232

singular beauty grows upon me, and my heart goes out in sympathy for her troubles, till it is beating ominously fast. "Yes," I say to myself, "this is more than Plato. I worship at the shrine of woman. No longer am I a sceptic!"

My sympathy can find no words; yet it must somehow take shape and reach this sorrowing divinity. I lay my hand upon hers and she—she lets me press her fingers silently, while a little smile begins to awake about the corners of her wilful mouth.

"Poor friend!" I exclaim, yet with gentle exclamation. "Yes, disillusionment is bitter!"

She gives her shoulders a shrug and her eye flashes into the fire.

"It is not that," she replies. "It's being made a beastly fool of."

For an instant I get a shock; but the spell of the moment and her beauty is too strong to be broken. It seems to me that I do but hear an evidence of her unconquerable spirit.

"You have a friend," I whisper, "who can never think you a fool. To me you are the ideal, the queen of women. You may have lost your own ardent faith in woman through this luckless experiment, but you have converted me!"

At this she gives me such a smile that all timidity vanishes. "Kate!" I exclaim, and the next moment she is in my arms.

For a silent five minutes I enjoyed all the raptures that a beautiful woman and a rioting imagination can bestow. Picture Don Quixote embracing a Dulcinea who should really be as fair of face as his fancy painted her. Would not the poor man conceive himself in heaven even though she never understood a word of all his passion? For the moment I shared some of the virtues of that paladin with a fairer reason for my blindness. Her soft face lay against mine, the dark lashes hid her eyes, her form yielded to every pressure. What I said to her I cannot remember, even if I were inclined to confess it now; I only know that my sentiments were flying very high indeed, when suddenly she laughed. I stopped abruptly.

"Why do you laugh?" I asked.

She raised her head and opened her eyes and I saw that there was certainly no trace of sentiment in them.

"You are getting ridiculous," she said. "Don't look so beastly serious!"

"Serious!" I gasped. "But — but what are you?"

She smiled at me again as kindly and provokingly as ever. But the veil of illusion was rent and it needed but another tear to pull it altogether from my eyes.

"You do not love me, then?" I asked, as calmly as I could.

"Love?" she smiled. "Don't be absurd!"

"Pardon!" I cried. "I see I have neglected my duties hitherto. I ought to have been kissing you all this time. That would have amused you better!"

Ah, I had roused her now, but to anger, not to love. She sprang back from me, her eyes flashing.

"You insult me!" she cried.

"Is it possible?" I asked, with a smile.

Her answer was brief, it was stormy, and it was not very flattering to myself; evidently she was genuinely indignant.

And I—yes, I was beginning to see the ordinary little bits of glass that had made so dazzling a kaleidoscope. I had been upbraiding Dulcinea with not being indeed the lady of Toboso; and that honest maiden was naturally incensed at my language.

I fear that in the polite apology I made her, I allowed this discovery to be too apparent. Again she was in arms, and this time with considerable dramatic effect.

"Oh, I know what you think!" she cried. "You think that because I don't make a fuss about *you*, I have no sentiments. If you were worth it you would see that I could be—"

She paused.

"What?" I asked.

With the privilege of woman, she slightly changed the line of argument.

"All men are alike," she said, contemptuously.

"Then you have had similar experiences before?"

"Yes," she replied, with a candor I could not help thinking was somewhat belated.

"In the Temple?" I asked.

"He made a fool of himself, just like you," she retorted.

"Yet you assured me there was no one—"

"What business had you with my confidence?" she interrupted.

"I see," I replied. "So you told what was not quite the truth? You were quite right; people are so apt to misunderstand these situations. In future I shall know better than to ask questions —because I shall be able to guess the answers. Good-bye."

She replied with a distant farewell, and that was the end of a pretty charade.

I went away vowing that I should never think of her again; I lunched at the gayest restaurant to assist me in this resolution; I planned a series of consolations that should make oblivion amusing, even if not very edifying; yet early in the afternoon I found myself in her uncle's apartments, watching the old gentleman put the finishing touches to "A portrait from memory of Miss Kate Kerry." That picture at least did not flatter! I had told him before of our ripening acquaintance and my engagement as secretary, and I think the General had enough martial spirit still left to divine the reason for my philanthropic ardor. To-day he quickly guessed that something unfortunate had happened.

"Had a row with Kate, eh?" he inquired.

"A row?" I said, endeavoring to put as humorous a face on it as possible. "General, I pulled a string, expecting warm water to flow, and instead I received a cold shower-bath."

I fear I must have smiled somewhat sadly, for it was in a very kindly voice that the old gentleman replied:

"I know, mossoo; I know what it feels like. I remember my feelings when a certain lady gave me the congé, as you'd say, in '62—was it?—or '63. Long time ago now, anyhow, but I haven't forgotten it yet. Only time I ever screwed my courage up to the proposing point; found afterwards she'd been engaged to another man for two years. She might have told me, hang it!—but I haven't died of broken heart, mossoo. You'll get over it, never fear."

"But it is not that she is engaged; it is not that she has repulsed me. She is your niece, General, but I fear her heart is of stone. She is a flirt, a—"

In my heat I was getting carried away; I recalled myself in time, and added:

"Pardon; I forget myself, General."

"I know, I know," he replied. "I've felt the same about her myself, mossoo. She's a fine girl; good feelings and all the rest of it, but a little—er

—unsatisfactory sometimes, I think. I've hoped for a little more myself now and then—a little—er —womanliness, and so on."

"I cannot understand her," I said. "I pictured her full of soul—and now!"

"I used to picture 'em full of soul, too," said the General, "till I learned that a bright eye only meant it wasn't shut and that you could get as heavenly a smile by tickling 'em as any other way."

"General!" I exclaimed. "Are you a cynic, then?"

"God forbid!" said the old boy, hastily. "I've seen too many good women for that. I only mean that you don't quite get the style of virtue you expect when you are — twenty-five, for instance. What you get in the best of 'em is a good wearing article, but not—er—the fancy piece of goods you imagine."

"In a word," I said, as I rose to leave him, "you ask for a pearl and you get a cheap but serviceable pebble."

"Well, well," he replied, good-humouredly, "we'll see what you say six weeks later."

"I have learned my lesson," I answered. "You will see that I shall remember it!"

The reader will also see, if his patience with the experimental philosopher and confident prophet is not yet quite exhausted.

Chapter XXV

"We won't go home till morning!"
—ENGLISH SONG.

"AND now for a 'burst'!" I said to myself. Adieu, fond fancies; welcome, gay reality!"

I dressed for the evening; I filled my purse; I started out to seek the real friends I had been neglecting for the sake of that imaginary one. But I had only got the length of opening my door when I smiled a cynical smile. There was Halfred in the passage playing the same farce with Aramatilda. They stood very close together, remarkably close together, talking in low tones.

"Thus woman fools us all," I thought.

With a little exclamation Miss Titch flew upstairs while Halfred turned to me with something of a convicted air.

"Miss Titch has been a-telling me, sir—" he began.

"I know; I saw her," I replied, eying him in a way that disconcerted him considerably. "She has been telling you that woman is worthy of your homage; and doubtless you believed her. Did you not?"

"No, sir. She ain't said that exactly," he answered; "though it wouldn't be surprising, either, to hear 'er usin' them kind of words, considering 'er remarkable heducation. Wot she said was—"

"That you will serve till she finds another," I interposed.

"Miss Titch, sir, ain't one of that kind," he replied, with an air of foolish chivalry I could not but admire in spite of myself.

"Pardon, Halfred. She is divine; I admit it. What did she say, then?"

"She says there's been a furriner pumpin' 'er about you, sir, this very hafternoon."

"Pumping?"

"Hasking questions like wot a Bobby does; as if 'e wanted hall the correct facts."

"Ha!" I said. "And he asked them of a woman!"

"Yes, sir; 'e comed up to 'er in the square and says 'e, 'You're Miss Titch, ain't you?' and 'e gets a-talkin' to 'er—a very polite gentleman 'e was, she says — and then 'e sorter gets haskin' about you, sir, and wot you was a-doing and 'oo your friends was, and about the General, too, sir—"

"And, in brief, he gossiped with her on every subject that would serve as an excuse," I said. "Halfred, if I were you and I felt interested in Miss Titch—I say, supposing I felt interested in Miss Titch, I should look out for that foreigner and practise my boxing upon him!"

"Then you don't think, sir—"

"I don't think it was me he was interested in."

"Well, sir," said my servant, with a disappoint-

"I should look out for that foreigner."

ed air, for he founded great hopes of melodrama upon me, "in that case I shall advise Miss Titch to take care of 'erself."

I laughed.

"Do not fear," I replied. "They all do that. It is we who need the caution! Yes, Halfred, my sympathy is with that poor foreigner."

I fear my servant put down this sentiment to

mere un-British eccentricity, but I felt I had done my duty by him.

As for the inquisitive foreigner, I smiled at the idea that he had really addressed the fair Aramatilda for the purpose of hearing news of me. I may mention that I had heard nothing more of Hankey; nothing from the league; nothing had followed the arrival of the packing-case; the French government seemed to have ignored my escapade; there were many foreigners in London unconnected with my concerns; so why should I suppose that this chance acquaintance of Aramatilda's had anything to do with me? "If I am wanted, I shall be sent for," I said to myself. "Till then, revelry and distraction!"

First, I sought out Teddy Lumme. We met for the first time since I left Seneschal Court, but at the first greeting it was evident that all resentment had passed from his mind as completely as it had from mine.

"Where the deuce have you been hiding?" he asked me, with his old geniality. "We wanted you the other night; great evening we had; Archie and me and Bobby and Tyler; box at the Empire, supper at the European, danced till six in the morning at Covent Garden; breakfast at Muggins; and the devil of a day after that. I'd have sent you a wire but I thought you'd left town. No one has seen you. Been getting up another conspiracy, what? Chap at the French embassy told me the other day their government expected your people to have a kick-up soon. By Jove, though, he told me not to tell any one! But you won't say anything about it, I dare say."

"I can assure you it is news to me," I replied, "but in any case I certainly should not discuss the matter indiscreetly."

"And now the question is," said Teddy, "where shall we dine and what shall we do afterwards?"

Ah, it may be elevating and absorbing to experiment in Plato and guide the operations of philanthropy, but when the head is not yet bald and the blood still flows fast, commend me to an evening spent with cheerful friends in search of some less austere ideal! This may not be the sentiment of an Aurelius — but then that is not my name.

We dined amid the glitter of lights and mirrors and fair faces and bright colors; a band thundering a waltz accompaniment to the soup, a mazurka to the fish; a babel of noise all round us — laughing voices, clattering silver, popping corks, stirring music; and ourselves getting rapidly into tune with all of this.

"By-the-way," I said, in a nonchalant tone, "have you seen Miss Trevor-Hudson again?"

"No," said Teddy, carelessly, and yet with a slightly uncomfortable air.

"Did you become friends again? Pardon me if I am indiscreet."

"Hang it! d'Haricot," he exclaimed; "I'm off women—for good this time."

"Then she was—what shall I say?"

"She kept me hanging on for a week," confessed Teddy, "and then suddenly accepted old Horley."

"Horley—the stout baronet? Why, he might be her father!"

"So Miss Horley thinks, I believe," grinned Teddy. "His family are sick as dogs about it."

"And hers?"

"Oh, Sir Henry has twenty thousand a year; they're quite pleased."

I smiled cynically at this confirmation of my philosophy.

"I say, have you got over your own penshant, as you'd call it, for the lady?" asked Teddy.

"My dear fellow," I said, lightly, "these affairs do not trouble me long. I give you a toast, Teddy —here is to man's best friend—a short memory!"

"And blow the expense!" added Teddy, somewhat irrelevantly, but with great enthusiasm.

"A short life and a merry one!" I exclaimed.

"Kiss 'em all, and no heel-taps!" cried Teddy. "Waiter, another bottle, and move about a little quicker, will you? Getting that gentleman's soup, were you? Well, don't do it again; d'ye hear?"

At this moment a piercing cry reached us from the other side of the room. It sounded like an elementary attempt to pronounce two words, "Hey,

Teddy! Hey, Teddy!" and to be composed of several voices. We looked across and saw four or five young men, most of them on their feet, and all waving either napkins or empty bottles.

On catching my friend's eye their enthusiasm redoubled, and on his part he became instantly excited.

"By Jove!" he exclaimed. "Excuse me one minute."

He rushed across the room and I could see that he was the recipient of a most hilarious greeting. Presently he came back in great spirits.

"I say, we're in luck's way," he said. "I'd quite forgotten this was the night of the match."

It then appeared that the universities of Oxford and Cambridge had been playing a football match that afternoon and that on the evening of the encounter it was an ancient custom for these seats of learning to join in an amicable celebration of the event.

"The very thing we want," said Teddy. "Come on and join these men—old pals of mine; dashed good chaps and regular sportsmen. Come on!"

"But," I protested, as I let him lead me to these "regular sportsmen," "I am neither of Oxford nor Cambridge."

"Oh, that doesn't matter. Hi!" (this was to call the attention of his friends to my presence). "Let me introduce Mr. Black, of Brasenose; Mr. Brown, of Balliol, Mr. Scarlett, of Magdalen; Mr. White, of Christchurch. This is my honorable and accomplished friend, Mr. Juggins, of Jesus!"

At this there was a roar of welcome and a universal shout of "Good old Juggins!"

"But indeed my friend flatters me!" I exclaimed. "I have not the honor to be the Juggins."

No use in disclaiming my new name, however. Juggins of Jesus I remained for the rest of that evening, and there was nothing for it but to live up to the character. And I soon found that it was not difficult. All I had to do was to shout whenever Mr. Scarlett or Mr. Black shouted, and wave my napkin in imitation of Mr. White or Mr. Brown. No questions were asked regarding my degree or the lectures I attended, and my perfect familiarity with Jesus College seemed to be taken for granted. I do not wish to seem vainglorious, but I cannot help thinking that I produced a favorable impression on my new friends.

"Juggins won the match for us," shouted Mr. White. "Good old Juggins!"

"I did, indeed. Vive la football! I won it by an innings and a goal!" I cried, adopting what I knew of their athletic terms.

"Juggins will make us a speech! Good old Juggins!" shouted Mr. Black.

"Fellow-students!" I replied, rising promptly at this invitation, "my exploits already seem known

GOOD Old Juggins!

to you, better even than to myself. How I hit the wicket, kick the goal, bowl the hurdle, and swing the oar, what need to relate? Good old Juggins, indeed! I give you this health—to my venerable college of Jesus, to the beloved colleges of you all, to my respectable and promising friend, Lumme, to the goal-post of Oxford, to love, to wine, to the Prince of Wales!"

Never was a speech delivered with more fervor or received with greater applause. After that I do not think they would have parted with me to save themselves from prison. And indeed it very nearly came to that alternative more than once in the course of the evening.

We hailed two hansoms, and drove, three in each, and all of us addressing appropriate sentiments to the passers-by, to a music-hall which, as I am now making my début as a distinguished sportsman, I shall call the "Umpire." I shall not give its real name, as my share in the occurrences that ensued is probably still remembered by the management. It was, however, not unlike the title I have given it.

My head, I confess, was buzzing in the most unwonted fashion, but I remember quite distinctly that as we alighted from our cabs there was quite a crowd about the doors, all apparently making as much noise as they could, and that as we pushed our way through, my eyes were fascinated by a bill bearing the legend "NEPTUNE—the Amphibious Marvel! First appearance to-night! All records broken!" And I wondered, in the seriously simple way one does wonder under such conditions, what in the world the meaning of this cryptogram might be.

We got inside, and, my faith! the scene that

addressing appropriate sentiments to the passers-by,

met our eyes! Apparently the football match was being replayed in the promenade and on the staircases of the Umpire. Three gigantic figures in livery—"the bowlers-out" as they are termed—were dragging a small and tattered man by the head and shoulders while his friends clung desperately to his lower limbs. Round this tableau seethed a wild throng shouting "Oxford!" "Cambridge!" and similar war-cries—destroying their own and each others' hats, and moved apparently by as incalculable forces as the billows in a storm. On the stage a luckless figure in a grotesque costume was vainly endeavoring to make a comic song audible; and what the rest of the audience were doing or thinking I have no means of guessing.

"Oxford! To the rescue!" shouted Mr. Black.

"Vive Juggins! Kick the football!" I cried, leading the onslaught and hurling myself upon one of the bowlers-out.

"Good old Juggins!" yelled my admirers, as they followed my spirited example, and in a moment the house rang with my new name. "Juggins!" could, I am sure, have been heard for half a mile outside.

The uproar increased; more bowlers-out hurried to the rescue; and I, thanks to my efficient use of my fists and feet, found myself the principal object of their attention. Had it not been for the loyal support of my companions I know not what my fate would have been, but their attachment seemed to increase with each fresh enemy who assailed me.

At last, panting and dishevelled, my opera-hat flattened and crushed over my eyes, the lining of my overcoat hanging out in a long streamer, like

dragging a small and tattered man

a flag of distress, I was dragged free by the united efforts of Mr. White and Mr. Scarlett, and for an instant had a breathing space.

I could see that the curtain was down and the performance stopped; that many people had risen in their places and apparently were calling for the assistance of the police, and that from the number of liveries in the mêlée the management were taking the rioters seriously in hand. In another moment two or three of these officials broke loose and bore down upon me with a shout of " That's 'im!"

"Bolt, Juggins!" cried Mr. Scarlett. "We'll give you a start."

The two intrepid gentlemen placed themselves between me and my pursuers. I stood my ground for a minute, but seeing that nothing could withstand the onset of my foes, and that Mr. White was already on the floor, I turned and fled. The chase was hot. I dashed down a flight of stairs, and then, by a happy chance, saw a door marked " private." Through it I ran and was making my way I knew not whither, but certainly in forbidden territory, when I was confronted by an agitated stranger. I stopped, and would have raised my hat had it not been so tightly jammed upon my head.

The man looked at me for a moment, and then seemed to think he recognized my face.

"You are Mr. Neptune?" said he.

"You have named me!" I cried, opening my arms and embracing him effusively.

"I am afraid you got into the crowd," said he, withdrawing, in some embarrassment, I thought. "I suppose that is why you are late."

"That is the reason," I replied, feeling mystified, indeed, but devoutly thankful that he did not recognize me as the hunted Juggins.

"Well," he said, "you had better go on at once, if you don't mind. There is rather a disturbance, I am afraid, and we have lowered the curtain; but perhaps your appearance may quiet them."

"My appearance?" I asked, glancing down at my torn overcoat, and wondering what sedative

"*You* have named me!"

effect such a scarecrow was likely to have. Besides, I had appeared and it had not quieted them; though this, of course, he did not know.

"I mean," he answered, "that the nature of your performance is so absorbing that we hope it may rivet attention somewhat."

A light dawned upon me. I now remembered

the bill outside the theatre. I was the "Amphibious Marvel!" Well, it would not do for the intrepid Juggins to refuse the adventure. For the honor of Jesus College I must endeavor to "break all records." My one hope was that, as it was to be my first appearance, anything strange in the nature of my performance might be received merely as a diverting novelty.

"The stage is set for you," said my unknown friend. "How long will it take you to change?"

"Change?" I replied. "This is the costume in which I always perform."

He looked surprised, but also relieved that there would be no further delay, and presently I found myself upon a huge stage, the curtain down in front, and no one there but myself and my conductor. What was I expected to do? I was sufficiently expert at gymnastics to make some sort of show upon the trapeze without more than a reasonable chance of breaking my neck. But there was no sign of any such apparatus. Was I, then, a strong man? I had always had a grave suspicion that those huge cannon-balls and dumb-bells were really hollow, and, in any case, I could at least roll them about. But there were neither cannon-balls nor dumb-bells. No, there was nothing but a high and narrow box of glass.

"It is all right, you will find," said my conductor, coming up to this.

I also approached it and gave a gasp.

The box was filled with water—water about six feet deep!

"I shouldn't care to dive into it myself," he said, jocularly. "But I suppose it is all a matter of practice."

"Do I dive in—from the roof?" I asked, a little weakly, I fear.

"Did you mean to?" he replied, evidently perturbed lest their arrangements had been insufficient.

"Not to-night," I said, with a sigh of relief. "But to-morrow night—ah, yes; you will see me then!"

He regarded me with undisguised admiration.

"You are all ready?" he asked.

"Quite," I replied.

We went into the wings and the curtain rose.

"I time you, of course," said my friend, taking out his watch. "You have stayed under five minutes in Paris, haven't you?"

I had discovered my vocation at last. The Amphibious Neptune was a record-breaking diver.

"Ten," I answered, carelessly, and with such an air as I thought appropriate to my reputation I walked onto the stage.

"Gentlemen and ladies!" shouted my friend, coming up to the foot-lights. "This is the world-famed Neptune, who has repeatedly stayed under water for periods of from eight to ten minutes! He is rightly styled—"

255

But at this point his voice was lost in such an uproar as, I flatter myself, greets the appearance of few Umpire artistes. "Good old Juggins!" they shouted. "Good old Juggins!" I was recognized now, and I must live up to my reputation

as the high-spirited representative of Jesus College, Oxford. Kissing my hand to my cheering audience I mounted the steps placed against the end of the tank, and with a magnificent splash leaped into the water—I cannot strictly say I dived, for, on surveying the constricted area of my aquatic operations, it seemed folly to risk cracking a valuable head.

Unluckily, I had omitted in my enthusiasm to remove even my top-coat, and either in the air or the water (I cannot say which) I drove my foot through the torn lining. Conceive now the situation into which my recklessness had plunged me—entangled in my overcoat at the bottom of six feet of water, struggling madly to free myself, with only a sheet of transparent glass between me and as dry a stage as any in England; drowning ridiculously in clear view of a full and enthusiastic house! My struggles can only have lasted for a few seconds, though to me they seemed longer than the ten minutes I had boasted of, and then—the good

into the
unwilling arms
of the
double-bass.

God be thanked!—I felt the side of my prison yield to my kicking, and in another moment I was seated in three inches of water, dizzily watching a miniature Niagara sweep the stage and foam over the foot-lights into the panic-stricken orchestra.

"Down with the curtain!" I heard some one cry from behind, but before it had quite descended the Amphibious Marvel had smashed his way out of his tank and leaped into the unwilling arms of the double-bass.

Ah! that was a night to be remembered—though not, I must frankly admit, to be repeated. Another mêlée with the exasperated musicians; a gallant rescue by Teddy and his friends; a triumphant exit from the Umpire borne on the shoulders of my cheering admirers; all the other events of that stirring night still live in the memory of "Good old Juggins." To my fellow undergraduates of an evening I dedicate this happy, disreputable reminiscence.

Chapter XXVI

"So you pushed that little snowball from the top? And now it has reached the bottom and become quite large? My faith! how sur-prising!"

—LA RABIDE.

T is an afternoon in December, gray and chilly and dark; neither the season nor the hour to exhilarate the heart. I am alone in my room, bending over my writing-table, endeavoring to relieve my depression upon paper.

Since my appearance upon the music-hall stage I have enjoyed the society of my Oxford friends while they remained in town; I have revelled with Teddy; I have had my "burst"; and now the reaction has come. The solace of my most real and intimate friend, Dick Shafthead, is denied me, for he has apparently left London for a time; at any rate, his rooms are shut up and he is not there. No company now but regrets and cynical reflec-

259

tions. . A short time ago what bright fancies were
visiting me!

"Woman gives and woman takes away," I said
to myself. "But she takes more than she gives!"
I felt indeed bankrupt.

Opening my journal and glancing back over
rose-tinted, deluded eulogies, I came to the inter-

A woman gives and
a woman takes away

rupted entry, "To d'Haricot from d'Haricot."
Ah, that I had profited by my own advice! "Foolish friend, beware!"—but he had not.

I took up my pen and continued the exhortation.

"What is woman? A false coin that passes
current only with fools! Art thou a fool, then?
No longer!"

Just then came a tap at the door, followed by
the comely face of Aramatilda.

"A lady to see you, sir," she said.

I started. Could it be—? Impossible!

"Who is she?" I asked, indifferently.

"She didn't give her name, sir."

"Show her in," I replied, closing my journal, but repeating its last words to myself.

Again the door opened. I rose from my seat.

Did Kate hope to befool me again? No, it was not Kate who entered and said, in a tone of perfect self-possession:

"Are you Mr. d'Haricot?"

She was rather small, she was young — not more than two-and-twenty. She had a very fresh complexion and a pretty, round little face saved from any dolliness by the steadiness of her blue eyes, the firmness of her mouth, and the expression of quiet self-possession. She reminded me of some one, though for the moment I could not think who.

"I am Mr. d'Haricot," I replied. "And you?"

"I am Miss Shafthead."

"Dick's sister!" I exclaimed.

"Yes," she said, with a pleasant glimpse of smile that accentuated the resemblance. "Have you seen him lately?"

"Unfortunately, no."

She gave me a quick, clear glance as if to test my truth, and then, as though she were satisfied, went on in the same quiet and candid voice:

"I tried to find my cousin Teddy Lumme, but, as he was out, I have taken the liberty of calling on you, because I know you are one of Dick's friends—and because—" She hesitated, though

without any embarrassment, and gave me the
same kind of glance again—just such a look as
Dick would have given, translated into a woman's
eye.

"Is anything the matter?" I asked, quickly.

"Yes," she said. "He has left home and we
don't know where he is."

"What has happened?" I exclaimed.

"He has told you of Agnes Grey, I think?" she
answered.

"He has given me his confidence."

"Dick came home a few days ago, and became
engaged to her. My father was angry about it
and now they have gone away."

She told me this in the same quiet, straightforward way, looking straight at me in a manner
more disconcerting than any suggestion of reproach. It was I—I, the misanthrope, the con-
temner of woman, who had urged him, exhorted
him to this reckless deed! And evidently she
knew what my counsel had been. I could have
shot myself before her eyes if I had thought that
step would have mended matters.

"Then they have run away together!" I cried.

"They have gone away," she repeated, quietly,
"and, I suppose, together. I am afraid my father
was very hard on them both."

"And doubtless you have learned what ridiculous advice I gave him?"

"Yes," she replied, "Dick told me."

"And now you abhor me."

"I should be much obliged if you would help me to find them," she answered, still keeping her steady eyes upon my distracted countenance.

"I ask your pardon," I said. "It is help you want, not my regrets — though, I assure you, I feel them. Have you been to his chambers?"

"Yes, I went and knocked, but I could get no answer."

"Perhaps they—I should say he—has returned by now. I shall go at once and see."

"Thank you," she replied, still quietly, but with a kinder look in her eyes.

"And you—will you wait here?"

"Oh, I shall come, too, of course," she said, and somehow I found this announcement pleasing.

As we drove together towards the Temple, I learned a few more particulars of Dick's escapade. When he told his father his intention of marrying Miss Grey, the indignation of the baronet evidently knew no bounds, for even his daughter admitted that he had been less than courteous to poor Agnes, and what he had said to Dick was discreetly left to my imagination. This all happened yesterday; Agnes had retired, weeping, to her bedroom, and Dick, swearing, towards the stables. The orders he gave the coachman were only discovered afterwards; but his plans were well laid, for it was not till the culprits were missing at dinner that any one discovered they had only waited till darkness fell and then driven straight to the station. No message was left, no clew to their whereabouts. You can picture the state of mind the family were thrown into.

Morning came, but no letter with it, and by the middle of the day Miss Shafthead could stand the suspense no longer, so, in the same business-like fashion as Dick, without a word to her parents, she had started in pursuit. The aunt she proposed to spend the night with was not as yet informed that she was to have a visitor; business first, and till that was accomplished my fair companion was simply letting fate take charge of her. "With fate's permission, I shall assist," I said to myself.

As we drew near to the Temple, she fell silent, and I felt sure that, despite her air of *sang-froid*, her sisterly heart was beating faster.

"Do you think they—I mean he—will have returned?" she said to me, suddenly, as we walked across the quiet court.

"Sooner or later he is sure to be in—if he is in London. May I ask you to say nothing as we ascend the stairs, and to permit me to make the inquiries?"

She gave her consent in a glance, and we tramped up the old wooden staircase till we stopped in silence before Dick's door. These chambers of the Temple are unprovided with any bells or other means of calling the inmates' attention beyond the simple method of knocking. If the heavy outer door of oak be closed, and he away from home, or disinclined to receive you, you may knock all afternoon without getting any satisfaction; and it was the latter alternative I feared. At this juncture I could imagine circumstances under which my friend might prefer to remain undisturbed.

For a moment I listened, and I was sure I could hear a movement inside. Then I knocked loudly. No answer. I knocked again, but still no answer.

"Stay where you are and make no sound," I whispered to my companion. "Like the badger, he must be drawn."

I fumbled at the letter-slit in the door as though I were the postman endeavoring to introduce a packet, and dropped my pocket-book on the floor outside. This I knew to be the habit of these officials when a newspaper proved too bulky. Then, quietly picking up the pocket-book, I descended the stairs with as much noise as possible, till I thought I was out of hearing, when I turned and ran lightly up again. Just as I was quietly approaching the top of the flight I saw the door open and the astonished Dick confront his sister. I stopped.

"Daisy!" he exclaimed, in a tone which seemed to be made up of several emotions.

"Dick!" she replied, her self-control just failing to keep her voice quite steady.

"Was it you who knocked?" he asked, more suspiciously than kindly.

265

"No, Dick; it was I who took that liberty," I answered, continuing my ascent.

He turned with a start, for he had not seen me.

"You?" he said, sharply. "It was a dodge, then, to—"

"To induce you to break from cover. Yes, my friend, to such extremities have you driven us."

"In what capacity have you come?" he asked, with ominous coolness.

the badger
must be drawn

"As friends," I replied. "Friends who have come to place ourselves at your service; haven't we, Miss Shafthead?"

"Yes," said she, "we are friends. Don't you believe me, Dick?"

"Who sent you?" he asked.

"I came myself."

"Does my father know?"

"No."

Dick's manner changed.

"It's very good of you, Daisy. Unfortunately—" here he hesitated in some embarrassment— "unfortunately, I am engaged — I mean I have some one with me."

At this crisis Miss Daisy rose to the occasion in a way that surprised me, even though I had done little but admire her spirit since we met.

"Of course," she replied, with a smile; "I was sure you would have, Dick, and I want to see you both."

"Come in, then," he said.

"And I?" I asked, with a becoming air of diffi-dence.

"As I acted on your advice," he answered, "you'd better see what you've done."

We entered, and there, standing in the lamp-light, we saw the cause of all this mischief. She was a little, slender figure with a pretty little oval face in which two very soft brown eyes made a mute appeal for sympathy. There was some-thing about her air, something about her demure expression, something about the simplicity of her dress and the Puritan fashion in which she wore her hair, that gave one an indescribably quaint and old-fashioned impression, and this impression was altogether pleasant. When she opened her lips, and in a voice that, I know not how, heightened this effect, and with an expression of sweetness and contrition said, simply: "Daisy, what must you think?" I forgot all my worldly wisdom and was ready, if necessary, to egg her lover on to still more gallant courses Daisy herself, however, capitulated more tardily. She did not, as I hoped, rush into the charming little sinner's arms, but only answered, kindly, indeed, yet as if holding her judgment in reserve:

"I haven't heard what has happened yet."

I gave a sign to Dick to be discreet in answering this inquiry, which he however read as merely calling attention to my presence.

"Oh, let me introduce Mr. d'Haricot — Miss Grey," he said.

So she was still Miss Grey—and they had fled together nearly four - and - twenty hours ago. I repeated my signal to be careful in making admissions.

"Where have you been?" said Daisy.

"I have some cousins — some cousins of my father's — in London," Agnes answered. "I am staying with them."

"And you are living here?" I said to Dick.

"Where else?" he replied, with a surprise that was undoubtedly genuine.

"The arrangement is prudence itself," I pronounced. "You see, Miss Shafthead, that these young people have tempered their ardor with a discretion we had scarcely looked for. I do not know what you intend to do, but, for myself, I kiss Miss Grey's hand and place my poor services at her disposal!"

And I proceeded to carry out the more immediately possible part of this resolution without further delay.

The little mademoiselle was evidently affected by my act of salutation, while Dick exclaimed, with great cordiality:

"Good old monsieur; by Jove! you're a sportsman!"

Still his sister hung back; in fact, my impetuosity seemed to have rather a damping effect upon her.

"What are you going to do, Dick?" she asked.

"We are going to get married."

"What, at once?"

"Almost immediately."

"Without father's consent?"

"After what he said to us both—to Agnes in particular—do you think I am going to trouble about his opinion?"

"But, Dick, supposing we can get him to change his mind?"

"Who is going to change it for him? for he won't do it himself—I know the governor well enough for that."

"If I try to, will you wait for a little?"

"It's no use," said Dick.

"Wait till we see, Dick!"

"Yes, we shall wait," said Agnes. "Dick, you will wait, won't you?"

"If you insist," replied Dick, though not very cordially.

"Then you will try?" said Agnes.

Daisy came to her side, took her hand, and kissed her at last.

"Oh yes, I'll do my very best!" she exclaimed.

There followed one of those little displays of womanly affection that are so charming yet so tantalizing when one stands outside the embraces and thinks of the improvement that might be effected by a transposition of either of the actors.

"What will you say?" asked Dick, in a minute.

"I don't quite know," replied Daisy, candidly. "I suppose I had better say that—"

She paused, as if considering.

"Say that this is one of the matches made in heaven!" I cried. "Say that not even a father has the right to stand between two people who love each other as these do!"

"By gad! Daisy," said Dick, "you ought to take the monsieur with you. I don't believe there'd be any resisting him."

"Let me come!" I exclaimed; "I claim the privilege. My rash counsels helped to cause this situation; permit me to try and make the atonement!"

Daisy looked at me, I am bound to say, rather doubtfully.

"He has a wonderful way with him," urged Dick. "We can't do that kind of eloquent appeal-to-the-feelings business in England, but it fetches us if it's properly managed. You see, I don't want to fall out with the governor. I know, Daisy, what a good sort he has been—but I am not going to give up Agnes."

"If you think Mr. d'Haricot would really do any good—" said Daisy.

"He can but try," I broke in.

"Please let him," said Agnes, softly.

Ah, I had not shown her my devotion in vain!

"All right," said Daisy.

And so it was arranged that we were to start upon our embassy next morning.

Chapter XXVII

"High Toryism, High Churchism, High Farming, and old port forever!"

—CORLETT.

HAT evening, when I came to meditate in solitude upon the appeal I purposed to make, my confidence began to evaporate in the most uncomfortable manner. Was I quite certain that I should be pleading a righteous cause? Ah, yes; I had gone too far now to question my cause; but how would my eloquence be received? Would it "fetch if properly managed"? I tried to picture the baronet, and the more my fancy laid on the colors, the more damping the prospect became.

"Ah, well; Providence must guide me," I said to myself at last. And in a way that I am sufficiently old-fashioned — superstitious — call it what you will—to think more than mere coincidence, Providence responded to my faith. I could scarcely guess that my friend, the old General, who came in to smoke a pipe with me, was an agent employed by Heaven, but so he proved.

"I want your advice," I said. "What should I say, what should I do, under the following perplexing circumstances?"

And, without giving him any names, I told him the story of Dick.

"Difficult business, mossoo, delicate affair and

An agent employed by Heaven

that sort of thing," he observed, when I had finished. "You say your friend is a pretty obstinate young fellow?"

"Dick Shafthead is obstinacy itself," I replied, letting his name escape by a most fortunate slip of the tongue.

"Shafthead!" said the General. "By Jove! Any relation to Sir Philip Shafthead?"

"Since you know his name, and can be trusted

not to repeat it, I may as well say you that Sir Philip is the stern father in question. Do you know him?"

"Knew his other son, Major Shafthead. He is the heir, isn't he?"

"Yes," I said. "Dick is the second son."

"Ever met Tommy Shafthead — as we called him—the Major, I mean?"

"No; he is stationed abroad, I believe."

"Heard about *his* marriage?"

"No," I replied. "Dick has seldom mentioned him."

"I wonder if he knows," said the General.

"What?" I asked.

"About Tommy's marriage."

"Is there a mystery?"

"Well," said the General, "it's a matter that has been kept pretty quiet; but in case it may be any good to you to know, I might as well tell you. Tommy was in my old regiment; that's how I know all about it. When he was only a subaltern he got mixed up with a girl much beneath him in station. His friends tried to get him out of it, but he was like your friend, pig-headed as the devil. He married her privately, lived with her for a year, found he'd made a fool of himself, and separated for good."

"They were divorced?" I asked.

"No such luck," said the General. "He can't get rid of her. She's behaving herself properly for the sake of getting the title, and naturally she's not going to divorce him. So that's what comes of marrying in haste, mossoo. Not that there isn't a good deal to be said for a young fellow who has—er—a warm heart and wants to do the right thing by the girl, and so forth. I am no Chesterfield, mossoo; right's right and wrong's wrong all the world over, but—er—there are limits, don't you know."

"Has Major Shafthead any family?" I inquired.

"No," said the General.

"Then Dick will succeed to the baronetcy one day?"

"Or his son."

"Ah," I reflected, "I see now why Sir Philip is so stern. He would not have a girl he dislikes the mother of future baronets, and he will not allow the younger son to follow, as he thinks, in the elder's steps."

At first sight this seemed only to increase my difficulties; but as I thought more over it, my spirits began to rise. Yes, I might make out a good case for Dick out of this buried story.

"Well, good-night, mossoo," said the old boy, rising. "Good luck to you."

"And many thanks to you, General."

The next morning broke very cold and gray. We were well advanced in December, and the frost was making us his first visit for the winter; indeed, it was cold enough to give Miss Daisy the opportunity of looking charming in a fur coat when I met her at the station. Dick came to see us off, and I must admit that I felt more responsibility than I quite liked in seeing the cheerful confidence he reposed in me.

"It is but a chance that I can do anything," I reminded him. "I may fail."

"No fear," he replied. "I expect a pardon by return of post. By-the-way, we got the manor of Helmscote in Edward the Third's time—Edward the Third, remember — and the baronetcy after Blenheim. The governor doesn't object to be reminded of that kind of thing if you do it neatly. But you know the trick."

"I should rather depend on your sister's eloquence," I suggested.

"Oh, she's like me; can't stand on her hind legs and catch cake," laughed Dick. "We are plain English."

"Not so very plain," I said to myself, glancing at my travelling companion's fresh little face nestling in a collar of fur.

She was very silent this morning, and I could now see that the experiment of taking down an advocate inspired her with considerably less confidence than it had Dick.

"Confess the truth, Miss Shafthead," I said to her, at last. "You fear I shall only make bad into worse."

"I don't know what you will do," she replied,

276

with a smile that was rather nervous than encouraging.

"Command me, then; I shall say what you please, or hold my tongue, if you prefer it."

can't stand on her hind legs and catch cake

"Oh no," she said, "you had better say something—now that you have come with me; only don't be too sentimental, please."

"I shall talk turnips till I see my opportunity; then I shall observe coldly that Richard is an affectionate lad in spite of his faults."

Daisy laughed.

"I think I hear you," she replied.

Well, at least, my jest served to make her a little more at her ease, and we now fell to planning our arrival. She had left a note before she started for

277

town, saying only that she would be away for the night, but giving no intimation of when , 'he might return, so that we expected no carriage at the station. This, we decided, was all the better. We should walk to Helmscote, attract as little notice as possible on entering the house, and then she would find out how the land lay before even announcing my presence; at least, if it were possible to keep me in the background so long.

"My father is rather difficult sometimes," she said.

"Hasty?" I asked.

"I'm afraid so."

"He may, then, decline to receive me?"

"It is quite possible."

The adventure began to assume a more and more formidable aspect. I agreed that great circumspection was required.

At last we alighted at a little way-side station in the heart of the country. We were the only travellers who descended, and when we had come out into a quiet road, and watched the train grow smaller and smaller, and rumble more and more faintly till the arms of the signals had all risen behind it, and the shining steel lines stretched still and uninhabited through the fields, we saw no sign of life beyond a cawing flock of rooks. The sun was bright, the hoar-frost only lay under the shadow of the hedge-rows, and not a breath of wind stirred the bare branches of the trees. After a word of protest I took the fur coat over my arm, and Daisy's bag in my hand, and we set out at a brisk pace to cover the two miles before us.

Presently a sleepy little village appeared ahead of us; before we reached it my guide turned off to the left.

"It is a little longer round this way," she said, "but I am afraid the people in the village might —well—"

"Exactly," I replied. "We are a secret embassy."

It was a narrow lane we were now in, winding in the shade of high beech-trees and littered with their brown cast leaves. Whether it was the charm of the place, or that we instinctively delayed the crisis now that it was so near, I cannot say, but gradually our pace slackened.

"I am afraid they will be rather anxious about me," said Daisy.

"If they value you as they ought," I replied.

She smiled a little, and then, in a minute, we rounded a corner, and she said, "That is Helmscote we see through the trees."

I looked, and saw a pile of chimneys and gables close before us and just a little distance removed from the lane. Along that side now ran a high, ancient-looking wall with a single door in it, opposite the house. Evidently this unostentatious postern was a back entrance, and the gates must open into some other road.

My fellow - ambassador paused and glanced in both directions, but there was no sign of any one but ourselves.

"I think it will be best if I leave you in the garden," she said, "while I go in and find mother."

"Yes, I think it will be wise," I answered.

She took out a key and opened the door in the wall, and I found myself in an old flower-garden screened by a high hedge of evergreens at the farther end.

"Give me my coat and bag," she said. "Many thanks for carrying them. Now just wait here. I shall be as quick as I can."

I lit a cigar and began to pace the gravel path, keeping myself concealed behind the bushes as far as I could. Decidedly this had a flavor of adventure, and the longer I paced, the more did a certain restlessness of nerves grow upon me. I took out my watch. She had been gone ten minutes. Well, after all, I could scarcely expect her to return so soon as that. I paced and smoked again, and again took out my watch. Twenty minutes now, and no sign of my fellow-ambassador. I began to grow impatient and also to feel less the necessity for caution. No one had discovered me so far and no one was likely to; why should I not explore this garden a little farther? I ventured down to the farther end, till I stood behind the hedge. It was charmingly quiet and restful and sunny, with high trees looking over the walls and rooks flapping and cawing about their tops, and a glimpse of the house beyond. This glimpse was so pleasing that I thought I should like to see more, and, spying a garden roller propped against the wall and a niche in the stone above it, I gave a wary look round, and in a moment more had scrambled up till my feet were in the niche and my head looking over the top.

Below me I saw a grass terrace and a broad walk, and beyond these the mansion of Helmscote. No wonder Dick showed a touch of pride and affection when (on very rare occasions, I admit) he had alluded to his home. It was an old brick house of the Tudor period, though some parts were apparently more ancient than that and had been built, I should say, by the first Shafthead who had settled there. The colors—the red with diagonal designs of black bricks through it, the stone of the mullioned windows, the old tiles on the roof, the gray of the ancient portions, even, I fancied, the green ivy—had all been softened and harmonized by time and by weather till the whole house had become a rich scheme that would have defied the most cunning painter to imitate it.

"I know Dick better since I have seen his home," I said to myself. "And his sister? Yes, I think I know her better, too, though not so well as I should like to. Pardieu! what has become of her?"

"Well, sir," said a voice behind me, "what are you doing there?"

I turned with a start, my grip of the wall slipped, and, with more precipitation than grace, I descended to the garden again to find myself confronted by a decidedly formidable individual. He was a gentleman of something over sixty years of age,

I descended to the garden

but tall and broad and upright far beyond the common, and even though his left arm was in a sling of black silk I should not have cared to try conclusions with him. His face was ruddy and fresh, his features aristocratic and well-marked, his eyes blue and very bright, and he was dressed in a shooting-suit and leather leggings. The air of proprietorship, the wounded left arm, and the family resemblance left me in no doubt as to who he was. I was, in fact, about to enjoy the interview with Sir Philip Shafthead for the sake of which I had entered his garden.

Yet, strange though it may seem, gratitude for this stroke of good luck was not my first sensation.

"Who the devil are you, and what are you doing here, sir?" he repeated, sternly.

He had not heard of my arrival, then, and on the instant the thought struck me that since he did not know who I was, I might make the experiment of feigning ignorance of him.

"I address a fellow-guest of Sir Philip's, no doubt?" I said, with as easy an air as is possible for a man who has just fallen from the top of a wall where he had no business to have climbed.

"Fellow-guest!" he repeated. "Do you mean to pretend you are visiting Helmscote?"

"I am about to; though I confess to you, sir, that Sir Philip is at present unaware of my intention."

"Indeed?" said he.

"Yes," I said. "You are doubtless a friend of Sir Philip's, sir?"

He emitted something that was between a laugh and an exclamation.

"More or less," he replied. "And who are you?"

283

"My name is d'Haricot, and I am a friend of his son, Dick Shafthead."

He started perceptibly, and looked at me with a different expression.

"I have heard your name," he said.

"As you are staying at Helmscote you have no doubt heard of Dick's imprudence?" I went on, boldly.

"I have," he replied, shortly. "Have you come to see Sir Philip about that?"

"Yes," I said. "I have travelled down with Miss Shafthead this morning; she left me here for a short time while she went in to see her parents, and while waiting I had the indiscretion to mount this wall, in order to obtain a better view of the beautiful old house. It is the finest mansion I have seen in England. No wonder, sir, that Dick is so attached to his home!"

"Yet, as you are aware, he has run away from it," said the baronet, dryly.

"Ah," I said, "you have doubtless heard the father's view of his escapade. Will you let me tell you the son's, while I am waiting?"

"Had you not better keep this for Sir Philip— that is, if he consents to hear you?"

"No," I said, eagerly. "I have no secrets to tell, and if I can persuade you that Dick has some excuse for his conduct, perhaps you, too, might say a word to Sir Philip in his favor."

"It is unlikely," said the baronet; "but go on."

284

At that moment I spied Daisy entering the garden, though fortunately her father's back was towards her. Swiftly I made a signal for her to go away, and after an instant's astonished pause she turned and slipped quietly out again. I had been given a better chance than I had dared to hope for.

Chapter XXVIII

*"At the journey's end a welcome;
For the wanderer a friend!"*

—CYD.

IR," I began, "I must tell you, in the first place, that there is this to be said for Dick Shafthead—and it is an argument he is too generous to use himself—he took counsel of a friend, who, perhaps rashly, urged him to follow the dictates of his heart."

"Indeed?" said the baronet.

"Yes; I can answer for it, because I was that friend; and that is one of the reasons why I was so eager to plead for him with Sir Philip."

"It sounds a damned poor one," said he. "May I ask why you advised a son to rebel against his father?"

"If I had thought his father would regard his marrying the girl he loved as an act of rebellion, I might—though I do not say I would—have ad-

286

vised him otherwise. But he had told me that
Sir Philip was a man of great sense and understanding; therefore I argued that he would not
take a narrow or prejudiced—"

"Prejudiced!" he exclaimed.

"Or a prejudiced view of his son's conduct. I
knew he was a good churchman; therefore, as a
follower of a Carpenter's Son, he could not seriously
let any blemish on a girl's pedigree stand between
his son and himself. Besides, he was so highly
placed that an alliance with his family would be
sufficient to ennoble. Furthermore, as he loves his
son, he would wish for nothing so much as his happiness. Lastly, being a great gentleman, Sir Philip
would give a lady's case every consideration."

But at this the baronet's feelings could no longer
be contained.

"By God, sir!" he exclaimed. "Do you mean
to say you preached this damnable sermon to
my—to Dick Shafthead?"

I had not preached this sermon, nor anything
very much like it; but these were undoubtedly
the arguments I ought to have used.

"I argued from what he had told me of his
father," I replied. "If I am incorrect in my esti-
mate of Sir Philip; if he is not a Christian, a gentleman, an affectionate father, and a man of sense,
then, indeed, I reasoned wrongly."

At this thrust beneath his guard, Sir Philip was
silent, and I hastened to follow up my attack.

"Another argument I used—and it seemed to me the strongest—was this: that as Dick had told me of the deep affection Sir Philip felt for Lady Shafthead, I knew his father had a heart which could love a woman devotedly, and he had but to turn back the pages of his own life to find himself reading the same words as his son."

"Sir Philip loved a lady of his own degree and station," he answered.

"And Dick a relative of that lady," I said. "A girl with the same blood in her veins, and a character which no one can impeach. Can Sir Philip?"

"Her character is beside the point," said he.

"Dick's father would not say so of his son's wife," I retorted.

Again the baronet seemed at a loss for a fitting answer; and from his expression I think he was on the point of revealing his identity, and sending me forthwith to the devil; but without a pause I hurried up the rest of my artillery.

"Even if Sir Philip remains deaf to all that I have hitherto said, there yet remains this, which must, at least, make him pause. He will be losing a son."

"And the son will be losing his father."

"Yes; and therefore Sir Philip will not only be suffering, but inflicting a misfortune."

"I may remind you, sir, that Dick has only to listen to reason."

"Dick's mind is made up; and can you, sir,

who know these Shaftheads, expect them to abandon their resolutions so easily? From whom has he inherited his firmness and tenacity? From his father, of course; and he from that long line of ancestors who have made the name of Shafthead honorable since the days of Edward the Third! The warrior who was ennobled on the field of Blenheim has not left descendants of milk and water!"

"I am perfectly aware that Dick is obstinate as the devil," replied the baronet, but this time in a tone that seemed to have in it a trace of something not unlike satisfaction.

"And so, sir, his father will be ruthlessly discarding a second daughter-in-law."

At these words the change that came over the baronet was so sudden and violent that I almost repented of having uttered them.

"What do you mean?" he exclaimed, in a stifled voice. "Dick didn't tell you? He does not know!"

"No," I replied. " I learned it through an old companion in arms of Major Shafthead."

For a moment there was a pause. Then he said, in a steadier voice:

"And does this seem to you an argument for permitting another son to commit an act of folly?"

"It does seem an argument for not breaking the last link with the generation to come."

The baronet turned round and walked a few paces away from me; then he turned back and said:

"Well, sir, if it is any satisfaction to you, I may tell you that you have already discharged your task. I am Sir Philip Shafthead."

"What!" I exclaimed, in simulated surprise. "Then I must indeed ask your pardon for the freedom with which I have spoken. My affection for your son is my only excuse."

"He is fortunate in his friends, sir," said Sir Philip, though with precisely what significance I could not be sure. "You will now have luncheon with us, I hope."

We walked in silence to the house, my host's face expressing nothing of what he thought or felt.

In a long, low room whose oak panelling and beams were black with age and whose windows tinged the sunshine with the colors of old coats of arms, I was introduced to Lady Shafthead. She was like her daughter, smaller and slighter than the muscular race of Shaftheads, gray-haired and very charming and simple in her manner. Daisy stood beside her, and both women glanced anxiously from one to the other of us. What those who knew him could read in Sir Philip's countenance, I cannot say. For myself, I merely professed my entire readiness for lunch and my appreciation of Helmscote, but, surreptitiously catching Daisy's eye, I gave her a glance that was intended to indicate a fair possibility of fine weather.

Evidently she read it as such, for she replied

by a smile from which all her distrust had vanished.

The meal passed off in outward calm and with no reference to the conversation of the morning. Indeed, Sir Philip scarcely spoke at all, and I was too afraid of making a discordant remark to say much myself.

"You will excuse me from joining you in the smoking-room at present," said the baronet, when we had finished. "Daisy, you will act as hostess, perhaps?"

Nothing could have suited me better than this arrangement, and for an hour we discussed our embassy and its prospects with the friendliness of two intimates who have shared an adventure.

Then Lady Shafthead entered and said with a smile towards us both,

"Sir Philip has written to Dick."

"He is forgiven?" I cried.

"He is told to come home."

"Alone?"

"Yes, alone."

My face fell for a little, but Lady Shafthead's air reassured me.

"For the present, at all events, alone," she said.

"And may the present be brief!" I replied. "And now his ambassador must regretfully return to town."

"Oh, but you are staying with us, I hope," said Lady Shafthead.

"With one collar, a tweed suit, and no razors?"

"Can't you send for your things?" suggested Daisy.

And that is precisely what I did.

The next day the prodigal returned and had a long interview with his stern parent. At the end of it he joined me in the smoking-room.

"Well?" I asked.

"An armistice is declared," said Dick. "For six months the matter is not to be mentioned."

"And that is all?"

"All at present."

"But six months, Dick! Can you wait?"

"Call it three weeks," said Dick. "I know the limit to the governor's patience. He never let a matter remain unsettled for one month in his life."

He filled his pipe deliberately, standing with his legs wide apart and his broad back to the fire, while an expression of amused satisfaction gathered upon his good-looking countenance.

"I say," he remarked, abruptly, "don't think I'm ungrateful. You did the trick, monsieur, and I won't forget it in a hurry."

As he said this he turned his back to me and took a match-box from the mantel-shelf, as though he had merely made a casual remark about the weather, but by this time I knew the value of such undemonstrative British thanks.

Another condition that Sir Philip had made was that his son should not return to London until the Christmas vacation was over, and, though this was a matter of merely two or three weeks, Dick found it harder than a six months' postponement of his marriage. But to me, I fear, it did not seem so unreasonable, for, as he could not have his sweetheart's company, he insisted on retaining mine; so, after a polite protest, which Lady Shafthead declared to be unnecessary and Daisy to be absurd, I settled down to spend my Christmas at Helmscote.

At that time there was no one else staying in the house, so that when I sat down at dinner that night, one of a friendly company of five, I felt almost as though I was a member of the family. And the Shaftheads, on their part, seemed bent on increasing this illusion. Once I cheerfully alluded to my exile—cheerfully, because at that moment the thought had no sting.

"An exile?" said Lady Shafthead, smiling at me as a good mother might smile. "Not here, surely. You must not feel yourself an exile here."

And, indeed, I did not. For the first time since I landed in this country, I felt no trace of strangeness, but almost as though I had begun to take root in the soil. Circumstances had not enabled me to enjoy any family life since I was a boy, and had I been given at that moment a free pardon and a ticket to Paris, I should have said, "Wait, please, for a few months, till I discover to which nation I really do belong. Here I am at home. Perhaps, if I return, I should now be lonely."

The very look of my room when I retired to bed impressed me further with this feeling. The fire was so bright, the curtains so warm, every little circumstance so soothing. I drew up the blind and looked out of a latticed casement-window into a garden bathed in moonlight, and my heart was filled with gratitude. Last thing before I went to sleep, I remember seeing the firelight playing on the walls and mingling with a long ray from the moon, and the fantastic designs seemed to form themselves into letters making a message of welcome. And this message was signed " Daisy Shafthead."

At what hour I woke I cannot say ; but I felt as though I had not been long asleep, and that something must have roused me. The fire had burned low, but the long beam of moonlight still fell across my bed and made a patch of light on the opposite wall. Suddenly it was obscured, and at the same moment I most distinctly heard a noise—a noise at the window. I turned on my pillow with that curious sensation in my breast that by the metaphysical may easily be distinguished from exhilaration. I had left the curtains a little apart with an oblong of blind showing light between them. Now there was a dark body moving stealthily either before or behind this.

For a moment I lay still, then, with a spring so violent as almost to suggest that I had exercised some compulsion upon my movements, I leaped

I leaped out of bed

out of bed. The next instant the body had disappeared, and I heard a scraping noise, apparently on the outside wall. I rushed to the window and drew aside the blind. The casement was certainly open, but then I had left it so. I put out my head and looked carefully over the garden. Not a movement anywhere, not a sound. I waited for a time, but nothing more happened, and then I went to bed again, first, I confess, closing and fastening the window; and in a little the whole incident was lost in oblivion.

With the prosaic entry of daylight and a servant to fill my bath, I began to wonder whether the whole thing was not a dream, and, in fact, I had almost persuaded myself that this was the case when I spied, lying on the floor below the window, a slip of paper. It was folded and addressed in pencil to "M. d'Haricot, confidential." I opened it and read these words:

"Beware how you betray! Lumme also is watched. Therefore be faithful, if it is not too late!"

"What the devil!" I said to myself, after reading these incomprehensible words two or three times. "Is this a practical joke—or can it be from—?" I hastily turned the scrap over, looked at it upside down, and against the light, but no, there was no mark to give me a clew.

So meaningless did the warning seem that before the day was far spent it had ceased to trouble me.

Chapter XXIX

"Enter Truculento brandishing a rapier.
Ordnance shot off without."
—OLD STAGE DIRECTION.

THAT day slipped by smoothly and swiftly as a draught of some delicious opiate, and every moment my fancy became anchored more securely to Helmscote. But upon the next morning I received a letter from my Halfred which, though it amused and moved me by the good fellow's own happiness, yet contained one perplexing piece of news. I give the epistle in his own words and spelling.

" DEAR SIR,—Hopping the close reached you safely i added the waterprove coat for shooting in rain supposing such happened. Miss Titch has concented to marry me some day but not now you being sir the objec of my attentions for the present hence i am happy beyond expreshon also she is and i hop you approve sir. Another

297

package has come for Mister Balfour not to be oppened and marked u d t which Mr. Titch says means undertake to return but I have done nothing hopping I am right yours obediently   ALFRED WINKES."

No, Halfred, U. D. T. did not mean "Undertake to return," but bore a much graver significance, and this news made me so thoughtful that at least one pair of bright eyes remarked it at breakfast.

"No bad news, I hope," said Daisy, as we went together to the door to inspect the weather.

"None that you cannot make me forget," I replied, with a more serious gallantry than I had yet shown towards her.

A little rise of color in her face did indeed make me forget all less absorbing matters.

"By the time you leave us, you perhaps won't find us still so consoling," she replied, with a smile.

"Don't remind me of that day," I said. "It is a long way off—a hundred years, I try to persuade myself!"

Little did I think how soon fate would laugh at my confidence.

To-day we were to shoot pheasants. The baronet had his arm out of the sling for the first time, and this so raised his spirits that I felt sure Dick's six months' probation were already divided by two, at least. Two friends were coming from a neighboring house, and the other gun was to be my second, Tonks, who was expected to stay for the night. Presently he appeared and greeted me with a friendly grin.

"You haven't got Lumme to fire at to-day," he remarked.

I drew him aside.

"Tonks," I said, "that incident is forgotten— also the cause of it. You understand?"

He had the uncomfortable perspicacity to glance over at Daisy as he replied:

"Right O; I won't spoil any one's sport."

This game of pheasant-shooting is played in England with that gravity and seriousness that the Briton displays in all his sports. No preparations are wanting, no precautions omitted. You stand in a specially prepared opening in a specially grown plantation, while a specially trained company of beaters scientifically drive towards you several hundred artificially incubated birds invigorated by a patent pheasant food. Owing to the regulated height of the trees and the measured distance at which you stand these birds pass over you at such a height (and, owing to the qualities of the patent food, at such a pace), and the shot is rendered what they call "sporting." Then, at a certain distance from his gun and a certain angle, the skilful marksman discharges both barrels, converts two pheasants into collapsed bundles of feathers, snatches a second gun from an attendant, and in precisely similar fashion accounts for two more. The flight of the bird is so calculated that

the bad shot has little chance of hitting anything
at all, so that the pheasant may return to his coop
and be preserved intact for another day. When
such a shot is firing, you will hear the host anxiously say to the keeper at the end of the day:

"Did he miss them all clean?"

And if the answer is in the affirmative, he will
add:

"Excellent! I shall ask him to shoot again."

A clean miss or a clean kill—that is what is demanded in order that you may strictly obey the
rules of the sport, and at my first stand, where I
was able to exhibit five severed tails, a mangled
mass which had received both barrels at three
paces, and seven swiftly running invalids, my enthusiasm was quickly damped by the face Sir
Philip pulled on hearing my prowess.

"Never mind," said Daisy, who had come to see
the sport, "you couldn't expect to get into it just
at first."

"Come and give me instruction," I implored her.

"Don't be in such a hurry!" she cried, as she
stood beside me at the next beat. "Look before
you shoot—that's what Dick always says you
ought to do. Now you've forgotten to put in
your—wait! Of course! No wonder nothing happened; you had forgotten to put in the cartridges.
Steady, now. Oh, but don't wait till it's past you!
Dick says— Good shot! Was that the bird you
aimed at?"

"Mademoiselle, it was the bird a far - seeing Providence placed within the radius of my shot. ' L'homme propose; Dieu dispose.' "

"I shouldn't trust to Providence *too* much," said she.

Well, between Heaven and Miss Shafthead, aided, I must say for myself, by a hand and eye that were naturally quick and not unaccustomed to exercises of skill, I managed by the end of the day to successfully uphold the honor of my country. The light was fading when we stopped the battue, the air was sharp, and the ground crisp with frost. My fair adviser had gone home a little time before, and, wrapped in pleasant recollections and meditations, I had fallen some way behind the others as we walked homeward across a stubble - field. The guns in front passed out through a gate into a lane, and I was just following them when a man stepped from the shadow of the hedge and said to me:

"A gentleman would speak to you."

I looked at him in astonishment.

He was an absolute stranger, and his manner was serious and impressive. Beyond him, in the opposite direction from that in which my friends had turned, stood a covered carriage, with another man wrapped in a cloak a few paces in front of it, and a third individual holding the horse's head.

"That is the gentleman," added the stranger, indicating the man in the cloak.

In considerable surprise I turned towards the carriage.

"M. d'Haricot," said the shrouded individual.

"M. le Marquis!" I cried, in astonishment.

It was indeed none other than he whom I have before mentioned under the name of F. 11, secretary of the league, conspirator by instinct and profession, by rank and name the Marquis de la Carrabasse.

"What are you doing here, my dear Marquis?" I exclaimed.

He regarded me with a fixed and searching expression.

"The hour is ripe," he said. "The moment has come to strike! Here is my carriage. Come!"

For a moment I was too astonished to reply. Then, in a reasonable tone, I said:

"Pardon, Marquis, but I must first take leave of my hosts."

"You cannot."

"That is to be seen," I replied, losing my temper a little.

Before I could make a movement the Marquis was covering me with a revolver, and from the corner of my eye I could see that the man who had first spoken to me had drawn one, too.

"Enter the carriage," said the Marquis. "I do not trust you."

"Since you give me no alternative between a somewhat prolonged rest in this ditch and the

pleasure of your society, I shall choose the latter,"
I replied, with as light an air as possible. "But
I warn you, Marquis, that this conduct requires
an explanation."

He continued to look sternly at me, holding his
revolver to my head, but making no reply, while,
in as easy a fashion as possible, I strolled up to
the carriage.

Then, to my surprise, I saw that they had employed one of the beaters to hold their horse, a
man whom I recognized at once as having carried
my cartridge-bag.

"You may now go," said the Marquis to this
man, handing him coin. "And for your own sake
be silent!"

I could have laughed aloud at the delightful
simplicity of thus hiring a stranger at random
to aid in an abduction and then expecting him
to keep his counsel, had I not seen in it an omen
of further failures. So certain was I that the news
of my departure would now reach Helmscote before night that I did not even trouble to send a
message by him.

The man who had first spoken to me jumped
upon the box and took the reins, the Marquis and
I entered the carriage, and through the dusk of that
winter evening I was carried off from Helmscote.

"Now, M. le Marquis," I said, sternly, "have
the goodness to explain your words and conduct
to me."

He looked at me intently for a moment and then answered:

"On your honor, are you still faithful?"

"What do you mean, monsieur?"

"Lumme has not betrayed us?"

"Lumme!" I exclaimed, in astonishment, and then suddenly remembered the warning paper. "Did you throw that paper into my bedroom?"

"An agent threw it for me. Did you obey the warning?"

"Again I must ask for an explanation. What has M. Lumme to do with it and what do you suspect me of?"

"M. Lumme is in the English Foreign Office," said the Marquis, with emphasis.

"And you suspect me of having betrayed my cause to him? On my honor, monsieur, even were I inclined to treason I should as soon think of confiding in that man whom you so rashly employed to hold your horse!"

"Sir Shafthead is in the English government," said the Marquis, unmoved by my sarcasm.

"Sir Philip Shafthead was at one time a member of Parliament, but is so no longer. But what of that?"

"You have told him nothing?"

"I have not."

"You have been watched," said he. "Every movement you have made is known to me."

"And why?" I exclaimed. "Why should you think it necessary to watch me?"

"Why did you not send me any report yourself?"

"You did not ask for one."

"I had not the honor to be informed of your address," said he.

"I wrote to you as soon as I was settled in London, and to this day have never received a reply."

"You wrote?" he exclaimed, with some sign of disturbance.

"I did," I repeated, and I quoted some words I remembered from my letter.

"Pardon!" said the Marquis, "I do remember now receiving that letter, but I must have mislaid it, and I certainly forgot that you had written."

"And, having forgotten an important communication, you proceed to suspect me of treason! This is excellent, M. le Marquis!"

"My dear friend," he replied, in an agitated voice, "you then assure me I was wrong in mistrusting you?"

"Absolutely!"

"Pardon me, my friend! I am overwhelmed with confusion!"

He was so genuinely distressed, and the sincerity of his contrition was so apparent, that what could I do but forgive him? But what carelessness, what waste of time in dogging the steps of a friend, what indications of mismanagement at every turn! And even at that moment I was apparently embarked under this leader upon some secret and hazardous undertaking. Well, there was nothing for it but to do my best so far as I was concerned.

"Ah, here is the station," said he. "The train should now be almost due."

"Train for London, sir?" said the porter. "Gone ten minutes ago. No, sir, no more trains to-night."

"Peste!" cried the Marquis. "Ah, well, my friend, we must look for some lodging for the night."

"But perhaps we might catch a train at another station," I suggested.

Yes, by driving ten miles we could just catch an express.

307

"Bravo!" said the Marquis. "You are full of ideas, my dear d'Haricot."

"And you?" I said to myself, with a shrug.

We arrived just in time, and on the platform were joined by our driver.

"Let me introduce Mr. Hankey," said the Marquis.

So this was the elusive Hankey. Well, I shall not take the trouble to describe him. Imagine a scoundrel, and you have his portrait. I was thankful he did not travel in the same compartment with us, but evidently regarded himself as in an inferior position.

"You trust that man implicitly?" I asked the Marquis, when we had started.

"Implicitly!" he replied, with emphasis.

"I do not," I said to myself.

By ten o'clock that night I was seated with the Marquis de la Carrabasse in my own rooms, thinking, I must confess, not so much of politics and dynasties as of the friends I had just lost for who could say how long.

Chapter XXX

"Conspiracy requireth a ready wit—and a readier exit."

—Francis Gallup.

HE Marquis de la Carrabasse, secretary of the U. D. T. League, and known in their circles as F. 11, enters this history so near its end that I shall not stop to give a prolonged account of him. Yet he was a person so remarkable as to merit a few words of description. The inheritor of an ancient title, but little money; a Royalist to the point of fanaticism; a man of wide culture and many ideas, and of the most perfect simplicity of character and honesty of purpose, he had devoted his whole life to the restoration of the monarchy, alternated during lulls in the political weather by an equally feverish zeal for scientific inventions of the most ambitious nature. Yet, owing to the excess of his enthusiasm and fertility of mind over the more

309

prosaic qualities that should regulate them, practical success had hitherto eluded this talented nobleman. His flying-machines had only once risen into the element for which they were intended, and then the subsequent descent had been so precipitate as to incapacitate the inventor for a month. His submarine vessel still reposed at the bottom of the Mediterranean, and the last I heard of his dynamite gun was that the fragments were to be found anywhere within a radius of three miles around its first discharge. As to his merits as a conspirator, my exile bears witness.

Yet he was a man for whom I could not but entertain a lively affection. Of medium height and slender figure, he had a large, well-shaped nose, a black mustache tinged with gray, whose vigorously upward curl had a deceptively truculent air at first sight, and a splendid dark eye, at times piercing and bright and at others dreamy as the eye of a somnambulist. Add to this a manner naturally courteous and simple, which, however, he was in the habit of artificially altering to one of decision and mystery, when he thought the rôle he was playing suited this transfiguration, and you have the Marquis de la Carrabasse, so far as I can sketch him.

We had only just seated ourselves in my room, when Halfred entered beaming with pleasure at the prospect of seeing me again.

" 'Appy to see you back, sir," he began, joyfully.

"A most hunexpected pleasure, sir. I thought as 'ow you wasn't comin' till hafter the festivities of Christmas, sir."

But at this point his eye fell upon my friend the Marquis, and his expression changed in the drollest manner. Halfred's British prejudices had become adjusted to me by this time, but evidently the very appearance of this stranger was altogether too foreign for him. He became abnormally solemn, and handed me a budget of letters that had come this evening, with no further comment, while his eye plainly said, "Have a care what company you keep!"

In the mean time my guest had been regarding him with a rapt and thoughtful gaze, and now he said, in the most execrable English:

"Vill you please get me a bread or biskeet?"

"Bread, sir?" replied Halfred, starting and looking hard at him. "Slice of 'am with it?"

"What did he say?" the Marquis asked me, in French.

I explained.

"Ah, yes; some pork; certain! Vich it vill also quite good and so to be."

What he meant by this riddle I cannot tell; but I can assure you he sent the honest Halfred from the room with a very perturbed countenance.

In a few minutes he had brought us some much-needed refreshments, and, with a last dark glance towards my unconscious visitor, retired for the night.

On our journey the Marquis had kept his counsel with that air of mystery he could assume so effectively, nor had I pressed him with questions;

" Vich it will also quite good "

but when our hunger was somewhat abated I began to consider it time that I was taken into his confidence. For I had gathered enough to feel sure that some coup was very shortly to be tried.

"M. le Marquis," I said, "have you nothing to tell me?"

"First, my dear friend, read your letters," he replied.

"But they can wait."

"I beseech you!"

A little struck by his tone, I opened the first, and as I read the contents I could not refrain from an exclamation of astonishment.

"You have unexpected news?" he said.

"'The Bishop of Battersea has much pleasure in accepting M. d'Haricot's kind invitation,'" I read, aloud. "Mon Dieu! I am to have a bishop to dinner in three days' time; and a bishop I have never invited!"

"Are you sure?"

"Positive!"

"Read your other letters. Possibly they will throw light upon this."

I opened the next, and cried in bewilderment:

"Sir Henry Horley has much pleasure also! But I have never asked him; I have only met him once at a country house!"

The Marquis smiled.

"Do not be too sure you have not asked these gentlemen," he said.

"But I swear—"

"Read this!"

He handed me an invitation-card on which, to my utter consternation, I saw these words engraved: "Monsieur d'Haricot requests the pleasure of —— company to dinner to meet—" and here followed a name it would be indecorous to reproduce in these frivolous memoirs, the name of that royal personage for whose cause we loyalists of France were striving!

"What!" I exclaimed. "It is true?"

"What is?"

"That *he* is to honor me with his company?"

"Scarcely, my dear d'Haricot," said the Marquis, with a smile. "But I have full authority to take what steps I choose."

"To employ this ruse?"

"Certainly, if I deem it advisable."

"But to what end?"

"Listen!" said he, his dark eyes glowing with enthusiasm and his face lighting up with patriotic ardor. "I have asked a party of your most influential friends to dine with you, inducing them by a prospect of this honor. You will tell them that his Highness cannot meet them there, but that he bids them, as they reverence their own sovereign, to assist his righteous cause. When they are inflamed with ardor, you will lead them from the table to the special train which I shall have waiting. A picked force will place themselves under our orders. By next morning the King shall be proclaimed in France."

For a minute I was too staggered to answer him.

"But, my dear Marquis," I replied, when I had recovered my breath, "*I* cannot induce these sober and law-abiding Englishmen to follow me, perhaps to battle."

"Not all, perhaps, but some, certainly. My dear friend, you have the gift of tongues; you can move, persuade, influence to admiration. I myself would try, but you know the English language better, I think, than I, and then I am unknown to these

314

gentlemen. Ah, you will not desert us, d'Haricot! Your King demands this service of you!"

"Of me?"

"Yes; he mentioned your name when I spoke to him of our schemes."

"He wished me to perform this act?"

"I had not then arranged it. But is it for you to choose the nature of your service?"

"If it is put to me thus, I shall endeavor to do my best," I replied. "But I confess I do not care for this scheme of yours."

No use in protesting; the Marquis rose and embraced me with such flattering words as I hesitate to reproduce.

"It is done! It is accomplished already!" he cried.

I disengaged myself and endeavored to reflect.

"This is all very well," I said. "But of what use to us is a bishop?"

"We wish the support of the English Church."

"And Sir Henry Horley?"

"Also of the nobility."

"But he is scarcely a nobleman, only a baronet," I explained. "And, besides, I only know him slightly. He is not my friend."

"Embrace him; make him your friend."

I fancied I saw myself; but what was the good in arguing with an enthusiasm like this?

I proceeded to read my other answers, and I did not know whether to feel more astonished at the list of guests or at the curious knowledge of my movements and acquaintances which my visitor must somehow have acquired. The acceptances included Lord Thane, with whom I had only the very slightest acquaintance, Mr. Alderman Guffin, at whose house I had once dined, one or two people of social position whom I had met through Lumme or Shafthead, and General Sholto.

"Ah, the General!" I said. "Well, he, at least, is an old soldier."

"Be kind to him; he is our brightest hope," said the Marquis.

I looked at him in astonishment. "What do you know of him?"

I could have sworn he blushed. "What do I not know of all your friends?" he replied.

Could it be from the inquiries of Hankey he had learned all this, and took so much interest in my gallant neighbor? I remembered now how the General had once met that disreputable individual. Yet it did not seem to me altogether a complete explanation.

But conceive of my astonishment when, among the few refusals, I found one from Fisher!

"What do you know of him?" I asked.

"He is a philanthropist. I regret that he cannot accept," said the Marquis, with an air of calm mystery, yet with another suggestion of flush in his face. He knew of my philanthropic escapade, then—and how?

316

"Well," I said, at last, "I am prepared to assist you in any way I can. In the two days left I shall arrange my affairs—and now I must send some explanation of my disappearance to Lady Shafthead."

He rose and grasped my arm.

"Not a word to her," he said. "I do not trust the member of Parliament. We must run no risk."

I protested, but no; he implored me—commanded me.

"A line to my friend Dick Shafthead, then?" I suggested. "He, at least, is beyond suspicion."

"My friend, we are serving the King," he replied.

"Very well," I said, though my heart sank a little at this sudden rupture with those kind friends.

My visitor rose to depart, and just then his eye fell on two immense packing-cases placed against the wall.

"Ah," he said, "they are safe, I see."

I took a lamp in my hand and came up to examine the latest arrived of those mysterious gifts, whose source I now plainly perceived.

"I should not let that lamp fall upon this box of bonbons," he remarked, lightly, and yet with a note of warning.

"Why not, Marquis?"

"The little packet may explode," he laughed.

317

Involuntarily I started.

"It contains, then—?"

"The munitions of war," he answered.

"And the other?"

"Was to try you, my dear friend. It contains only bricks. Forgive me for putting you to this test. I should not have doubted you."

"But to try me?" I said. "How would you have known if I had called in a detective?"

The Marquis looked at me.

"I had not thought of that," he confessed.

It was my turn to look at him, and, I fear, not altogether with a flattering eye.

"Why was it addressed to Mr. Balfour?" I asked.

"A ruse," he replied, with his air of confident mystery returning somewhat. "A mere ruse, my dear friend."

"I perceive," I said, a little dryly. "Well, you can trust me for my own sake not to explode this box; also to make the preparations for this dinner."

"My friend, I make them."

"You?"

"Read your invitation again."

I looked at the card sent out in my name, and then I noticed that an address was placed in one corner, "Twenty-two Beacon Street, Strand."

"What is the meaning of this?"

"It is a house I have hired for two weeks," he

replied. "The dinner, as you see, takes place there. Hankey and I make all preparations."

"And I do nothing?"

"You prepare yourself for the hour of action. Brave friend, au revoir!"

"Au revoir, Marquis."

Chapter XXXI

"So you are actuated by the best motives?
Poor devil! Have you tried strychnine?"
—LA RABIDE.

THE next morning I called in Mr. and Mrs. Titch, Aramatilda, and Halfred, and, in a voice from which I could not altogether banish my emotion, I told them that I must give up my rooms and that they might never see me again. From Halfred's manner I could not but suspect he was prepared for ominous news; he had evidently concluded that a man who introduced after dark such a visitor as I had entertained last night must stand on the brink either of insanity or crime. Yet his stoical look as he heard my announcement said, better than words: "You may disgust my judgment, but you cannot shake my fidelity. Through all your errors I am prepared to stand by you, and brush your trousers even on the morning of your execution."

320

Mr. Titch's sorrow was, I fear, somewhat tinctured by regret at the loss of a profitable tenant, though I am sure it was none the less sincere on that account.

"What 'as to 'appen, 'as to come about, as it were, sir," he said, clearing his throat for a further flight of imagery. "You will 'ave our good wishes even in furrin parts, if I may say so, which people which has been there tells me is enjoyable to such as knows the language, and 'as the good fortune for to be able to digest their vittles. We will 'old your memory, sir, in respectful hestimation, and forward letters as may be required."

Mrs. Titch being, as I have said before, a lady of no ideas and a kindly heart, confined her remarks to observing:

"As Mr. Titch says, what has to be is such as we will hendeavor to hestimate regretfully, sir."

As for Aramatilda, she looked as though she would have spoken very kindly, indeed, had the occasion been more private. That, at least, was the sentiment which a wide experience enabled me to read in her brown eye.

"My dear Miss Titch," I said to her, "I leave you in good hands. Next to having the felicity myself, I should sooner see you solaced by my good friend Halfred than by any one I can think of."

"Oh, sir," she replied, with a most becoming blush, "you are very kind. But that won't be till you don't require him no longer."

"Right you are," said her lover, regarding her with an approving eye. "And Mr. d'Haricot ain't done with me yet."

"I fear that I shall be in two days more," I replied, with a sadness that brought a sympathetic tear to Aramatilda's eye.

"That's to be seen, sir," said Halfred, with resolution.

Well, I dismissed these good people with a sadder heart than I cared to allow, and had turned to arranging my papers and collecting my bills, when I was interrupted by the entry of the Marquis in person.

He was busy, he told me, busy about many things; and his manner was mystery itself. Yet even a conspirator is human, and evidently he had other interests in London besides our plot. From one or two sighs and tender allusions I shrewdly guessed the nature of these.

"You are not in love?" he asked me, suddenly.

"In love!" I exclaimed, in astonishment, for his previous sentence, though uttered with a melancholy air, had referred to the merits of a new rifle.

"In love with a dark lady?"

I started. Could he refer to Kate? Yes, of course, now I come to think of it, he or his agents must have seen us together.

"No, Marquis, I give you my word I am not in love either with black or brown," I answered, gayly.

"I am glad, my dear friend," he replied, "for I would not do you an injury."

"An injury?" I exclaimed, with a laugh. "Would you be my rival?"

"No, no," he said, though with some confusion. "I meant, my friend, that I would not like to tear you from her."

"The conspirator must conspire," I said, with a smile.

"True; true, indeed," he replied, with a sigh.

Used as I was to the complex nature of my friend, I could not help thinking that this was indeed a sentimental mood for one who was about to undertake as mad and desperate an enterprise as ever patriot devised.

"To-morrow morning I shall not be available," he told me as he left; "but after that—the King!"

"You do not, then, prepare my dinner to-morrow morning?"

"No, monsieur, not in the morning."

By that night I had made the few preparations that were necessary before striking my tent and leaving England, perhaps forever. The next day found me idle and restless, and suddenly I said to myself:

"The most embarrassing part of this wild enterprise is being thrown upon me. I want a friend by my side, and if the Marquis de la Carrabasse objects, let the devil take him!"

Ah, if I could have summoned Dick Shafthead!

But, having undertaken not to do this, I selected that excellent sportsman, his cousin Teddy
Lumme. His courage I had proved, his wisdom I
felt sure was not sufficient to deter him from mix-
ing himself up with the business, and as for any
harm coming to him, I promised myself to see
that he did not accompany me too far.

I went to him, and having sworn him to secrecy,
I told him of the dinner. He, of course, knew that
his father, the venerable bishop, was to be of the
party, and when he heard the part that the guests
were afterwards expected to play you should have
seen his face.

"Of course they will not listen to me for a moment," I said. "The idea is absurd. But I am
bound to carry out my instructions, and afterwards
to start upon this reckless expedition myself. I
only ask you, as my friend, to come to the dinner,
and keep me in countenance, and afterwards take
my farewells to your cousins—I should say, to all
my English friends. Will you?"

"Like a shot," said Teddy. "I wouldn't miss
the fun for anything. By Jove! I think I see my
governor's face! I say, you Frenchies are good,
old-fashioned sportsmen. You're going to swim
the channel, of course?"

His mirth, I confess, jarred a little upon me.

"I am serving my King," I reminded him.

"Oh, I know, I'd do the same myself if these
dashed Radicals got into power over here. A

man can't be too loyal, I always say. All right; I'll come. What time?"

"Eight o'clock."

In the afternoon a decidedly disquieting incident occurred. Much more to my surprise than pleasure, I received a brief visit from Mr. Hankey. I had disliked the thought of this individual ever since my burgling experience, and now that I saw him in the flesh I disliked him still more.

"Do you come from the Marquis de la Carrabasse?" I asked.

"His Lordship has directed me to remove the packing-case to-night."

"Take it," I said. "My faith! I prefer its room to its company! The Marquis is at Beacon Street at present, I suppose?"

"His Lordship is engaged."

"Engaged?"

"Rather more than that," said Mr. Hankey, with a peculiar look. "But he will call upon you to-morrow and give you your orders."

"My orders!" I exclaimed, with some annoyance.

"His Lordship used that expression."

Mr. Hankey looked at me as if to see how I liked this, and then, in a friendly tone which angered me still further, remarked:

"It's a risky job, is this."

"A man must take some risks now and then."

"If the police were to hear?" he suggested.

"Who is to tell them?"

"It might be worth somebody's while."

"And whom do you suspect of being that traitor?" I exclaimed.

With a very abject apology for giving any offence, Mr. Hankey withdrew.

"They still suspect me!" I said to myself, indignantly.

Then another suspicion, still more unpleasant, struck me. Was Mr. Hankey making an over-

"My orders!"

ture to me? I tried to dismiss it, but my spirits were not very high that night, not even after the explosive packing-case had been removed.

Before retiring to bed on the last night which I was going to spend in this land, a sudden and happy idea struck me. Not to write a single line of explanation to my late hosts was ungrateful and unbecoming in one who boasted of belonging

326

to the politest nation in Europe. I had only promised not to write to Lady Shafthead and Dick. Well, then, there was nothing to hinder me from writing to Daisy. I admit that Sir Philip also was exempt, but this alternative did not strike me so forcibly. If I posted my letter in the morning, she would not get it till it was too late to take any steps that might interfere with our plans. I seized my pen and sat down and wrote:

" DEAR MISS SHAFTHEAD,—Truly you must think me the most ungrateful and unmannerly of guests; but, believe me, gratitude and kind recollections are not what have been lacking. I am prevented from explaining fully, but I may venture to tell you this—since the occasion will be past even when you read these lines; I am again in the service of one who has the first call upon my devotion. Without naming him, doubtless you can guess who I mean. Silence towards the kind Lady Shafthead and towards my dear friend Dick has been enjoined upon me; but since you were not specifically mentioned I cannot resist the impulse to assure you of my eternal remembrance of your kindness and of yourself. Convey my adieus to Sir Philip and to Lady Shafthead, and assure them that their hospitality and goodness will never be forgotten by me.

" Tell Dick that I shall write to him later if fate permits me. If not, he can always assure himself that I was ever his most affectionate and devoted friend.

" I leave England to-night on an adventure which I cannot but allow seems hopeless and desperate enough, but, as I once said to you on a less serious occasion, 'l'homme propose, Dieu dispose.' The cause calls, I can but obey! I know not what English customs permit me to sign myself, but in the language of sincerity and of the heart, I am, yours eternally and gratefully."

And then I signed my name, lingering a little over it to delay the curtain which seemed to descend when I folded my letter and placed it in its envelope.

Chapter XXXII

"Farewell, my friends, farewell!
We have had some brave days together!"
—Boulevardé.

THE momentous day had come. Looking out of my bedroom window in the morning, I saw the sunshine smiling on the bare trees and the frosted grass of the park. At that hour the shadows were long, and Rotten Row quiet as a lonely sea-shore, so that a lively flock of sparrows seemed to fill the whole air with their cheerful discussions, and I fancied they were debating whether they could let me go away and leave forever this little home that I had made.

"I would stay," I said to them; "I would stay if I could."

But, alas! it was to be my last day in England, the land I had first regarded as so alien, and then come to love so well. And there was no use standing here letting my spirit run down at heel.

Yet, when I came into my sitting-room and saw the bareness that had already been made by my preparations for departure, the absence of little things my eye had before fallen upon without noticing, and the presence of a half-packed box in one corner, my heart began to feel an emptiness again.

"I feel as a man must when he is going to get married," I said to myself, and endeavored to smile gayly at my humor.

Hardly had I finished my breakfast, endeavoring as I read as usual my morning paper to forget that I was leaving all this, when I heard a quick step in the passage, and with a brisk, "Bon jour, monsieur!" the Marquis entered.

"Ah," I thought, "he is in his element. No regrets with him."

Yet, after the first alertness of his entry, I observed, to my surprise, a certain air of sentiment about him, which, if it was not regret, was at least not martial keenness.

"You did your business yesterday?" I said.

"I did," he replied, in a grave tone, and with something like a tender look in his eye. "I did some private business of an unforgettable and momentous nature, my dear d'Haricot. But not now; I shall not tell you now. To-night you shall know."

Then, making a gesture as if to banish this mood, he threw himself into a chair, and, bending his brows in a keen look at me, said:

"But to business, my friend; to the business we are embarked upon."

"Precisely," I said. "I await it."

"In this house where you dine are two entrances. Your guests come in by one, and you await them in the rooms I have set apart for you. In the rest of the house I operate."

"And what do you do?"

"I gather our force. Men picked by my agents are to be invited to enter by the other door. I offer them refreshments. They follow, or, rather, precede me. In a lane at the back of the house is yet another door; against it is drawn up a great van, a van used for removing furniture, a van of colossal size. You see?"

"Hardly; I fear I am stupid."

"You do not see? Ah, my dear d'Haricot, eloquence is your gift, contrivance mine. I have not invented a flying-machine, a submarine vessel, and a dynamite gun for nothing. These men enter this van; the door is closed upon them; it is driven to the station, put on board my special train, and taken to the coast. They then emerge; I address them in such terms as will make it impossible for them to withdraw, even if they wish —and they are to be desperate, picked men; we arm them, and then to France! On the coast of Normandy we will be met by five regiments of foot, two of cavalry, and six batteries of artillery which I am assured will declare for the King.

Paris is ripe for a revolution. Vive le Roi! Why are you silent? Is it not well thought of, my friend?"

"It is indeed ingenious," I replied. "But the carrying of it out I foresee may not be so easy."

"Nothing can fail. My confidence is implicit. Was I ever deceived?"

I might with truth have retorted "always," but I saw that I should only enrage him.

I shrugged my shoulders and asked:

"You superintend the affair?"

"In the house. Hankey makes the arrangements at the station. Much is to be done. One man to one task."

"And I? What do I do?"

"You bring your friends to the station. At eleven precisely the train starts. Do not be late."

"But if they will not accompany me?"

"If all else fails, we go to France together. At least our brave countrymen will not be afraid, whatever these colder islanders may do."

"You may depend on me for that," I answered. "By-the-way, I should tell you that I bring a friend of my own to dinner—M. Lumme."

"Lumme!" cried the Marquis. "You can trust him?"

"Implicitly."

"And I trust you. Bring him if he is brave."

There was a minute's pause; he had suddenly fallen silent.

"Is that all?" I asked.

"All for the present, my brave friend; au revoir! We meet at the station at eleven precisely! Do not forget!"

He leaped up with that surprising vivacity that marked his movements, and before I had time to accompany him even as far as the door he had closed it and gone. In a moment, however, I heard his voice outside, apparently engaged in altercation with some one, and then followed some vigorous expletives and a brisk sound of scuffling.

I rushed into the passage, and there, to my consternation, beheld my friend retreating towards me before a vigorous onslaught by Halfred, who was flourishing his fists and exclaiming, "Come out, you beastly mounseer! Come out into the square and I'll paste your hugly mug inter a cocked 'at!"

"Diable!" cried the Marquis. "Leetle bad man stop short! Mon Dieu! What can it was?"

"Halfred!" I cried, indignantly. "Cease! What is the meaning of this?"

"Beg pardon, sir," said Halfred, desisting, but unabashed at my anger. "You told me yourself, sir, as 'ow I was to do it."

"I told you? Explain! Come into my room."

I brought the two combatants in, closed the door, and repeated, sternly:

"Explain, sir!"

"This is the furriner as haccosted Miss Titch,

sir," said Halfred, doggedly, "and you said as
'ow I'd better practise my boxing on 'im. I didn't
spot 'im the other night, but Miss Titch she seed
'im this morning and told me."

"I know not the meaning you mean when you
speak so fast!" cried the Marquis. "But I see

"small beast, to damn
with you!"

you are intoxicate, foddled and squiff. Small
beast, to damn with you!"

"You just wait till I gets you outside," said
Halfred, ominously. "I'll give you something to
talk German about!"

"German!" shrieked the Marquis, catching at
the only word he understood. "If you was gentleman not as could be which I then should—ha!"
And he stamped his foot and made a gesture
of lunging my retainer through the chest.

"Oh, you're ready to begin, are you?" said
Halfred, mistaking this movement for the pre-

liminary to a box and throwing himself into the proper attitude.

"With your permission, sir."

"Stop!" I said. "You certainly have not my permission! I shall dismiss you if you strike my guest again!"

Yet I fear I was unable to keep my countenance as severe as it should have been. I then turned to the livid and furious Marquis and explained the cause of the assault.

"Address that girl!" cried he. "It was to ask her questions—questions about you, monsieur, when I wrongly distrusted you. This is a scandalous charge!"

"But you see how liable your action was to misconstruction?"

"I see, I do see!" he exclaimed. "He was right to feel jealous! I have given many good cause, yes, I confess it. Explain to him."

I told Halfred of his mistake.

"Well, sir," he said, "I takes your word, sir."

"Good young man," said the Marquis, turning to him with his finest courtesy. "I forgive. I admire. You have right. Many have I love, but your mistress is not admired of me. She is preserve! Good-night, young man; good-night, monsieur."

And off he marched as briskly as ever.

Halfred shook his head darkly.

"Him being a friend of yours, sir, I says nothing," he observed, but his abstinence from further comment was more eloquent than even his candid opinion would have been.

I posted my letter, I smoked, I read a book to pass the time, and at last, as the afternoon was wearing on, I went to my bedroom and packed a bag containing a change of clothes and other essentials, for I remembered that I should have to drive straight from the dinner-table to the train. I looked out into the street; dusk was falling, the lamps were lit, the lights of a carriage and the rattle of horses passed now and then, the steady hum of London reached my ears. It was still cheerful and inviting, but now my nerves were tighter strung and I felt rather excitement than depression.

"Monsieur! You in there?"

The voice came from my sitting-room. I started, I rushed towards the welcome sound, and the next moment I was embracing Dick Shafthead. He looked so uncomfortable at this un-English salutation that I had to begin with an apology.

"Never before and never again, I assure you!" I said. "For the instant I forgot myself; that is the truth. Tell me, what good angel has sent you?"

For I knew his sister could not yet have received my letter.

"We were afraid you'd got into the hands of the police again, and I've come prepared to bail you out. What the deuce happened to you?"

"You heard the circumstances of my departure?"

"We heard a cock-and-bull story from a thick-headed yokel — something about a pistol and a villain with a mustache and a carriage and pair; but as we learned that you'd appeared at the station safe and sound, we divided the yarn by five. I must say, though, I've been getting a little worried at hearing no news of you—that's to say, the women folk got in a flutter."

"Did they?" I cried, with a pleasant excitement I could not quite conceal.

"Naturally, we are not accustomed to have our guests vanish like an Indian juggler. I've come to see what's up."

I told him then the whole story, letting the Marquis's prohibition go to the winds. He listened in amused astonishment.

"Well," he said, at last, "it seems I've just come in time for the fair. You've napkins enough to feed another conspirator, I suppose?"

"You are the one man I want!"

"That's all right, then," said Dick. "I'd better be off to my rooms to dress. Where shall we meet?"

"I will call for you soon after half-past seven. The house is not far from the Temple, I believe."

So now, thanks to Providence, I would have both my best friends by my side. My spirits rose high, and I began to look forward gayly even to urging a bishop to start by a night train with a repeating-rifle.

Soon after seven Teddy appeared, immaculate and garrulous as ever, and in high spirits at the thought of the shock his reverend father would get on finding him included among the select party.

"The governor's looking forward to having a great night of it," said this irreverend son. "Scratching his head when I last saw him, trying

scratching his
head to remember
stories he tells to Dooks.

to remember the stories he generally tells to dooks and royalties. I told him he'd better get up a few spicy ones to tickle a Frenchie, don't you know."

"My faith!" I exclaimed; "how disappointed they will all be! I scarcely have the face to meet them."

"Rot," said Teddy. "Do 'em good. Hullo! what's this bag for? Oh, I see, you cross to-night, don't you? Is Halfred going with you?"

I also looked at my servant in surprise. He

was dressed in his overcoat, and stood holding my bag in one hand and his hat in the other.

"Going to take your bag down for you, sir," he explained.

"But I do not need you, my good Halfred. I was just going to say farewell to you this moment."

"I'm a-coming," he persisted.

"Even against my wishes?"

"Beg pardon, sir, but that there furriner, 'e's in this show, ain't he?"

"Why should you think so?"

"I smells a rat, sir, as soon as I sees 'im. I don't mean no offence, but you don't know Hengland as well as I do. I'll come along, sir, and if you happens to be thinking of a trip across the channel, I was thinking, sir, a change of hair wouldn't do me no 'arm."

"But I cannot allow you! There is danger!"

"Just as I thought, sir; but I'm ready for 'em."

And, laying down the bag, he showed me the butt of an immense pistol in his overcoat-pocket.

"Halfred," I cried, "you may not glitter, but you are of gold! Come, then, my brave fellow, if you will!"

"Good sportsman, isn't he?" said Teddy, as we drove off together.

At a quarter to eight we three, Teddy and Dick and I, alighted at number Twenty-two Beacon Street, Strand, to find Halfred and the bag awaiting us outside the door. A waiter with a mysterious air showed us up a narrow staircase into a small, well-furnished reception-room. Beyond this, through folding-doors, opened a dining-room of moderate size, where we found the table laid and ready. The man closed the door and disappeared, and the four of us were left to await the arrival of my guests.

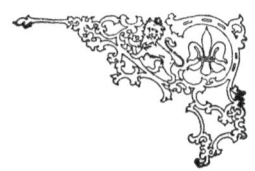

Chapter *XXXIII*

" The time has come, the very hour has struck
When deeds most unforgettable are due."
—BEN VERULAM.

UARTER - PAST eight, and no sign of a guest!" I exclaimed.

"You are sure you asked 'em for eight and not eight-thirty?" said Dick.

"Positive; it was on the card. I noticed particularly."

"Perhaps they've gone to your rooms," suggested Teddy.

"Scarcely. Some of them do not know my address, and this house was also engraved upon the card."

We were sitting round the anteroom fire while Halfred waited in the dining-room.

"Beg pardon, sir," he observed, putting his head through the door-way. "But perhaps they've smelled a rat, like as I do."

341

Another quarter of an hour passed, and then we heard the sound of heavy footsteps on the stairs; it sounded like several people. Then came a knock. I opened the door and saw the waiter who had shown me in, and behind him a number of as disreputable-looking fellows as I have ever met.

"*Your visitors, sir.*"

"Your visitors, sir," said the waiter, in his mysterious voice, though with an evident air of surprise, and, I think, of disgust.

"Mine?"

"Yes, sir; Mr. Horleens, they wants."

"But I am not Mr. Horleens. There is some mistake here."

I addressed a few questions to one of the men, but he was so abashed at the well-dressed appearance of myself and my two guests that, muttering something about "being made a blooming fool of," the whole party turned and descended again.

"It was the right word, sir," said the waiter to me. "Some of 'em was to ask for Mr. Horleens."

"What do you make of that?" I exclaimed, when they had all gone.

"They've mistaken the house, o' course," said Teddy.

"Horleens, Horleens," repeated Dick, thoughtfully. "I have it! They meant Orleans. They must be some of your gay sportsmen."

"Of course!" I cried. "That must have been the password. Well, no doubt they have found the proper door by this time. But I fear, gentlemen, that we are to have this dinner all to ourselves."

"Let's eat it anyhow," said Dick. "I've a twist like a pig's tail."

This sentiment being heartily applauded by Teddy, I rang for the waiter, and we sat down to as excellent a dinner as you could wish to taste. Certainly, whatever miscalculations the Marquis had made, this part of his programme was successfully arranged and enthusiastically carried through. We ate, we drank, we laughed, we jested; you would have thought that the night had nothing more serious in store for any of us. Halfred, who helped to wait upon us, nearly dropped the dishes more than once in his efforts to control his mirth at some exuberant sally. It was not possible to have devised a merrier evening for my last.

"Here's to your guests for not turning up!" cried Teddy. "They'd only have spoiled the fun."

"And the average of bottles per man," added Dick.

"Yes. Thank God I am not making an inflammatory speech to Sir Henry Horley and the Bishop of Battersea!" I said. "But, my dear friends"—and here I pulled out my watch—"I fear I shall have to make a little speech as it is, a farewell oration to you. It is now half-past ten. I leave you in a few minutes."

"The devil you do," said Dick. "Teddy, the monsieur proposes to dismiss us. What shall we do?"

"The monsieur be blanked!" cried Teddy, using a most unnecessarily strong expression. "O' course we're coming, too."

"But I shall not permit—"

"Silence!" said Dick. "Messieurs, let us put on our coats! Halfred, load that pistol of yours; the expedition is starting."

No use in protesting. These two faithful comrades hilariously cried down all resistance, and the four of us set off for the station.

In a remote, half-lit corner of that huge, draughty building, we found the special train standing; an engine, two carriages, and the great colored van already mounted upon a truck. The Marquis met me with a surprised and disappointed look.

"Is this all the aid you bring?" he asked.

"All!" I exclaimed. "I do not know what mistake you have made, but my guests never appeared."

"Is that the truth?"

"M. le Marquis!"

"Pardon. I see; there must have been some error. Well, it cannot be helped now. I, at least, have been more successful; I have got my men. Who are these two?"

I introduced my two friends, and we walked down the platform. As we passed the furniture van I started to hear noises proceeding from inside.

"Do not be alarmed," said the Marquis. "I have explained that I am conveying a menagerie."

We stopped before a first-class compartment. He opened the door and invited us to enter.

"Do not think me impolite if I myself travel in another carriage," he said to me. "I have a companion."

"M. Hankey?"

"He also is here," he replied, I thought evasively.

Just before we started, Halfred put his head through our window and said, with a mysterious grin:

"The furriner's got a lady with him!"

But he had to run to his own carriage before he had time to add more. The next moment the engine whistled and the expedition had started.

"I don't quite know what the penalty is for this sort of thing," said Dick, as we clanked out over the

"The furriner's got a lady with him!"

dark Thames and the constellations of the Embankment. "Hard labor if we're caught on this side of the channel, and hanging on the other, I suppose; so cheer up, Teddy!"

At this quite unnecessary exhortation, Teddy forthwith burst into song. You would have thought that these two young men, travelling in their evening clothes and laughing gayly, were bound for some ball or carnival. Yet they knew quite well they were running a very serious risk for a cause they had no interest in whatever, and that seemed only to increase their good-humor.

"What soldiers they would make!" I said to myself.

But in the course of an hour or two our talk and laughter ceased, not that our courage oozed away, but for the prosaic reason that we were all becoming desperately sleepy. How long we took to make that journey I cannot say. The lines seemed to be consecrated to goods traffic at that hour of the night and our train moved by fits and starts, now running for half an hour, then stopping for it seemed twice as long. At last I awoke from a doze to find the train apparently entering a station, and at the same instant Dick started up.

"We must be nearly there," I said.

"My dear fellow," he replied, seriously. "Are you really going on with this mad adventure?"

"I have no choice; but you—"

"Oh, I'm coming with you if you persist. But think twice before it's too late."

"Hey!" cried Teddy, starting from his slumbers. "Where are we?"

Dick and I looked at each other, and, seeing that we were resolute, he smiled and then yawned, while I let down the window and looked out.

Yes, we were entering a station, and in a minute or two more our journey was at an end.

"There will be a little delay while we get the van off the train and the horses harnessed," said the Marquis, coming up to me. "In the mean

347

time there is some one to whom I wish to present you."

He led me to his carriage and there I saw a veiled lady sitting. Even with her veil down I started, and when she raised it I became for the instant petrified with utter astonishment. It was Kate Kerry!

"I believe you have met this lady," said the Marquis, in his stateliest manner, "but not previously as my wife."

"Your wife!" I exclaimed. "I have, then, the honor of addressing the Marchioness de la Carrabasse?"

"You have," said Kate, with a smile and a flash of those dark eyes that had once thrilled me so.

"We were married yesterday morning," said the Marquis. "That was the business I was engaged upon. And now for the moment I leave you; the general must attend to his command!"

I entered the carriage, and there, from her own lips, I heard the story of this extraordinary romance. The Marquis, she told me, had obtained an introduction to her (I did not ask too closely how, but, knowing his impetuous methods, I guessed what this phrase meant); this had been just after the end of the mission, and his object at first was to obtain information about me from one whom (I also guessed) he regarded as probably my mistess; but in a very short time from playing the

348

detective he had become the lover; his suit was pressed with irresistible vigor, and now I beheld the result.

"May I ask a delicate question?" I said.

"Yes," she replied, with all her old haughty assurance.

"What was it that moved your heart, that so suddenly made you love the Marquis?"

"He attracted my sympathy."

"Your sympathy only?"

"And my admiration. He is serving a noble cause."

Truly, my friend had infected his wife with his own enthusiasm in the most remarkable way.

"Does your uncle know?"

"No."

"He might not approve of my friend."

"My husband is a marquis," she replied, with an air of pride and satisfaction that seemed to me to throw more than a little light on the complex motives of this young lady.

"And now you propose to accompany him on this dangerous adventure?"

"Certainly I do! Where else should I be?"

"He is fortunate, indeed," I said, politely.

Now I understand how my friend F. 11 had obtained all his information regarding my movements and my friends and my different escapades, for in the days of Plato I had talked most frankly with his fair Marchioness. In fact, I perceived

clearly several things that had been obscure before.

But our talk was soon interrupted by the return
of the happy husband.

"All is ready! Come!" he said.

Undoubtedly, with his eyes burning with the
excitement of action, his effective gestures and
distinguished air, his dramatic speech, not to speak
of that little title of marquis, I could well fancy
his charming a girl who delighted in the unusual,
and was ready, as her uncle said, to fill in the picture from her own imagination.

"And so my dethroned divinity is the Marchioness de la Carrabasse!" I said to myself. "Mon
Dieu! I shall be curious to see the offspring of
this remarkable union!"

Chapter XXXIV

"Et Balbus bellum horridum fecit."
—Convulsius.

HE Marquis led us from the station into a road, where we found the van already under way and two carriages awaiting us. In one Dick and Teddy were already installed; the Marquis and Kate entered the other. I joined my friends, and Halfred sprang upon the box; and off we set for a destination which our leader, after his habit, kept till the last a profound secret. So far as I could see, our force consisted of the party I have named, the men in the van, and the three drivers. Hankey, I presumed, must be one of the last. Where we were to find a ship, and how soon we were to find our French allies, I had no notion at all.

That drive seemed as interminable as the railway journey, and certainly it was far more uncomfortable. We were all three too sleepy to talk

351

much, but, to my constant wonder and delight, I found my two companions as ready as ever to go ahead and take their chance of what might befall them.

"I say," said Teddy, in a drowsy tone, "do you think there's any chance of getting a bath before we begin?"

"The despised sandwich would come in handy, too," added Dick. "I say, monsieur, why didn't you bring a flask?"

"I did," I replied, "and here it is."

"He is another Napoleon," said Dick. "Nothing is forgotten."

Meantime the day began to break, and, though the sun had not yet risen, it was quite light when we felt our carriage stop.

"Alight!" said the voice of the Marquis. "We have arrived!"

We were in a side track that ran through the fields of a sheltered valley; on one side a grove of trees concealed us; on the other, through the end of the valley and only at a little distance off, I saw something that roused me with a thrill of excitement. It was the open, gray sea, with a small steamboat lying close inshore.

"Peste!" cried the Marquis, taking me aside. "Hankey is not here!"

"Not with us?"

"No; he must have been left at the station. It is a nuisance!"

"It seems to me worse than that."

"Yes, for we cannot wait; we must leave him behind. It is a great loss. And now, my brave comrade, the drama commences—the drama of the restoration! You will open the van, and as the men come out I shall address them."

"In English?" I asked.

"Yes; I have prepared and learned by heart an oration. It will not be long, but it will be moving. Ah, you will see that I can be eloquent!"

With his wife at his side, and the drivers a few paces behind him, he drew himself up and threw out his chest, while I unlocked the door of the van.

Throwing it open I stepped back, curious to see the desperadoes he had collected, and wondering how they would regard the business, while the Marquis cleared his throat.

A moment's expectant pause, and then—conceive my sensations—out stepped, first, the burly form of Sir Henry Horley, then the upright figure of General Sholto, next the benevolent countenance of the Bishop of Battersea, and after him the remainder of my invited guests. The Marquis had kidnapped the wrong men!

"What the devil!" began Sir Henry, glancing round him to see in what country and company he found himself; but before there was time for a word of explanation, the Marquis had launched upon his passionate appeal. As the original manuscript afterwards came into my possession,

I am able to give the exact words of this remarkable oration.

"Brave, gallant men," he cried; "you have come
to share adventures stupendous, miraculous, which
you will enjoy! I lead you, my good Britannic
sportsmen, whither or why obviously can be seen,
to establish the anointed and legal King in his
right country! To die successfully is glorious!
But you will not; you will live forever conquer-
ing, and gratefully recollected in France!

"You" [here he waved his hand towards the
astonished baronet] "will enjoy drink of all beers
and spirits that an English proverbially adores
ever after and always! Also you" [here he indicated the dumfounded bishop] "will enjoy women,
the most lively and sporting in the wide world,
always and ever after! Also you" [pointing
towards the substantial form of Mr. Alderman
Guffin] "shall bask and revel in the land of song,
of music, of light fantastic toes, amid all which
once and more having been never stopping again
bravo and hip, hip, my sportsmen! Once, twice,
thrice, follow me to victory!"

He stopped and looked eagerly for the fruits of
this appeal, and his Britannic sportsmen returned
his gaze with interest. I am free to confess that
long before this my two companions and I had
shrunk from publicity behind the door of the van,
awaiting a more fitting moment to greet our
friends.

"Is this a dashed asylum, or a dashed nightmare?" demanded Sir Henry.

Not quite comprehending this, but seeing that these recruits displayed no great alacrity, the Marquis again raised his voice and cried:

"Are you afraid, brave garçons?"

But now an unexpected light was thrown on their captors.

"Kate!" exclaimed General Sholto in a bewildered voice.

That the unfortunate General should have his domestic drama played in public was more than I could bear. I stepped forward, and I may honestly say that I effectually distracted attention. It was not a pleasant process, even when assisted by the explanations of Teddy to his father and the loyal assurances of Dick; but it at least cleared the air. As for the unfortunate Marquis, his chagrin was so evident that, diabolically unpleasant as he had made my own position, I could not but feel sorry for him.

"And so," he said to me, sadly, "Heaven has been unkind to me again. I acted for the best, my dear d'Haricot, believe me! But I fear I do not excel so much in carrying out details as in conceiving plans. I see, it was my fault! I allowed these gentlemen to enter that house by the wrong door. Well, if they will not follow us —and I fear they are reluctant, though I do not understand all they say—we three must go alone!"

355

"Three?" I asked.

"My wife and you and I. Say farewell to your friends and come! The vessel awaits us and our forces in France will at all events be ready."

But Heaven was to prove still more unkind to our unfortunate leader.

"Who are these?" I exclaimed.

"The English police!" he cried. "We are betrayed!"

And indeed we were. A force of mounted policemen swept round the corner of the wood and trotted up to us, and in the midst of them we recognized the double-faced Hankey.

"What do you want, gentlemen?" asked the Marquis, calmly, though his eyes flashed dangerously at the traitor.

"We come in the Queen's name!" replied the officer in command. "Are you the Marquis de la Carrabasse?"

"I am."

"I have a warrant, then, for your arrest."

But now, for the first time, fortune turned in the Marquis's favor, though I fear it seemed to that zealous patriot a poor crumb of consolation that she threw.

Instead of finding, as our betrayer had calculated, a crew of suspicious-looking adventurers, he beheld a small party of middle-aged gentlemen attired in evening clothes and anxious only to find their way home again; and, to add to our good luck, when they came to look for our case of arms and ammunition it appeared that the Marquis had forgotten to bring it. Also, these same elderly gentlemen showed a very marked disinclination to have their share in the adventure appear in the morning papers, even in the capacity of witnesses.

And, finally, as the French government had been informed of our plans for some weeks past, so that we were absolutely powerless for mischief, the police decided to overlook my share altogether and make a merely formal matter of my friend's arrest.

"What will my King say?" cried the poor Marquis. "Oh, d'Haricot, I am disgraced, and my honor is lost! Tell me not that I am unfortunate; for what difference does that make? Such misfortunes must not be survived! Adieu, my friend! Pardon my suspicions!"

Before I could prevent him, the unfortunate man quickly thrust his hand into his pistol-pocket, and in that same instant would have blown out those ingenious, unpractical brains. But, with a fresh look of despair, he stopped, petrified, his hand still in his pocket.

"My revolver also is forgotten!" he exclaimed. "I am neither capable of living nor of dying!"

"Thank Heaven who mislaid that pistol," I replied. "Had you forgotten your bride, too?"

"Mon Dieu! I had! I thank you for reminding me. Ah, yes, I have some consolation in life left me!"

But though the Marchioness no doubt consoled him later, she was at that moment in anything but a sympathetic mood.

"Well, my dear," I overheard the General saying to her, "as you make your bed so you must lie in it. This—er—Marquis, doesn't he call himself?—of yours hasn't started very brilliantly, but, I dare say, by the time he has been before the magistrate and cooled down, and had a shave and so forth, he will do better. I shouldn't let him mix himself up in any more of these plots of his, though, if I were you."

She tossed her head, and the defiant flash of her eyes told her uncle plainly to mind his own business; but I fear his words had stung her more than he intended, for when her husband said to her, dramatically, "My love, we have failed!" she merely replied, with a sarcastic air, "Naturally; what else could you have expected?"

She beamed upon me with contrasting kindness, lingered to say farewell to the admiring Teddy, who had just been presented to her, went by her uncle with a disdainful glance, and then the happy couple passed out of this story.

"A devilish fine woman!" said Teddy.

"Others have made the same reflection," I replied.

"And now, monsieur," said Dick, "I think it's

about time we were getting back to London, bath, and breakfast."

"Carriage is ready, sir," said the voice of Halfred.

"Whose carriage?"

"Carriage as we came down in, sir. I've give the driver the tip, and he's waiting behind them trees."

"But what about all these unfortunate gentlemen?"

"Thought as 'ow they might prefer travelling in the van they comed in," he replied, with a semblance of great gravity.

But I had not the hardihood to do this, and concerning my journey to town with my dinnerless, sleepless, and breakfastless guests, I should rather say as little as possible.

I confess I envied the Marquis accompanying his escort of constables.

Chapter XXXV

"Adieu! I never wait till my friends have yawned twice."

—HERCULE D'ENVILLE.

ELL, I am back in London after all, amid the murmur of millions of English voices, the rumble of millions of wheels, the painted omnibus, and the providential policeman—all the things to which I bade a long farewell last night. And my reader, if indeed he has kept me company so far, now fidgets a little for fear I am about to mix myself in further complications and pour more follies into the surfeited ear. But no! I have rambled and confessed enough, and in a few more pages I, like the Indian juggler Dick compared me to, shall throw a rope into the sky, and, climbing up it, disappear — into heaven? Again no! It may be a surprise to many, but it was not there that these memoirs were written.

To round up and finish off a narrative that has

360

no plot, no moral, and only the most ridiculous hero, is not so easy as I thought it was going to be. Probably the best plan will be not to say too much about this hero and just a little about his friends.

As I had given up and dismantled my rooms, Dick insisted that I must return to Helmscote with him that same day and finish my Christmas visit, and need it be said that I accepted this invitation?

At the station, upon our arrival in London, I parted with Teddy Lumme and General Sholto.

"By-bye," said Teddy, cheerfully; "I must trot along and look after the governor; he's in a terrible stew; I don't suppose he has missed two meals running before in his life—poor old beggar! It'll do him good, though; don't you worry, old chap."

And with a friendly wave of his hand this filial son drove off with the still muttering Bishop.

The General wrung my hand, hoped he would see me again soon, and then, without more words, left us. He was not so cheerful, for that final escapade of his niece had hurt him more than he would allow. Still, it was a fine red neck and a very erect back that I last saw marching down the platform.

"And now, my good Halfred," I said, "I suppose you fly to Miss Titch and happiness? Lucky fellow!"

"I 'aven't been dismissed yet, sir," he replied, solemnly, and with no answering smile, "but if you gives me the sack, o' course I'll 'ave to go."

"Then you think I need your watchful eye on me a little longer?"

From the expression of that watchful eye it was evident that he was very far from disposed to let me take my chance of escaping the consequences of my errors without his assistance. Indeed, to this day he firmly holds the opinion that it was his vigilance alone that insured so harmless an end to our desperate expedition, and that if he had not stood by me I should have conspired again within a week.

"I puts hit to Mr. Shafthead," he replied, casting a glance at my friend which might be compared to a warning in cipher addressed to some potentate by an allied sovereign.

"You certainly had better come down with us, Halfred," said Dick. "The Lord only knows what the monsieur would be up to without you."

And accordingly Halfred went with us to Helmscote.

Behold me now once more beneath the ancient, hospitable roof, the kind hostess smiling graciously, the genial baronet roaring with unrestrained mirth at the tale of our adventures—and Daisy? She was not looking directly at me; but her face was smiling, with pleasure a little, I thought, as well as amusement. At night the same welcoming chamber and a fire as bright as before; only this time no missives thrown through the casement window. Next morning I am severely left alone;

362

Dick has been summoned by his father. Half an hour passes, and then, with an air of triumph, he returns.

"You'll have to look after yourself to-day, monsieur," he says. "I'm off to town to bring her back with me."

"Her!" So the stern parent has relented, and some day in the distant future, I suppose, Agnes Grey will be Lady Shafthead and rule this house. What Dick added regarding my own share in this issue I need not repeat, though I confess it will always be a satisfaction for me to think of one headlong performance, unguided even by Halfred, which resulted so prosperously.

Being thus bereft of Dick, what more natural than that I should be entertained by his sister?

She speaks of Dick's happiness witn a bright gleam in her eye.

"He should feel very grateful to you," she says.

I should have preferred "we" to "he," but, unluckily, I have no choice in the matter.

"I envy him," I reply, with meaning in my voice.

Her face is composed and as demure as ever, only her color seems to me to be a little higher and her eye certainly does not meet mine as frankly as usual.

Suddenly I am emboldened to exclaim:

"I do not mean that I envy him Miss Grey, but his happiness in being loved!"

And then I tell her whose love I myself covet.

She is embarrassed, she is kind, she is not offended, but her look checks me.

"How often have you felt like this within the last
few months—towards some one or other?" she asks.

Alas! How dangerous a thing to let the brother
of the adored one know too much! Dick meant
no harm; he never knew how his tales would affect
me; but evidently he has jested at home about my
amours, and now I am regarded by his sister either
as a Don Juan or a perpetually love-sick sentimen-
talist. And the worst of it is that there are some
superficial grounds for either theory.

"Ah," I cry, "you have heard then of my wan-
derings in search of the ideal? But I have only
just found it!"

"How can you be sure of that?" she asks, a little
smile appearing in her eye like a sudden break in a
misty sky. "You haven't known me long enough
to say. In a month you may make a jest of me."

"I am serious at last. I swear it!"

"I am afraid you will have to remain serious for
some time to make me believe it," she replies, the
smile still lingering. "When any one has treated
women, and everything else, flippantly so long as
you, I—"

She hesitated.

"You do not trust them?"

"No," she confesses.

"If I am serious for six months will you trust
me then?"

"Perhaps," she allows at last.

It means a good deal, does that word, said in such circumstances, but I am not going to drag you through the experiences of a faithful lover, sustained by a "perhaps." *Mon Dieu!* You have the privations of Dr. Nansen on his travels to read if that is the literature you admire.

No; in the words of Halfred on the eve of his nuptials with Aramatilda, "I ain't what you'd call solemn nat'rally, but this here matrimonial business do make a man stop talkin' as free as he'd wish."

I also shall stop talking, and, with the blotting-pad already in my hand, pray Heaven to grant my readers an indulgent and a not too solemn spirit.

F I N  I S